U0141703

UNVEILNG GREEK MYTHOLOGY

邂逅希臘神話
英文讀本

James Baldwin 著

羅慕謙 譯

Preface

Homer and His Guide

Perhaps no other stories have ever been told so often or listened to with so much pleasure as the classic tales of ancient Greece. For many ages they have been a source of delight to young people and old, to the ignorant and the learned, to all who love to hear about and contemplate things mysterious, beautiful, and grand.

They have become so incorporated into our language and thought, and so interwoven with our literature, that we could not do away with them now if we would. They are a portion of our heritage from the distant past, and they form perhaps as important a part of our intellectual life as they did of that of the people among whom they originated.

I have here attempted to tell a few stories of Jupiter and his mighty company and of some of the old Greek heroes, *simply as stories*, nothing more.

I have carefully avoided every suggestion of interpretation. Attempts at analysis and explanation will always prove fatal to a reader's appreciation and enjoyment of such stories.

To inculcate the idea that these tales are merely descriptions of certain natural phenomena expressed in narrative and poetic form, is to deprive them of their highest charm; it is like turning precious gold into utilitarian iron: it is changing a delightful romance into a dull scientific treatise. The wise teacher will take heed not to be guilty of such an error.

It will be observed that while each of the stories in this volume is wholly independent of the others and may be read without any knowledge of those which precede it, there is nevertheless a certain continuity from the first to the last, giving to the collection a completeness like that of a single narrative.

In order that the young people of our own country and time may be the better able to read these stories in the light in which they were narrated long ago, I have told them in simple language, keeping the supernatural element as far as possible in the background, and nowhere referring to Jupiter and his mighty company as gods.

I have hoped thus to free the narrative still more from everything that might detract from its interest simply as a story.

J.B.

CONTENTS

目錄

God and Goddess
in Greek and Roman Mythology

	Greek	Roman	
1	Zeus	Jupiter	‣ principal god of the Greek pantheon ‣ ruler of the heavens ‣ king of the sky and the earth
2	Hera	Juno	‣ principal goddess of the Pantheon ‣ queen of the Gods ‣ goddess of marriage
3	Poseidon	Neptune	‣ king of the sea, earthquakes, and horses
4	Hades	Pluto	‣ god of the dead ‣ ruler of the underworld
5	Persephone		‣ queen of the Dead, grain-goddess
6	Demeter	Ceres	‣ goddess of the earth, flowers, plants, and harvest
7	Prometheus		‣ a Titan, brother of Atlas
8	Heracles	Hercules	‣ a divine hero

9	Dionysus	Bacchus	‣ god of wine and sensual pleasures
10	Pan	Faunus	‣ god of woods, fields, and flocks
11	Ares	Mars	‣ god of war
12	Hermes	Mercury	‣ god of commerce, invention, travelers and shepherds ‣ messenger of the gods
13	Hephaestus	Vulcan	‣ god of fire and metalworking
14	Athena	Minerva	‣ goddess of wisdom and war
15	Aphrodite	Venus	‣ goddess of love and beauty
16	Apollo	Phoebus Apollo	‣ god of the sun, poetry, music, dance, medicine, and oracles
17	Artemis	Diana	‣ goddess of the hunt, the moon, virginity, animals, and childbirth
18	Eros	Cupid	‣ god of love
19	Muses		‣ sisterhood of goddesses ‣ embody the arts, inspire the creation
20	Hebe	Juventas	‣ goddess of youth and spring
21	Pandora		‣ the first woman

1 Jupiter and His Mighty Company

Jupiter & Juno
on Mount Ida

 A long time ago, when the world was much younger than it is now, people told and believed a great many wonderful stories about wonderful things which neither you nor I have ever seen.

They often talked about a certain Mighty[1] Being[2] called Jupiter, or Zeus, who was king of the sky and the earth; and they said that he sat most of the time amid the clouds on the top of a very high mountain where he could look down and see everything that was going on in the earth beneath.

Jupiter and Thetis

He liked to ride on the storm-clouds and hurl[3] burning thunderbolts[4] right and left among the trees and rocks; and he was so very, very mighty that when he nodded[5], the earth quaked, the mountains trembled[6] and smoked, the sky grew black, and the sun hid his face.

1 mighty ['maɪti] (a.) of great strength and power 強大有力的
2 being ['biːɪŋ] (n.) a person or thing that exists 生物；人；生命
3 hurl [hɜːrl] (v.) to throw forcefully 猛力投擲
4 thunderbolt ['θʌndərboʊlt] (n.) a flash of lightning and the sound of thunder together 雷電；霹靂
5 nod [nɑːd] (v.) move head in agreement 點頭
6 tremble ['trembəl] (v.) to shake involuntarily 搖動

The Horses
of Neptune

🎧002   Jupiter had two brothers, both of them terrible fellows, but not nearly so great as himself. The name of one of them was Neptune, or Poseidon, and he was the king of the sea. He had a glittering[7], golden palace far down in the deep sea-caves where the fishes live and the red coral[8] grows.

And whenever he was angry the waves would rise mountain high, and the storm-winds would howl[9] fearfully, and the sea would try to break over the land; and men called him the Shaker of the Earth.

---

7 glittering ['glɪtərɪŋ] (a.) to shine brightly, with sparkling or lustrous reflected light 閃閃發光的
8 coral ['kɑːrəl] (n.) a rock-like substance, formed in the sea by groups of particular types of small animal 珊瑚
9 howl [haʊl] (v.) to make a long whining sound 怒吼

The Abduction of Persephone by Hades

The other brother of Jupiter was a sad pale-faced being, whose kingdom was underneath the earth, where the sun never shone and where there was darkness and weeping and sorrow all the time. His name was Pluto, or Aidoneus, and his country was called the Lower World, or the Land of Shadows, or Hades.

Men said that whenever any one died, Pluto would send his messenger, or Shadow Leader, to carry that one down into his cheerless kingdom; and for that reason they never spoke well of him, but thought of him only as the enemy of life.

A great number of other Mighty Beings lived with Jupiter amid the clouds on the mountain top,—so many that I can name a very few only.

The Birth of Venus

003   There was Venus, the queen of love and beauty, who was fairer by far than any woman that you or I have ever seen.

There was Athena, or Minerva, the queen of the air, who gave people wisdom and taught them how to do very many useful things.

There was Juno, the queen of earth and sky, who sat at the right hand of Jupiter and gave him all kinds of advice. There was Mars, the great warrior, whose delight was in the din[10] of battle.

---

10 din [dɪn] (n.) a loud continued noise 喧囂 ; 嘈雜聲

There was Mercury, the swift[11] messenger, who had wings on his cap and shoes, and who flew from place to place like the summer clouds when they are driven before the wind.

Mercury and Paris

There was Vulcan, a skillful blacksmith, who had his forge[12] in a burning mountain and wrought[13] many wonderful things of iron and copper[14] and gold. And besides these, there were many others about whom you will learn by and by, and about whom men told strange and beautiful stories.

---

11 swift [swɪft] (a.) moving very rapidly 快捷的
12 forge [fɔ:rdʒ] (n.) metal workshop 煉冶場
13 work [wɜ:rk] (v.) to exert physical or mental effort to make or accomplish something (pp. form: wrought) 做出；操作
14 copper ['kɑ:pər] (n.) reddish brown metal 銅

Venus at the Forge of Vulcan

They lived in glittering, golden mansions, high up among the clouds— so high indeed that the eyes of men could never see them. But they could look down and see what men were doing, and oftentimes they were said to leave their lofty[15] homes and wander[16] unknown across the land or over the sea.

And of all these Mighty Folk[17], Jupiter was by far the mightiest.

---

15 lofty ['lɔːfti] (a.) rising to a great height 高聳的
16 wander ['wɑːndər] (v.) to move about with no purpose or plan, or at no definite pace 漫遊
17 folk [foʊk] (n.) people, especially those of a particular group or type 某一民族、種族或社會階層中的廣大成員

2 The Titans and the Golden Age

005 Jupiter and his Mighty Folk had not always dwelt[1] amid the clouds on the mountain top. In times long past, a wonderful family called Titans had lived there and had ruled over all the world. There were twelve of them—six brothers and six sisters—and they said that their father was the Sky and their mother the Earth. They had the form and looks of men and women, but they were much larger and far more beautiful.

The name of the youngest of these Titans was Saturn; and yet he was so very old that men often called him Father Time. He was the king of the Titans, and so, of course, was the king of all the earth besides.

Men were never so happy as they were during Saturn's reign[2]. It was the true Golden Age then. The springtime lasted all the year. The woods and meadows[3] were always full of blossoms, and the music of singing birds was heard every day and every hour.

It was summer and autumn, too, at the same time. Apples and figs[4] and oranges always hung ripe from the trees; and there were purple grapes on the vines[5], and melons and berries of every kind, which the people had but to pick and eat.

The Golden Age

Of course nobody had to do any kind of work in that happy time. There was no such thing as sickness or sorrow or old age.

Men and women lived for hundreds and hundreds of years and never became gray or wrinkled[6] or lame[7], but were always handsome and young.

---

1 dwell [dwel] (v.) to live or stay as a resident; reside 居住
2 reign [reɪn] (n.) to possess or exercise sovereign power 統治
3 meadow ['medoʊ] (n.) grassy field 草地
4 fig [fɪg] (n.) a pear-shaped fruit 無花果
5 vine [vaɪn] (n.) climbing plant 藤蔓
6 wrinkled ['rɪŋkəld] (a.) facial line from aging 有皺紋的
7 lame [læm] (a.) walking unevenly; disabled 跛足的

"Nobody has to do any kind of work in that happy time."

They had no need of houses, for there were no cold days nor storms nor anything to make them afraid.

Nobody was poor, for everybody had the same precious things—the sunlight, the pure air, the wholesome[8] water of the springs, the grass for a carpet, the blue sky for a roof, the fruits and flowers of the woods and meadows. So, of course, no one was richer than another, and there was no money, nor any locks or bolts[9]; for everybody was everybody's friend, and no man wanted to get more of anything than his neighbors had.

---

8 wholesome ['hoʊlsəm] (a.) good for the health 有益於身心健康的
9 bolt [boʊlt] (n.) bar for fastening door 閂；門栓

When these happy people had lived long enough they fell asleep, and their bodies were seen no more. They flitted[10] away through the air, and over the mountains, and across the sea, to a flowery land in the distant west.

And some men say that, even to this day, they are wandering happily hither and thither[11] about the earth, causing babies to smile in their cradles[12], easing the burdens of the toilworn[13] and sick, and blessing mankind everywhere.

10 flit [flɪt] (v.) to pass quickly 輕快地飛過
11 hither and thither: from one place or situation to another 到處
12 cradle ['kreɪdl] (n.) a small bed for an infant 搖籃
13 toilworn ['tɔɪl,wɔrn] (a.) showing wear or fatigue 疲憊的

What a pity it is that this Golden Age should have come to an end! But it was Jupiter and his brothers who brought about[14] the sad change.

Saturn Conquered
by Amor Venus and Hope

It is hard to believe it, but men say that Jupiter was the son of the old Titan king, Saturn, and that he was hardly a year old when he began to plot how he might wage[15] war against his father.

As soon as he was grown up, he persuaded his brothers, Neptune and Pluto, and his sisters, Juno, Ceres, and Vesta, to join him; and they vowed[16] that they would drive[17] the Titans from the earth.

---

14 bring about: cause to occur or exist 引起
15 wage [weɪdʒ] (v.) to engage in; to carry on 進行
16 vow [vaʊ] (v.) a solemn promise to perform an act 發誓
17 drive [draɪv] (v.) to cause to move by force; push 驅逐

Then followed a long and terrible war. But Jupiter had many mighty helpers. A company of one-eyed monsters called Cyclopes were kept busy all the time, forging thunderbolts in the fire of burning mountains.

Cyclopes

Three other monsters, each with a hundred hands, were called in to throw rocks and trees against the stronghold[18] of the Titans; and Jupiter himself hurled his sharp lightning darts[19] so thick and fast that the woods were set on fire and the water in the rivers boiled with the heat.

Of course, good, quiet old Saturn and his brothers and sisters could not hold out always against such foes[20] as these. At the end of ten years they had to give up and beg for peace.

---

18 stronghold ['strɔːŋhoʊld] (n.) a place dominated by a particular group 據點；大本營
19 dart [dɑːrt] (n.) a short arrow thrown with the hand 鏢；標槍
20 foe [foʊ] (n.) a personal enemy 仇敵

The Battle Between the Gods and the Titans

011 They were bound in chains of the hardest rock and thrown into a prison in the Lower Worlds; and the Cyclopes and the hundred-handed monsters were sent there to be their jailers and to keep guard over them forever.

The Clash of the Titans

"Instead of peace, there was war."

Then men began to grow dissatisfied with their lot. Some wanted to be rich and own all the good things in the world. Some wanted to be kings and rule over the others. Some who were strong wanted to make slaves of those who were weak.

Some broke down the fruit trees in the woods, lest others should eat of the fruit. Some, for mere sport, hunted the timid animals which had always been their friends. Some even killed these poor creatures and ate their flesh for food.

"Instead of happiness, there was misery."

At last, instead of everybody being everybody's friend, everybody was everybody's foe.

So, in all the world, instead of peace, there was war; instead of plenty, there was starvation[21]; instead of innocence[22], there was crime[23]; and instead of happiness, there was misery[24].

And that was the way in which Jupiter made himself so mighty; and that was the way in which the Golden Age came to an end.

---

21 starvation [stɑːrˈveɪʃən] (n.) the act of starving or condition of being starved 飢餓
22 innocence [ˈɪnəsəns] (n.) freedom from guilt 無罪；清白
23 crime [kraɪm] (n.) something done against the law 罪行
24 misery [ˈmɪzəri] (n.) someone who is often very unhappy and is always complaining about things 不幸；痛苦

3 The Story of Prometheus

How Fire Was Given to Men

013 In those old, old times, there lived two brothers who were not like other men, nor yet like those Mighty Ones who lived upon the mountain top. They were the sons of one of those Titans who had fought against Jupiter and been sent in chains to the strong prison-house of the Lower World[1].

Prometheus Brings Fire to Mankind

The name of the elder of these brothers was Prometheus, or Forethought[2]; for he was always thinking of the future and making things ready for what might happen tomorrow, or next week, or next year, or it may be in a hundred years to come[3].

The younger was called Epimetheus, or Afterthought[4]; for he was always so busy thinking of yesterday, or last year, or a hundred years ago, that he had no care at all for what might come to pass[5] after a while.

For some cause Jupiter had not sent these brothers to prison with the rest of the Titans.

Prometheus did not care to live amid the clouds on the mountain top. He was too busy for that. While the Mighty Folk were spending their time in idleness, drinking nectar[6] and eating ambrosia[7], he was intent upon plans for making the world wiser and better than it had ever been before.

He went out amongst men to live with them and help them; for his heart was filled with sadness when he found that they were no longer happy as they had been during the golden days when Saturn was king.

1 lower world: the dwelling place of the dead 陰曹地府
2 forethought ['fɔːrθɔːt] (n.) thought for future 事先的考量
3 to come: (in the) future 未來的
4 afterthought ['æftərθɔːt] (n.) something not thought of but added afterward 事後的想法
5 come to pass: happen 實現；發生
6 nectar ['nɛktər] (n.) the drink of the gods 神酒；瓊漿玉液
7 ambrosia [æm'brouʒə] (n.) the food eaten by god
神仙食品；仙饌

The Myth of
Prometheus

015   Ah, how very poor and wretched[8] they were! He
found them living in caves and in holes of the earth,
shivering[9] with the cold because there was no fire, dying
of starvation, hunted by wild beasts and by one another—
the most miserable of all living creatures.

"If they only had fire," said Prometheus to himself, "they
could at least warm themselves and cook their food; and
after a while they could learn to make tools and build
themselves houses. Without fire, they are worse off[10] than
the beasts."

Then he went boldly to Jupiter and begged him to
give fire to men, that so they might have a little comfort
through the long, dreary[11] months of winter.

"Not a spark[12] will I give," said Jupiter. "No, indeed! Why,
if men had fire they might become strong and wise like
ourselves, and after a while they would drive us out of our
kingdom. Let them shiver with cold, and let them live like
the beasts. It is best for them to be poor and ignorant[13],
that so we Mighty Ones may thrive[14] and be happy."

Prometheus made no answer; but he had set his heart on helping mankind, and he did not give up. He turned away, and left Jupiter and his mighty company forever.

As he was walking by the shore of the sea he found a reed[15], or, as some say, a tall stalk[16] of fennel[17], growing; and when he had broken it off he saw that its hollow center was filled with a dry, soft pith[18] which would burn slowly and keep on fire a long time. He took the long stalk in his hands, and started with it towards the dwelling of the sun in the far east.

8 wretched ['retʃɪd] (a.) unhappy; miserable 不幸的
9 shiver ['ʃɪvər] (v.) to tremble or shake involuntarily 顫抖
10 worse off: to be poorer or in a more difficult situation 每況愈下的
11 dreary ['drɪri] (a.) causing sadness or gloom 陰鬱的
12 spark [spɑːrk] (n.) a hot and glowing material thrown off by burning wood 火花；火星
13 ignorant ['ɪgnərənt] (a.) without knowledge or education 無知的
14 thrive [θraɪv] (v.) to grow, develop or be successful 繁榮；興旺
15 reed [riːd] (n.) a tall water plant 蘆葦
16 stalk [stɔːk] (n.) plant stem 花柄；莖
17 fennel ['fɛnl] (n.) a perennial European herb 茴香
18 pith [pɪθ] (n.) the soft white inner part of the stem of some plants 木髓

"The glowing, golden orb was rising from the earth and beginning his daily journey through the sky."

016

"Mankind shall have fire in spite of the tyrant who sits on the mountain top," he said.

He reached the place of the sun in the early morning just as the glowing, golden orb[19] was rising from the earth and beginning his daily journey through the sky. He touched the end of the long reed to the flames, and the dry pith caught on fire and burned slowly. Then he turned and hastened back to his own land, carrying with him the precious spark hidden in the hollow center of the plant.

He called some of the shivering men from their caves and built a fire for them, and showed them how to warm themselves by it and how to build other fires from the coals[20]. Soon there was a cheerful blaze[21] in every rude home in the land, and men and women gathered round it and were warm and happy, and thankful to Prometheus for the wonderful gift which he had brought to them from the sun.

---

19 orb [ɔːrb] (n.) a sphere or globe 球狀物
20 coal [koʊl] (n.) black rock used as fuel 煤
21 blaze [bleɪz] (n.) a large strong fire 火焰;熊熊燃燒

It was not long until they learned to cook their food and so to eat like men instead of like beasts. They began at once to leave off their wild and savage habits; and instead of lurking[22] in the dark places of the world, they came out into the open air and the bright sunlight, and were glad because life had been given to them.

After that, Prometheus taught them, little by little, a thousand things. He showed them how to build houses of wood and stone, and how to tame[23] sheep and cattle and make them useful, and how to plow[24] and sow[25] and reap[26], and how to protect themselves from the storms of winter and the beasts of the woods.

Then he showed them how to dig in the earth for copper and iron, and how to melt the ore[27], and how to hammer[28] it into shape and fashion from it the tools and weapons which they needed in peace and war; and when he saw how happy the world was becoming he cried out:

"A new Golden Age shall come, brighter and better by far than the old!"

---

22 lurk [lɜːrk] (v.) to be hidden; to sneak about 偷偷地行動
23 tame [teɪm] (v.) to make a wild animal tame 馴養
24 plow [plaʊ] (v.) to cut or turn over by using a plow 耕田；犁田
25 sow [soʊ] (v.) to plant seed for 播種
26 reap [riːp] (v.) to gather or take a crop, harvest, etc. 收割
27 ore [ɔːr] (n.) rock from which metal can be obtained 礦石
28 hammer ['hæmər] (v.) to hit or strike with a hammer 錘打

2 The First Woman: Pandora

018 Things might have gone on very happily indeed, and the Golden Age might really have come again, had it not been for Jupiter. But one day, when he chanced to look down upon the earth, he saw the fires burning, and the people living in houses, and the flocks feeding on the hills, and the grain ripening in the fields, and this made him very angry.

"Who has done all this?" he asked.

And some one answered, "Prometheus!"

"What! that young Titan!" he cried. "Well, I will punish him in a way that will make him wish I had shut him up in the prison-house with his kinsfolk[1]. But as for those puny[2] men, let them keep their fire. I will make them ten times more miserable than they were before they had it."

Of course it would be easy enough to deal with Prometheus at any time, and so Jupiter was in no great haste about it. He made up his mind to distress[3] mankind first; and he thought of a plan for doing it in a very strange, roundabout[4] way.

In the first place, he ordered his blacksmith Vulcan, whose forge was in the crater[5] of a burning mountain, to take a lump[6] of clay which he gave him, and mold[7] it into the form of a woman.

---

1 kinsfolk ['kɪnzfoʊk] (n.) somebody's relatives （總稱）親人
2 puny ['pjuːnɪ] (a.) small and weak 弱小的
3 distress [dɪ'strɛs] (v.) upset somebody 使悲痛；使苦惱
4 roundabout ['raʊndəbaʊt] (a.) indirect 繞道的；迂迴的
5 crater ['kreɪtər] (n.) volcano summit 火山口
6 lump [lʌmp] (n.) a large piece of something without definite shape 一堆；一團
7 mold [moʊld] (v.) become moldy 塑造成……

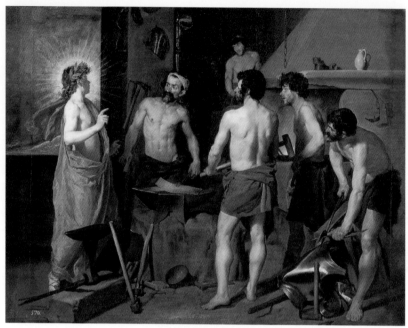

The Forge of Vulcan

〔019〕 Vulcan did as he was bidden[8]; and when he had finished the image, he carried it up to Jupiter, who was sitting among the clouds with all the Mighty Folk around him. It was nothing but a mere lifeless body, but the great blacksmith had given it a form more perfect than that of any statue[9] that has ever been made.

"Come now!" said Jupiter, "let us all give some goodly gift to this woman;" and he began by giving her life.

Then the others came in their turn, each with a gift for the marvelous creature. One gave her beauty; and another a pleasant voice; and another good manners; and another a kind heart; and another skill in many arts; and, lastly, some one gave her curiosity.

Then they called her Pandora, which means the all-gifted, because she had received gifts from them all.

"They called her Pandora, which means the all-gifted."

8 bid [bɪd] (v.) order somebody 吩咐
9 statue ['stætʃuː] (n.) a sculpture representing a human or animal雕像

Pandora was so beautiful and so wondrously gifted that no one could help loving her. When the Mighty Folk had admired her for a time, they gave her to Mercury, the light-footed; and he led her down the mountain side to the place where Prometheus and his brother were living and toiling[10] for the good of mankind.

He met Epimetheus first, and said to him: "Epimetheus, here is a beautiful woman, whom Jupiter has sent to you to be your wife."

Prometheus had often warned his brother to beware of any gift that Jupiter might send, for he knew that the mighty tyrant could not be trusted; but when Epimetheus saw Pandora, how lovely and wise she was, he forgot all warnings, and took her home to live with him and be his wife.

10 toil [tɔɪl] (v.) work hard 努力工作

3 Pandora's Box

Pandora's Box

(021) Pandora was very happy in her new home; and even Prometheus, when he saw her, was pleased with her loveliness. She had brought with her a golden casket[1], which Jupiter had given her at parting[2], and which he had told her held many precious things; but wise Athena, the queen of the air, had warned her never, never to open it, nor look at the things inside.

---

1 casket ['kæskɪt] (n.) a small decorated box in which you keep jewellery 首飾盒
2 parting ['pɑːrtɪŋ] (n.) leaving 離別

"They must be jewels," she said to herself; and then she thought of how they would add to her beauty if only she could wear them. "Why did Jupiter give them to me if I should never use them, nor so much as look at them?" she asked.

The more she thought about the golden casket, the more curious she was to see what was in it; and every day she took it down from its shelf and felt of the lid, and tried to peer³ inside of it without opening it.

"Why should I care for what Athena told me?" she said at last. "She is not beautiful, and jewels would be of no use to her. I think that I will look at them, at any rate. Athena will never know. Nobody else will ever know."

She opened the lid a very little, just to peep inside. All at once there was a whirring⁴, rustling⁵ sound, and before she could shut it down again, out flew ten thousand strange creatures with death-like faces and gaunt⁶ and dreadful forms, such as nobody in all the world had ever seen.

They fluttered[7] for a little while about the room, and then flew away to find dwelling-places wherever there were homes of men. They were diseases and cares; for up to that time mankind had not had any kind of sickness, nor felt any troubles of mind, nor worried about what the morrow[8] might bring forth.

These creatures flew into every house, and, without any one seeing them, nestled down in the bosoms of men and women and children, and put an end to all their joy.

3 peer [pɪr] (v.) look searchingly 盯著看
4 whir [wɜːr] (v.) make a swishing sound 呼呼作聲地飛或轉
5 rustle ['rʌsəl] (v.) make a dry crackling sound 沙沙作響
6 gaunt [gɔːnt] (a.) very thin especially from disease 憔悴的
7 flutter ['flʌtər] (v.) to flap the wings rapidly 振翼；拍翅
8 morrow ['mɔːroʊ] (n.) next day 翌日

How Diseases of Cares
Came Among Men

And ever since that day they have been flitting[9] and creeping[10], unseen and unheard, over all the land, bringing pain and sorrow and death into every household.

If Pandora had not shut down the lid so quickly, things would have gone much worse. But she closed it just in time to keep the last of the evil creatures from getting out. The name of this creature was *Foreboding*[11], and although he was almost half out of the casket, Pandora pushed him back and shut the lid so tight that he could never escape.

If he had gone out into the world, men would have known from childhood just what troubles were going to come to them every day of their lives, and they would never have had any joy or hope so long as they lived.

And this was the way in which Jupiter sought to make mankind more miserable than they had been before Prometheus had befriended them.

---

9 flit [flɪt] (v.) to move quickly from place to place 輕快地掠過
10 creep [kriːp] (v.) move quietly 不知不覺地到來
11 foreboding [fɔːrˈboʊdɪŋ] (n.) a feeling of evil to come
    不祥的預感

4 How Prometheus Was Punished

〔025〕　The next thing that Jupiter did was to punish Prometheus for stealing fire from the sun. He bade two of his servants, whose names were Strength and Force, to seize the bold Titan and carry him to the topmost peak of the Caucasus Mountains. Then he sent the blacksmith Vulcan to bind him with iron chains and fetter[1] him to the rocks so that he could not move hand or foot.

1　fetter ['fɛtər] (v.) put fetters on somebody 上腳鐐

Prometheus Being Chained by Vulcan

026 Vulcan did not like to do this, for he was a friend of Prometheus, and yet he did not dare to disobey. And so the great friend of men, who had given them fire and lifted them out of their wretchedness and shown them how to live, was chained to the mountain peak.

And there he hung, with the storm-winds whistling always around him, and the pitiless hail[2] beating in his face, and fierce[3] eagles shrieking[4] in his ears and tearing his body with their cruel claws. Yet he bore all his sufferings without a groan[5], and never would he beg for mercy or say that he was sorry for what he had done.

Prometheus Punished
for His Gift to Man

Year after year, and age after age, Prometheus hung there. Now and then old Helios, the driver of the sun car, would look down upon him and smile; now and then flocks of birds would bring him messages from far-off lands; once the ocean nymphs[6] came and sang wonderful songs in his hearing; and oftentimes men looked up to him with pitying eyes, and cried out against the tyrant who had placed him there.

2 hail [heɪl] (n.) small balls of ice and hardened snow that fall like rain 冰雹
3 fierce [fɪrs] (a.) raging and savage 兇猛的
4 shriek [ʃriːk] (v.) make shrill sound 尖叫
5 groan [groʊn] (n.) an utterance expressing pain 呻吟聲
6 nymph [nɪmf] (n.) a minor nature goddess 居於山林水澤的仙女

5 How Prometheus Was Rescued

Then, once upon a time, a white cow passed that way,—a strangely beautiful cow, with large sad eyes and a face that seemed almost human. She stopped and looked up at the cold gray peak and the giant body which was chained there. Prometheus saw her and spoke to her kindly:

"I know who you are," he said. "You are Io who was once a fair and happy maiden in distant Argos; and now, because of the tyrant Jupiter and his jealous queen, you are doomed[1] to wander from land to land in that unhuman form. But do not lose hope. Go on to the southward and then to the west; and after many days you shall come to the great river Nile. There you shall again become a maiden, but fairer and more beautiful than before; and you shall become the wife of the king of that land, and shall give birth to a son, from whom shall spring[2] the hero who will break my chains and set me free. As for me, I bide in patience the day which not even Jupiter can hasten or delay. Farewell!"

---

1 doom [du:m] (v.) make certain of the failure or destruction 注定
2 spring [sprɪŋ] (v.) be descended from a person or family 出現

Heracles Rescuing Prometheus

Poor Io would have spoken, but she could not. Her sorrowful eyes looked once more at the suffering hero on the peak, and then she turned and began her long and tiresome journey to the land of the Nile.

Ages passed, and at last a great hero whose name was Hercules came to the land of the Caucasus. In spite of Jupiter's dread thunderbolts and fearful storms of snow and sleet³, he climbed the rugged⁴ mountain peak.

---

3 sleet [sliːt] (n.) partially melted snow 凍雨
4 rugged ['rʌgɪd] (a.) rocky and steep 崎嶇的

Hercules Wrestling With Death

He slew[5] the fierce eagles that had so long tormented[6] the helpless prisoner on those craggy[7] heights; and with a mighty blow, he broke the fetters of Prometheus and set the grand old hero free.

"I knew that you would come," said Prometheus. "Ten generations ago I spoke of you to Io, who was afterwards the queen of the land of the Nile."

"And Io," said Hercules, "was the mother of the race from which I am sprung."

---

5 slay [sleɪ] (v.) kill intentionally 殺死
6 torment ['tɔ:rment] (v.) treat cruelly 折磨
7 craggy ['krægi] (a.) rocky and steep 崎嶇的

4 The Flood and the Creation of Humans

The Flood:
Destroying All Humans

029 In those very early times there was a man named
Deucalion, and he was the son of Prometheus. He was only
a common man and not a Titan like his great father, and
yet he was known far and wide for his good deeds and the
uprightness[1] of his life. His wife's name was Pyrrha, and
she was one of the fairest of the daughters of men.

After Jupiter had bound Prometheus on Mount
Caucasus and had sent diseases and cares into the world,
men became very, very wicked. They no longer built
houses and tended[2] their flocks and lived together in
peace; but every man was at war with his neighbor, and
there was no law nor safety in all the land.

　Things were in much worse case now than they had been before Prometheus had come among men, and that was just what Jupiter wanted. But as the world became wickeder and wickeder every day, he began to grow weary of seeing so much bloodshed[3] and of hearing the cries of the oppressed and the poor.

"These men," he said to his mighty company, "are nothing but a source of trouble. When they were good and happy, we felt afraid lest[4] they should become greater than ourselves; and now they are so terribly wicked that we are in worse danger than before. There is only one thing to be done with them, and that is to destroy them every one."

So he sent a great rain-storm upon the earth, and it rained day and night for a long time; and the sea was filled to the brim[5], and the water ran over the land and covered first the plains and then the forests and then the hills. But men kept on fighting and robbing, even while the rain was pouring down and the sea was coming up over the land.

1　uprightness ['ʌpraɪtnɪs] (n.) honest and moral 正直
2　tend [tend] (v.) to care for something or someone 照料
3　bloodshed ['blʌdʃed] (n.) killing and violence 殺人；流血
4　lest [lest] (conj.) for fear that 擔心
5　brim [brɪm] (n.) top edge of a container（容器的）邊緣

No one but Deucalion, the son of Prometheus, was ready for such a storm. He had never joined in any of the wrong doings of those around him, and had often told them that unless they left off their evil ways there would be a day of reckoning[6] in the end. Once every year he had gone to the land of the Caucasus to talk with his father, who was hanging chained to the mountain peak.

"The day is coming," said Prometheus, "when Jupiter will send a flood to destroy mankind from the earth. Be sure that you are ready for it, my son."

And so when the rain began to fall, Deucalion drew from its shelter[7] a boat which he had built for just such a time. He called fair Pyrrha, his wife, and the two sat in the boat and were floated safely on the rising waters.

Day and night, day and night, I cannot tell how long, the boat drifted[8] hither and thither. The tops of the trees were hidden by the flood, and then the hills and then the mountains; and Deucalion and Pyrrha could see nothing anywhere but water, water, water—and they knew that all the people in the land had been drowned.

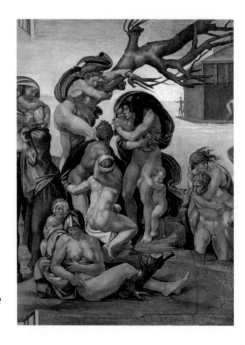

After a while the rain stopped falling, and the clouds cleared away, and the blue sky and the golden sun came out overhead. Then the water began to sink very fast and to run off the land towards the sea; and early the very next day the boat was drifted high upon a mountain called Parnassus, and Deucalion and Pyrrha stepped out upon the dry land.

After that, it was only a short time until the whole country was laid bare, and the trees shook their leafy branches in the wind, and the fields were carpeted with grass and flowers more beautiful than in the days before the flood.

But Deucalion and Pyrrha were very sad, for they knew that they were the only persons who were left alive in all the land. At last they started to walk down the mountain side towards the plain, wondering what would become of them now, all alone as they were in the wide world.

6 day of reckoning: time of punishment or retribution 果報現前的時候
7 shelter ['ʃɛltər] (n.) protection from danger 避難處
8 drift [drɪft] (v.) be carried along 漂流

2 The Creation of Human Beings

🎧 **033** While they were talking and trying to think what they should do, they heard a voice behind them. They turned and saw a noble young prince standing on one of the rocks above them.

He was very tall, with blue eyes and yellow hair. There were wings on his shoes and on his cap, and in his hands he bore[1] a staff[2] with golden serpents[3] twined[4] around it. They knew at once that he was Mercury, the swift messenger of the Mighty Ones, and they waited to hear what he would say.

"Is there anything that you wish?" he asked. "Tell me, and you shall have whatever you desire."

"We should like, above all things," said Deucalion, "to see this land full of people once more; for without neighbors and friends, the world is a very lonely place indeed."

"Go on down the mountain," said Mercury, "and as you go, cast[5] the bones of your mother over your shoulders behind you;" and, with these words, he leaped into the air and was seen no more.

"What did he mean?" asked Pyrrha.

"Surely I do not know," said Deucalion. "But let us think a moment. Who is our mother, if it is not the Earth, from whom all living things have sprung? And yet what could he mean by the bones of our mother?"

"Perhaps he meant the stones of the earth," said Pyrrha. "Let us go on down the mountain, and as we go, let us pick up the stones in our path and throw them over our shoulders behind us."

"It is rather a silly thing to do," said Deucalion; "and yet there can be no harm in it, and we shall see what will happen."

And so they walked on, down the steep[6] slope[7] of Mount Parnassus, and as they walked they picked up the loose stones in their way and cast them over their shoulders; and strange to say, the stones which Deucalion threw sprang up as full-grown men, strong, and handsome, and brave; and the stones which Pyrrha threw sprang up as full-grown women, lovely and fair.

1 bear [ber] (v.) have 佩帶
2 staff [stæf] (n.) a rod carried as a symbol 權杖
3 serpent ['sɜːrpənt] (n.) a snake 大蛇
4 twine [twaɪn] (v.) to wrap round an object several times 盤繞
5 cast [kæst] (v.) to throw something 投擲
6 steep [stiːp] (a.) rising or falling at a sharp angle 陡峭的
7 slope [sloʊp] (n.) side of hill or mountain 坡

Deucalion and Pyrrha

035 When at last they reached the plain they found themselves at the head of a noble company of human beings, all eager[8] to serve them.

So Deucalion became their king, and he set them in homes, and taught them how to till[9] the ground, and how to do many useful things; and the land was filled with people who were happier and far better than those who had dwelt there before the flood. And they named the country Hellas, after Hellen, the son of Deucalion and Pyrrha; and the people are to this day called Hellenes.

But we call the country GREECE.

---

8 eager ['iːgər] (a.) wanting very much to do or have something 渴望的

9 till [tɪl] (v.) to prepare and use land for growing crops 耕種

5 The Story of Io

Changing Io
Into a White Cow

036 In the town of Argos there lived a maiden[1] named Io. She was so fair and good that all who knew her loved her, and said that there was no one like her in the whole world. When Jupiter, in his home in the clouds, heard of her, he came down to Argos to see her.

Jupiter and Io

She pleased him so much, and was so kind and wise, that he came back the next day and the next and the next; and by and by he stayed in Argos all the time so that he might be near her. She did not know who he was, but thought that he was a prince from some far-off land; for he came in the guise[2] of a young man, and did not look like the great king of earth and sky that he was.

But Juno, the queen who lived with Jupiter and shared his throne[3] in the midst of the clouds, did not love Io at all.

When she heard why Jupiter stayed from home so long, she made up her mind to do the fair girl all the harm that she could; and one day she went down to Argos to try what could be done.

Jupiter saw her while she was yet a great way off, and he knew why she had come. So, to save Io from her, he changed the maiden to a white cow. He thought that when Juno had gone back home, it would not be hard to give Io her own form again.

But when the queen saw the cow, she knew that it was Io.

"Oh, what a fine cow you have there!" she said. "Give her to me, good Jupiter, give her to me!"

Jupiter did not like to do this; but she coaxed[4] so hard that at last he gave up, and let her have the cow for her own. He thought that it would not be long till he could get her away from the queen, and change her to a girl once more.

1 maiden ['meɪdn] (n.) a girl or young woman 少女
2 guise [gaɪz] (n.) deceptive outward appearance 偽裝
3 throne [θroʊn] (n.) the special chair used by a ruler 寶座
4 coax [koʊks] (v.) persuade gently 哄誘

Juno
Discovering
Jupiter With Io

🎧 038   But Juno was too wise to trust him. She took the cow by her horns, and led her out of the town.

"Now, my sweet maid[5]," she said, "I will see that you stay in this shape as long as you live."

Then she gave the cow in charge of a strange watchman named Argus, who had, not two eyes only, as you and I have, but ten times ten. And Argus led the cow to a grove[6], and tied her by a long rope to a tree, where she had to stand and eat grass, and cry, "Moo! moo!" from morn[7] till night; and when the sun had set, and it was dark, she lay down on the cold ground and wept, and cried, "Moo! moo!" till she fell asleep.

---

5   maid [meɪd] (n.) young unmarried woman 未婚少女
6   grove [groʊv] (n.) group of trees 小樹林
7   morn [mɔːrn] (n.) morning 早晨

2 Argus and Peacock

But no kind friend heard her, and no one came to help her; for none but Jupiter and Juno knew that the white cow who stood in the grove was Io, whom all the world loved.

Day in and day out, Argus, who was all eyes, sat on a hill close by and kept watch; and you could not say that he went to sleep at all, for while half of his eyes were shut, the other half were wide awake, and thus they slept and watched by turns.

Jupiter was grieved[1] when he saw to what a hard life Io had been doomed, and he tried to think of some plan to set her free.

---

1 grieved [griːvd] (a.) feeling very sad 傷心的

Mercury, Argus and Io

🎧 040 　One day he called sly[2] Mercury, who had wings on his shoes, and bade him go and lead the cow away from the grove where she was kept.

Mercury went down and stood near the foot of the hill where Argus sat, and began to play sweet tunes on his flute[3]. This was just what the strange watchman liked to hear; and so he called to Mercury, and asked him to come up and sit by his side and play still other tunes.

Mercury did as he wished, and played such strains[4] of sweet music as no one in all the world has heard from that day to this.

2　sly [slaɪ] (a.) seeming to know secrets 悄悄的
3　flute [fluːt] (n.) a tube-shaped musical instrument 笛子
4　strain [streɪn] (n.) a musical theme or melody 曲子；旋律

And as he played, queer[5] old Argus lay down upon the grass and listened, and thought that he had not had so great a treat in all his life. But by and by those sweet sounds wrapped him in so strange a spell[6] that all his eyes closed at once, and he fell into a deep sleep.

Mercury Piping to Argus

This was just what Mercury wished. It was not a brave thing to do, and yet he drew a long, sharp knife from his belt and cut off the head of poor Argus while he slept. Then he ran down the hill to loose the cow and lead her to the town.

---

5 queer [kwɪr] (a.) strange or unusual 古怪的
6 spell [spɛl] (n.) words with supposed magical power 咒語

Juno Receiving the Head of Argos

041 But Juno had seen him kill her watchman, and she met him on the road. She cried out to him and told him to let the cow go; and her face was so full of wrath[7] that, as soon as he saw her, he turned and fled, and left poor Io to her fate.

Juno was so much grieved when she saw Argus stretched dead in the grass on the hilltop, that she took his hundred eyes and set them in the tail of a peacock; and there you may still see them to this day.

7 wrath [ræθ] (n.) strong anger 憤怒

3 Gadfly and Bosphorus

Then she found a great gadfly[1], as big as a bat, and sent it to buzz[2] in the white cow's ears, and to bite her and sting her so that she could have no rest all day long.

Poor Io ran from place to place to get out of its way; but it buzzed and buzzed, and stung and stung, till she was wild with fright and pain, and wished that she were dead.

Day after day she ran, now through the thick woods, now in the long grass that grew on the treeless plains, and now by the shore of the sea.

By and by she came to a narrow neck of the sea, and, since the land on the other side looked as though she might find rest there, she leaped into the waves and swam across; and that place has been called Bosphorus—a word which means the Sea of the Cow—from that time till now, and you will find it so marked on the maps which you use at school.

---

1 gadfly ['gædflaɪ] (n.) any of various large flies
  that annoy livestock 牛虻
2 buzz [bʌz] (v.) make steady humming sound 嗡嗡叫

4 Meeting Prometheus

After a time she came to a place where there were high mountains with snow-capped[1] peaks which seemed to touch the sky. There she stopped to rest a while; and she looked up at the calm, cold cliffs[2] above her and wished that she might die where all was so grand[3] and still.

But as she looked she saw a giant form stretched upon the rocks midway between earth and sky, and she knew at once that it was Prometheus, the young Titan, whom Jupiter had chained there because he had given fire to men.

"My sufferings are not so great as his," she thought; and her eyes were filled with tears.

Then Prometheus looked down and spoke to her, and his voice was very mild and kind.

"I know who you are," he said; and then he told her not to lose hope, but to go south and then west, and she would by and by find a place in which to rest.

She would have thanked him if she could; but when she tried to speak she could only say, "Moo! moo!"

Then Prometheus went on and told her that the time would come when she should be given her own form again, and that she should live to be the mother of a race of heroes.

"As for me," said he, "I bide the time in patience, for I know that one of those heroes will break my chains and set me free. Farewell!"

---

1 snow-capped ['snoʊkæpt] (a.) capped with a covering of snow
   積雪蓋頂的
2 cliff [klɪf] (n.) a high steep rock or ice face 懸崖
3 grand [grænd] (a.) splendid in style and appearance
   高貴的；堂皇的

5 Coming to Egypt

045 Then Io, with a brave heart, left the great Titan and journeyed, as he had told her, first south and then west. The gadfly was worse now than before, but she did not fear it half so much, for her heart was full of hope.

For a whole year she wandered, and at last she came to the land of Egypt in Africa. She felt so tired now that she could go no farther, and so she lay down near the bank of the great River Nile to rest.

All this time Jupiter might have helped her had he not been so much afraid of Juno. But now it so chanced that when the poor cow lay down by the bank of the Nile, Queen Juno, in her high house in the clouds, also lay down to take a nap.

As soon as she was sound asleep, Jupiter like a flash[1] of light sped over the sea to Egypt.

Jupiter and Io

---

1 flash [flæʃ] (n.) sudden burst of light 閃光

He killed the cruel gadfly and threw it into the river. Then he stroked the cow's head with his hand, and the cow was seen no more; but in her place stood the young girl Io, pale and frail[2], but fair and good as she had been in her old home in the town of Argos. Jupiter said not a word, nor even showed himself to the tired, trembling maiden.

He hurried back with all speed to his high home in the clouds, for he feared that Juno might waken and find out what he had done.

---

2 frail [freɪl] (a.) weak or unhealthy 身體虛弱的

The people of Egypt were kind to Io, and gave her a home in their sunny land; and by and by the king of Egypt asked her to be his wife, and made her his queen; and she lived a long and happy life in his marble palace on the bank of the Nile.

Ages afterward, the great-grandson of the great-grandson of Io's great-grandson broke the chains of Prometheus and set that mighty friend of mankind free.

The name of the hero was Hercules.

Hercules

6 The Wonderful Weaver

Arachne:
The Boastful Weaver

047 There was a young girl in Greece whose name was Arachne. Her face was pale but fair, and her eyes were big and blue, and her hair was long and like gold. All that she cared to do from morn till noon was to sit in the sun and spin[1]; and all that she cared to do from noon till night was to sit in the shade and weave.

And oh, how fine and fair were the things which she wove in her loom[2]! Flax[3], wool, silk—she worked with them all; and when they came from her hands, the cloth which she had made of them was so thin and soft and bright that men came from all parts of the world to see it.

1 spin [spɪn] (v.) create yarn from raw materials 紡紗
2 loom [luːm] (n.) a textile machine for weaving yarn into a textile 織布機
3 flax [flæks] (n.) fiber of the flax plant 亞麻

And they said that cloth so rare could not be made of flax, or wool, or silk, but that the warp⁴ was of rays of sunlight and the woof⁵ was of threads⁶ of gold.

Then as, day by day, the girl sat in the sun and span, or sat in the shade and wove, she said: "In all the world there is no yarn⁷ so fine as mine, and in all the world there is no cloth so soft and smooth, nor silk so bright and rare."

"Who taught you to spin and weave so well?" some one asked.

---

4 warp [wɔ:rp] (n.) threads running lengthwise〔紡〕經紗
5 woof [wʊf] (n.) a woven fabric, or its texture〔紡〕緯紗
6 thread [θrɛd] (n.) (a length of) a very thin fiber 線
7 yarn [jɑ:rn] (n.) thread used for making cloth or for knitting 紗線

"No one taught me," she said. "I learned how to do it as I sat in the sun and the shade; but no one showed me."

"But it may be that Athena, the queen of the air, taught you, and you did not know it."

"Athena, the queen of the air? Bah!" said Arachne. "How could she teach me? Can she spin such skeins[8] of yarn as these? Can she weave goods like mine? I should like to see her try. I can teach her a thing or two."

She looked up and saw in the doorway a tall woman wrapped in a long cloak[9]. Her

Athena

face was fair to see, but stern[10], oh, so stern! and her gray eyes were so sharp and bright that Arachne could not meet her gaze[11].

"Arachne," said the woman, "I am Athena, the queen of the air, and I have heard your boast[12]. Do you still mean to say that I have not taught you how to spin and weave?"

"No one has taught me," said Arachne; "and I thank no one for what I know;" and she stood up, straight and proud, by the side of her loom.

"And do you still think that you can spin and weave as well as I?" said Athena.

Arachne's cheeks grew pale, but she said: "Yes. I can weave as well as you."

"Then let me tell you what we will do," said Athena. "Three days from now we will both weave; you on your loom, and I on mine. We will ask all the world to come and see us; and great Jupiter, who sits in the clouds, shall be the judge. And if your work is best, then I will weave no more so long as the world shall last; but if my work is best, then you shall never use loom or spindle[13] or distaff[14] again. Do you agree to this?"

"I agree," said Arachne.

"It is well," said Athena. And she was gone.

---

8 skein [skeɪn] (n.) a length of wool or thread loosely wound into the shape of a ring（紗、線等的）一束

9 cloak [kloʊk] (n.) a loose sleeveless outer garment that fastens at the neck 斗篷；披風

10 stern [stɜːrn] (a.) serious and strict 嚴峻的

11 gaze [geɪz] (n.) a long fixed look 注視

12 boast [boʊst] (n.) excessively proud statement 自誇

13 spindle ['spɪndl] (n.) a part of a machine around which something turns 紡錘

14 distaff ['dɪstæf] (n.) rod for unspun thread 紡紗桿

2 The Contest in Weaving

051 When the time came for the contest in weaving, all the world was there to see it, and great Jupiter sat among the clouds and looked on.

Arachne had set up her loom in the shade of a mulberry¹ tree, where butterflies were flitting and grasshoppers chirping² all through the livelong³ day. But Athena had set up her loom in the sky, where the breezes were blowing and the summer sun was shining; for she was the queen of the air.

---

1 mulberry ['mʌlberi] (n.) a small soft purple fruit 桑樹
2 chirp [tʃɜːrp] (v.) a short high-pitched sound, especially as made by a bird（小鳥）啁啾
3 livelong ['lɪvlɔːŋ] (a.) long and tedious 漫長的

Then Arachne took her skeins of finest silk and began to weave. And she wove a web of marvelous beauty, so thin and light that it would float in the air, and yet so strong that it could hold a lion in its meshes[4]; and the threads of warp and woof were of many colors, so beautifully arranged and mingled one with another that all who saw were filled with delight.

"No wonder that the maiden boasted of her skill," said the people.

And Jupiter himself nodded.

Then Athena began to weave. And she took of the sunbeams that gilded[5] the mountain top, and of the snowy fleece[6] of the summer clouds, and of the blue ether[7] of the summer sky, and of the bright green of the summer fields, and of the royal purple of the autumn woods,—and what do you suppose she wove?

4 mesh [mɛʃ] (n.) net 羅網；陷阱
5 gild [ɡɪld] (v.) cover something with gold 塗上金色
6 fleece [fliːs] (n.) the wool of a sheep 羊毛
7 ether [ˈiːθər] (n.) the clear sky; the upper air 蒼穹

The web which she wove in the sky was full of enchanting[8] pictures of flowers and gardens, and of castles and towers, and of mountain heights, and of men and beasts, and of giants and dwarfs[9], and of the mighty beings who dwell in the clouds with Jupiter. And those who looked upon it were so filled with wonder and delight, that they forgot all about the beautiful web which Arachne had woven.

And Arachne herself was ashamed and afraid when she saw it; and she hid her face in her hands and wept.

"Oh, how can I live," she cried, "now that I must never again use loom or spindle or distaff?"

And she kept on, weeping and weeping and weeping, and saying, "How can I live?"

Then, when Athena saw that the poor maiden would never have any joy unless she were allowed to spin and weave, she took pity on her and said:

---

8 enchanting [ɪn'tʃæntɪŋ] (a.) very pleasant 迷人的
9 dwarf [dwɔːrf] (n.) a person who is abnormally small 小矮人

"I would free you from your bargain if I could, but that is a thing which no one can do. You must hold to your agreement never to touch loom or spindle again. And yet, since you will never be happy unless you can spin and weave, I will give you a new form so that you can carry on your work with neither spindle nor loom."

Then she touched Arachne with the tip of the spear which she sometimes carried; and the maiden was changed at once into a nimble[10] spider, which ran into a shady place in the grass and began merrily[11] to spin and weave a beautiful web.

I have heard it said that all the spiders which have been in the world since then are the children of Arachne; but I doubt whether this be true. Yet, for aught I know, Arachne still lives and spins and weaves; and the very next spider that you see may be she herself.

---

10 nimble ['nɪmbəl] (a.) fast and light in movement 敏捷的
11 merrily ['merɪli] (adv.) in a joyous manner 快樂地

7 Apollo: the Lord of the Silver Bow

Leto's Escape and Dolphin

054 Long before you or I or anybody else can remember, there lived with the Mighty Folk on the mountain top a fair and gentle lady named Leto. So fair and gentle was she that Jupiter loved her and made her his wife.

But when Juno, the queen of earth and sky, heard of this, she was very angry; and she drove Leto down from the mountain and bade all things great and small refuse to help her.

So Leto fled[1] like a wild deer from land to land and could find no place in which to rest. She could not stop, for then the ground would quake under her feet, and the stones would cry out, "Go on! go on!" and birds and beasts and trees and men would join in the cry; and no one in all the wide land took pity on her.

One day she came to the sea, and as she fled along the beach she lifted up her hands and called aloud to great Neptune to help her.

---

1 flee [fl:i] (v.) run away quickly 逃走

Neptune

055 Neptune, the king of the sea, heard her and was kind to her. He sent a huge fish, called a dolphin, to bear her away from the cruel land; and the fish, with Leto sitting on his broad[2] back, swam through the waves to Delos, a little island which lay floating on top of the water like a boat.

There the gentle lady found rest and a home; for the place belonged to Neptune, and the words of cruel Juno were not obeyed there. Neptune put four marble pillars under the island so that it should rest firm upon them; and then he chained[3] it fast, with great chains which reached to the bottom of the sea, so that the waves might never move it.

2 broad [brɔːd] (a.) wide 寬闊的

3 chain [tʃeɪn] (v.) fasten something or somebody with chain 用鎖鏈拴住

2 The Birth of Apollo and Diana

By and by twin babes were born to Leto in Delos. One was a boy whom she called Apollo, the other a girl whom she named Artemis, or Diana.

When the news of their birth was carried to Jupiter and the Mighty Folk on the mountain top, all the world was glad. The sun danced on the waters, and singing swans flew seven times round the island of Delos. The moon stooped[1] to kiss the babes in their cradle; and Juno forgot her anger, and bade all things on the earth and in the sky be kind to Leto.

The two children grew very fast. Apollo became tall and strong and graceful; his face was as bright as the sunbeams; and he carried joy and gladness with him wherever he went.

Jupiter gave him a pair of swans and a golden chariot[2], which bore him over sea and land wherever he wanted to go; and he gave him a lyre[3] on which he played the sweetest music that was ever heard, and a silver bow with sharp arrows which never missed the mark[4].

When Apollo went out into the world, and men came to know about him, he was called by some the Bringer of Light, by others the Master of Song, and by still others the Lord of the Silver Bow.

Apollo

Diana

057 Diana was tall and graceful, too, and very handsome. She liked to wander in the woods with her maids, who were called nymphs; she took kind care of the timid deer and the helpless creatures which live among the trees; and she delighted in hunting wolves and bears and other savage beasts. She was loved and feared in every land, and Jupiter made her the queen of the green woods and the chase.

---

1 stoop [stuːp] (v.) bend over or down 屈身；彎腰
2 chariot ['tʃæriət] (n.) ancient two-wheeled vehicle 雙輪戰車
3 lyre [laɪr] (n.) a harp used by ancient Greeks 七弦豎琴
4 mark [mɑːrk] (n.) target 靶子；目標

3 The Center of the World: Parnassus

 058 "Where is the center of the world?"

This is the question which some one asked Jupiter as he sat in his golden hall. Of course the mighty ruler of earth and sky was too wise to be puzzled[1] by so simple a thing, but he was too busy to answer it at once.

So he said: "Come again in one year from today, and I will show you the very place."

Then Jupiter took two swift eagles which could fly faster than the storm-wind, and trained them till the speed of the one was the same as that of the other.

At the end of the year he said to his servants: "Take this eagle to the eastern rim of the earth, where the sun rises out of the sea; and carry his fellow to the far west, where the ocean is lost in darkness and nothing lies beyond. Then, when I give you the sign, loosen both at the same moment."

The servants did as they were bidden, and carried the eagles to the outermost[2] edges of the world.

---

1   puzzled ['pʌzəld] (a.) confused 搞糊塗的
2   outermost ['aʊtərmoʊst] (a.) farthest away 最外邊的

Then Jupiter clapped his hands. The lightning flashed, the thunder rolled, and the two swift birds were set free.

One of them flew straight back towards the west, the other flew straight back towards the east; and no arrow ever sped faster from the bow than did these two birds from the hands of those who had held them.

On and on they went like shooting stars[3] rushing to meet each other; and Jupiter and all his mighty company sat amid the clouds and watched their flight. Nearer and nearer they came, but they swerved[4] not to the right nor to the left.

Nearer and nearer—and then with a crash like the meeting of two ships at sea, the eagles came together in midair and fell dead to the ground.

"Who asked where is the center of the world?" said Jupiter. "The spot where the two eagles lie—that is the center of the world."

They had fallen on the top of a mountain in Greece which men have ever since called Parnassus.

"If that is the center of the world," said young Apollo, "then I will make my home there, and I will build a house in that place, so that my light may be seen in all lands."

---

3 shooting star: meteor ['miːtiər] (n.) 流星
4 swerve [swɜːrv] (v.) to turn suddenly to one side 突然轉向

4 The Serpent Python and The City of Delphi

🎧060 So Apollo went down to Parnassus, and looked about for a spot in which to lay the foundations[1] of his house. The mountain itself was savage and wild, and the valley below it was lonely and dark. The few people who lived there kept themselves hidden among the rocks as if in dread of some great danger.

They told Apollo that near the foot of the mountain where the steep cliff seemed to be split in two there lived a huge serpent called the Python. This serpent often seized sheep and cattle, and sometimes even men and women and children, and carried them up to his dreadful den and devoured[2] them.

"Can no one kill this beast?" said Apollo.

And they said, "No one; and we and our children and our flocks shall all be slain[3] by him."

---

1 foundations [faʊnˈdeɪʃəns] (n.) (pl.) base 地基
2 devour [dɪˈvaʊr] (v.) to eat something quickly and hungrily 吞噬
3 slay [sleɪ] (v.) kill (slay-slew-slain) 殺死

Apollo Slays Python

Then Apollo with his silver bow in his hands went up towards the place where the Python lay. When he caught sight of Apollo, he uncoiled[4] himself, and came out to meet him.

The Python saw that his foe was no common man, and turned to flee. Then the arrow sped from the bow— and the monster was dead.

"Here I will build my house," said Apollo.

Close to the foot of the steep cliff, and beneath the spot where Jupiter's eagles had fallen, he laid the foundations; and soon where had been the lair of the Python, the white walls of Apollo's temple arose among the rocks.

Then the poor people of the land came and built their houses near by; and Apollo lived among them many years, and taught them to be gentle and wise, and showed them how to be happy. The mountain was no longer savage and wild, but was a place of music and song.

"What shall we call our city?" the people asked.

"Call it Delphi, or the Dolphin," said Apollo; "for it was a dolphin that carried my mother across the sea."

---

4 uncoil [ʌnˈkɔɪl] (v.) release from being coiled 解開

5 Apollo Chasing Daphne And Laurel

(062) In the Vale of Tempe, which lies far north of Delphi, there lived a young girl whose name was Daphne. She was a strange child, wild and shy as a fawn[1], and as fleet[2] of foot as the deer that feed on the plains. But she was as fair and good as a day in June, and none could know her but to love her.

Daphne spent the most of her time in the fields and woods, with the birds and blossoms and trees; and she liked best of all to wander along the banks of the River Peneu. Very often she would sing and talk to the river as if it were a living thing, and could hear her. The good people who knew her best said: "She is the child of the river."

"Yes, dear river," she said, "let me be your child."

1 fawn [fɔːn] (n.) young deer 幼鹿
2 fleet [fliːt] (a.) moving very fast 敏捷的

The river smiled and answered her in a way which she alone could understand; and always, after that, she called it "Father Peneus."

One day when the sun shone warm, and the air was filled with the perfume of flowers, Daphne wandered farther away from the river than she had ever gone before.

Beyond her were other hills, and then the green slopes and wooded top of great Mount Ossa. Ah, if she could only climb to the summit of Ossa, she might have a view of the sea, and of other mountains close by, and of the twin peaks of Mount Parnassus, far, far to the south!

"Good-by, Father Peneus," she said. "I am going to climb the mountain; but I will come back soon."

By and by she came to the foot of a wooded slope where there was a pretty waterfall and the ground was bespangled[3] with thousands of beautiful flowers; and she sat down there a moment to rest.

Then from the grove on the hilltop above her, came the sound of the loveliest music she had ever heard. She stood up and listened. Some one was playing on a lyre, and some one was singing.

3　bespangle [bɪˈspæŋgəl] (v.) decorate with spangles 飾以閃亮之物

Apollo and the Muses

064 She was frightened; and still the music was so charming that she could not run away.

Then, all at once, the sound ceased, and a young man, tall and fair and with a face as bright as the morning sun, came down the hillside towards her.

"Daphne!" he said; but she did not stop to hear. She turned and fled like a frightened deer, back towards the Vale of Tempe.

"Daphne!" cried the young man. She did not know that it was Apollo; she only knew that the stranger was following her, and she ran as fast as her fleet feet could carry her. No young man had ever spoken to her before, and the sound of his voice filled her heart with fear.

"She is the fairest maiden that I ever saw," said Apollo to himself. "If I could only look at her face again and speak with her, how happy I should be."

Through brake[4], through brier[5], over rocks and the trunks of fallen trees, down rugged slopes, across mountain streams, leaping, flying, panting[6], Daphne ran.

Apollo and Daphne

   She looked not once behind her, but she heard the swift
footsteps of Apollo coming always nearer; she heard the
rattle[7] of the silver bow which hung from his shoulders;
she heard his very breath, he was so close to her.

4 brake [breɪk] (n.) an area of dense undergrowth or brush 草叢
5 brier ['braɪər] (n.) tangled mass of prickly plants 荊棘
6 pant [pænt] (v.) breathe noisily 氣喘吁吁
7 rattle ['rætl] (n.) a rapid series of short loud sounds 咯咯聲

At last she was in the valley where the ground was smooth and it was easier running, but her strength was fast leaving her. Right before her, however, lay the river, white and smiling in the sunlight.

Apollo and Daphne

She stretched out her arms and cried: "O Father Peneus, save me!"

Then it seemed as though the river rose up to meet her. The air was filled with a blinding mist[8]. For a moment Apollo lost sight of the fleeing maiden. Then he saw her close by the river's bank, and so near to him that her long hair, streaming behind her, brushed his cheek.

He thought that she was about to leap into the rushing, roaring waters, and he reached out his hands to save her. But it was not the fair, timid Daphne that he caught in his arms; it was the trunk of a laurel[9] tree, its green leaves trembling in the breeze.

---

8 mist [mɪst] (n.) thin fog 霧
9 laurel ['lɔːrəl] (n.) tree or bush resembling bay 月桂樹

066 "O Daphne! Daphne!" he cried, "is this the way in which the river saves you? Does Father Peneus turn you into a tree to keep you from me?"

Whether Daphne had really been turned into a tree, I know not; nor does it matter now—it was so long ago. But Apollo believed that it was so, and hence he made a wreath of the laurel leaves and set it on his head like a crown, and said that he would wear it always in memory of the lovely maiden.

And ever after that, the laurel was Apollo's favorite tree, and, even to this day, poets and musicians are crowned with its leaves.

6 Coronis and Crow

Apollo and the Muses

067 Apollo did not care to live much of the time with his mighty kinsfolk on the mountain top. He liked better to go about from place to place and from land to land, seeing people at their work and making their lives happy.

When men first saw his fair boyish face and his soft white hands, they sneered[1] and said he was only an idle, good-for-nothing fellow. But when they heard him speak, they were so charmed that they stood, spellbound[2], to listen; and ever after that they made his words their law.

---

1 sneer [snɪr] (v.) smile contemptuously 輕蔑地笑
2 spellbound ['spelbaʊnd] (a.) having your attention completely held by something 入迷的

Apollo and the Muses

They wondered how it was that he was so wise; for it seemed to them that he did nothing but stroll[3] about, playing on his wonderful lyre and looking at the trees and blossoms and birds and bees.

But when any of them were sick they came to him, and he told them what to find in plants or stones or brooks that would heal them and make them strong again.

They noticed that he did not grow old, as others did, but that he was always young and fair.

In a mountain village beyond the Vale of Tempe, there lived a beautiful lady named Coronis. When Apollo saw her, he loved her and made her his wife; and for a long time the two lived together, and were happy.

3 stroll [stroʊl] (v.) to walk in a relaxed manner 蹓躂

By and by a babe was born to them,—a boy with the most wonderful eyes that anybody ever saw,—and they named him Aesculapius.

One day Apollo left Coronis and her child, and went on a journey to visit his favorite home on Mount Parnassus.

"I shall hear from you every day," he said at parting. "The crow will fly swiftly every morning to Parnassus, and tell me whether you and the child are well, and what you are doing while I am away."

For Apollo had a pet crow which was very wise, and could talk. The bird was not black, like the crows which you have seen, but as white as snow. Men say that all crows were white until that time, but I doubt whether anybody knows.

Apollo's crow was a great tattler[4], and did not always tell the truth. It would see the beginning of something, and then, without waiting to know anything more about it, would hurry off and make up a great story about it.

All went well for several days. Every morning the white bird would wing its way over hills and plains and rivers and forests until it found Apollo, either in the groves on the top of Parnassus or in his own house at Delphi. Then it would alight upon his shoulder and say, "Coronis is well! Coronis is well!"

One day, however, it had a different story. It came much earlier than ever before, and seemed to be in great haste.

---

4 tattler ['tætlər] (n.) somebody who gossips, reveals secrets, or talks idly 多嘴饒舌的人

"Cor—Cor—Cor!" it cried; but it was so out of breath that it could not speak her whole name.

"What is the matter?" cried Apollo, in alarm. "Has anything happened to Coronis? Speak! Tell me the truth!"

"She does not love you! she does not love you!" cried the crow. "I saw a man—I saw a man,—" and then, without stopping to take breath, or to finish the story, it flew up into the air, and hurried homeward again.

Apollo, who had always been so wise, was now almost as foolish as his crow. He fancied that Coronis had really deserted[5] him for another man, and his mind was filled with grief and rage[6]. With his silver bow in his hands he started at once for his home.

After a time, he came to the village where he had lived happily for so many years, and soon he saw his own house half-hidden among the dark-leaved olive trees. In another minute he would know whether the crow had told him the truth.

---

5 desert [dɪˈzɜːrt] (v.) leaving someone and not come back 拋棄
6 rage [reɪdʒ] (n.) extreme or violent anger 盛怒

Delator coruus, transfixâ Virgine Phœbi
Præmia nigrorem garrulitatis habet.

Ein Rab verschwäkt Coronis that,
Drum sie Apollo tödet hat. 22.

🎧 071 He heard the footsteps of some one running in the grove. He caught a glimpse[7] of a white robe among the trees. He felt sure that this was the man whom the crow had seen, and that he was trying to run away. He fitted an arrow to his bow quickly. He drew the string. Twang[8]! And the arrow which never missed sped like a flash of light through the air.

Apollo heard a sharp, wild cry of pain; and he bounded[9] forward through the grove. There, stretched dying on the grass, he saw his dear Coronis. She had seen him coming, and was running gladly to greet him, when the cruel arrow pierced[10] her heart.

7 glimpse [glɪmps] (n.) a quick or incomplete look 一瞥
8 twang [twæŋ] (n.) sound of tight string vibrating 撥弦聲
9 bound [baʊnd] (v.) to move quickly with large jumping movements 跳起
10 pierce [pɪrs] (v.) to penetrate through 刺穿

Apollo was overcome with grief. He took her form in his arms, and tried to call her back to life again. But it was all in vain[11]. She could only whisper his name, and then she was dead.

A moment afterwards the crow alighted[12] on one of the trees near by. "Cor—Cor—Cor," it began; for it wanted now to finish its story. But Apollo bade it begone[13].

"Cursed bird," he cried, "you shall never say a word but 'Cor—Cor—Cor!' all your life; and the feathers of which you are so proud shall no longer be white, but black as midnight."

And from that time to this, as you very well know, all crows have been black; and they fly from one dead tree to another, always crying, "Cor—cor—cor!"

---

11 in vain: to no avail 徒勞
12 alight [ə'laɪt] (v.) to land or settle after a flight 飛落
13 begone [bɪ'gɔːn] (v.) go away 走開

7 Grieving for the Dead Son Aesculapius

 Soon after this, Apollo took the little Aesculapius in his arms and carried him to a wise old schoolmaster named Cheiron, who lived in a cave under the gray cliffs of a mountain close by the sea.

"Take this child," he said, "and teach him all the lore[1] of the mountains, the woods, and the fields. Teach him those things which he most needs to know in order to do great good to his fellowmen."

---

1 lore [lɔːr] (n.) knowledge handed down verbally 學問

And Aesculapius proved to be a wise child, gentle and sweet and teachable; and among all the pupils of Cheiron he was the best loved. He learned the lore of the mountains, the woods, and the fields. He found out what virtue[2] there is in herbs and flowers and senseless stones; and he studied the habits of birds and beasts and men.

But above all he became skillful in dressing[3] wounds[4] and healing[5] diseases; and to this day physicians[6] remember and honor him as the first and greatest of their craft[7]. When he grew up to manhood his name was heard in every land, and people blessed him because he was the friend of life and the foe of death.

2 virtue ['vɜːrtʃuː] (n.) advantage or benefit 效用
3 dress [drɛs] (v.) cover wound 敷藥
4 wound [wuːnd] (n.) a damaged area of the body 傷口
5 heal [hiːl] (v.) to cure somebody 治癒
6 physician [fɪ'zɪʃən] (n.) medical doctor 醫生
7 craft [kræft] (n.) skill and experience 技術

A Sick Child Brought Into the Temple of Aesculapius

075 As time went by, Aesculapius cured[8] so many people and saved so many lives that Pluto, the pale-faced king of the Lower World, became alarmed.

"I shall soon have nothing to do," he said, "if this physician does not stop keeping people away from my kingdom."

And he sent word to his brother Jupiter, and complained that Aesculapius was cheating him out of what was his due[9]. Great Jupiter listened to his complaint, and stood up among the storm clouds, and hurled his thunderbolts at Aesculapius until the great physician was cruelly slain.

---

8 cure [kjʊr] (v.) to restore a sick person 治癒
9 due [duː] (n.) owed as a debt or as a right 應得權益

Then all the world was filled with grief, and even the beasts and the trees and the stones wept because the friend of life was no more.

When Apollo heard of the death of his son, his grief and wrath[10] were terrible. He could not do anything against Jupiter and Pluto, for they were stronger than he; but he went down into the smithy[11] of

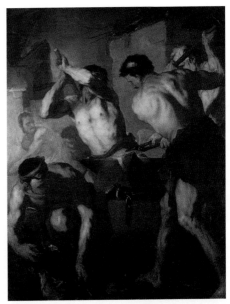

The Forge of Vulcan

Vulcan, underneath the smoking mountains, and slew the giant smiths who had made the deadly thunderbolts.

---

10 wrath [ræθ] (n.) extreme anger 狂怒
11 smithy ['smɪθi] (n.) the place where a blacksmith works 鍛冶場

Then Jupiter, in his turn, was angry, and ordered Apollo to come before him and be punished for what he had done.

He took away his bow and arrows and his wonderful lyre and all his beauty of form and feature; and after that Jupiter clothed him in the rags[12] of a beggar and drove him down from the mountain, and told him that he should never come back nor be himself again until he

Apollo With His Lyre

had served some man a whole year as a slave.

And so Apollo went out, alone and friendless, into the world; and no one who saw him would have dreamed that he was once the sun-bright Lord of the Silver Bow.

---

12 rags [ræɡz] (n.) (pl.) clothes that are old and torn 破爛衣衫

8 Cadmus and Europa

Europa and the White Bull

078 In Asia there lived a king who had two children, a boy and a girl. The boy's name was Cadmus, and the girl's name was Europa.

The king's country was a very small one. He could stand on his house top and see the whole of it. Yet he was very happy in his own little kingdom, and very fond of his children. And he had good reason to be proud of them; for Cadmus grew up to be the bravest young man in the land, and Europa to be the fairest maiden that had ever been seen. But sad days came to them all at last.

One morning Europa went out into a field near the seashore to pick flowers. Her father's cattle were in the field, grazing[1] among the sweet clover[2]. They were all very tame, and Europa knew every one of them by name.

That morning she noticed that there was a strange bull with the herd. He was very large and as white as snow; and he had soft brown eyes which somehow made him look very gentle and kind.

At first he did not even look at Europa, but went here and there, eating the tender grass which grew among the clover. But when she had gathered her apron full of daisies[3] and buttercups[4], he came slowly towards her.

He came close to her, and rubbed her arm with his nose to say "Good-morning!"

She stroked his head and neck, and he seemed much pleased. Then she made a wreath of daisies, and hung it round his neck. Europa then made a smaller wreath, and climbed upon his back to twine it round his horns. But all at once he sprang up, and ran away so swiftly that Europa could not help herself.

1 graze [greɪz] (v.) eat grass in fields（牛羊等）吃草
2 clover ['kloʊvər] (n.) plant with three-lobed leaves 苜蓿
3 daisy ['deɪzi] (n.) a tall flowering plant 雛菊
4 buttercup ['bʌtərkʌp] (n.) wild plant with yellow flowers 毛茛屬植物

She did not dare to jump off while he was going so fast, and all that she could think to do was to hold fast to his neck and scream very loud.

Rape of Europa

The herdsman under the tree heard her scream, and jumped up to see what was the matter. He saw the bull running with her towards the shore.

He ran after them as fast as he could, but it was of no use. The bull leaped into the sea, and swam swiftly away, with poor Europa on his back.

Several other people had seen him, and now they ran to tell the king. The king sent out his fastest ship to try to overtake the bull. The sailors rowed far out to sea, much farther than any ship had ever gone before; but no trace[5] of Europa could be found. When they came back, everybody felt that there was no more hope.

---

5   trace [treɪs] (n.) a sign that something has happened or existed
    痕跡

2 Searching for Europa

081 All the women and children in the town wept for the lost Europa. The king shut himself up in his house, and did not eat nor drink for three days. Then he called his son Cadmus, and bade him take a ship and go in search of his sister; and he told him that, no matter what dangers might be in his way, he must not come back until she was found.

Cadmus was glad to go. He chose twenty brave young men to go with him, and set sail the very next day. It was a great undertaking; for they were to pass through an unknown sea, and they did not know what lands they would come to.

Indeed, it was feared that they would never come to any land at all. Ships did not dare to go far from the shore in those days. But Cadmus and his friends were not afraid. They were ready to face any danger.

In a few days they came to a large island called Cyprus. Cadmus went on shore, and tried to talk with the strange people who lived there. They were very kind to him, but they did not understand his language.

082 At last he made out by signs to tell them who he was, and to ask them if they had seen his little sister Europa or the white bull that had carried her away. They shook their heads and pointed to the west.

Then the young men sailed on in their little ship. They came to many islands, and stopped at every one, to see if they could find any trace of Europa; but they heard no news of her at all.

At last, they came to the country which we now call Greece. It was a new country then, and only a few people lived there, and Cadmus soon learned to speak their language well. For a long time he wandered from one little town to another, always telling the story of his lost sister.

3 Pythia, the Priestess of Apollo at Delphi

One day an old man told Cadmus that if he would go to Delphi and ask the Pythia, perhaps she could tell him all about Europa. Cadmus had never heard of Delphi or of the Pythia, and he asked the old man what he meant.

"I will tell you," said the man. "Delphi is a town, built near the foot of Mount Parnassus, at the very center of the earth. It is the town of Apollo, the Bringer of Light; and there is a temple there, built close to the spot where Apollo killed a black serpent, many, many years ago. The temple is the most wonderful place in the world. In the middle of the floor there is a wide crack[1], or crevice[2]; and this crevice goes down, down into the rock, nobody knows how deep. A strange odor[3] comes up out of the crevice; and if any one breathes much of it, he is apt to fall over and lose his senses."

---

1 crack [kræk] (n.) thin break 裂縫
2 crevice ['krɛvɪs] (n.) a narrow crack or opening 裂縫；裂隙
3 odor ['oʊdər] (n.) a smell, often unpleasant 氣味

"But who is the Pythia that you spoke about?" asked Cadmus.

"I will tell you," said the old man. "The Pythia is a wise woman, who lives in the temple. When anybody asks her a hard question, she takes a three-legged stool[4], called a tripod[5], and sets it over the crevice in the floor. Then she sits on the stool and breathes the strange odor; and instead of losing her senses as other people would do, she talks with Apollo; and Apollo tells her how to answer the question. Men from all parts of the world go there to ask about things which they would like to know. The temple is full of the beautiful and costly gifts which they have brought for the Pythia. Sometimes she answers them plainly[6], and sometimes she answers them in riddles[7]; but what she says always comes true."

---

4 stool [stuːl] (n.) a seat without any support for the back or arms 凳子
5 tripod ['traɪpɑːd] (n.) a three-legged seat 三腳凳
6 plainly ['pleɪnli] (adv.) clearly or obviously 明確地
7 riddle ['rɪdl] (n.) word puzzle 謎語

So Cadmus went to Delphi to ask the Pythia about his lost sister. The wise woman was very kind to him; and when he had given her a beautiful golden cup to pay her for her trouble, she sat down on the tripod and breathed the strange odor which came up through the crevice in the rock.

Then her face grew pale, and her eyes looked wild, and she seemed to be in great pain; but they said that she was talking with Apollo. Cadmus asked her to tell him what had become of Europa. She said that Jupiter, in the form of a white bull, had carried her away, and that it would be of no use to look for her any more.

"But what shall I do?" said Cadmus. "My father told me not to turn back till I should find her."

"Your father is dead," said the Pythia, "and a strange king rules in his place. You must stay in Greece, for there is work here for you to do."

"What must I do?" said Cadmus.

"Follow the white cow," said the Pythia; "and on the hill where she lies down, you must build a city."

Cadmus did not understand what she meant by this; but she would not speak another word.

"This must be one of her riddles," he said, and he left the temple.

4 The City Location and The Fierce Dragon

When Cadmus went out of the temple, he saw a snow-white cow standing not far from the door. She seemed to be waiting for him, for she looked at him with her large brown eyes, and then turned and walked away.

Cadmus thought of what the Pythia had just told him, and so he followed her. All day and all night he walked through a strange wild country where no one lived; and two of the young men who had sailed with Cadmus from his old home were with him.

When the sun rose the next morning, they saw that they were on the top of a beautiful hill, with woods on one side and a grassy meadow on the other. There the cow lay down.

"Here we will build our city," said Cadmus.

Then the young men made a fire of dry sticks[1], and Cadmus killed the cow.

They thought that if they should burn some of her flesh, the smell of it would go up to the sky and be pleasing to Jupiter and the Mighty Folk who lived with him among the clouds; and in this way they hoped to make friends with Jupiter so that he would not hinder[2] them in their work.

---

1 stick [stɪk] (n.) a small thin branch of a tree 柴枝
2 hinder ['hɪndər] (v.) get in way of 妨礙

But they needed water to wash the flesh and their hands; and so one of the young men went down the hill to find some. He was gone so long that the other young man became uneasy and went after him.

Cadmus waited for them till the fire had burned low. He waited and waited till the sun was high in the sky. He called and shouted, but no one answered him. At last he took his sword[3] in his hand and went down to see what was the matter.

He followed the path which his friends had taken, and soon came to a fine stream of cold water at the foot of a hill. He saw something move among the bushes[4] which grew near it.

It was a fierce dragon, waiting to spring upon him. There was blood on the grass and leaves, and it was not hard to guess what had become of the two young men.

The beast sprang at Cadmus, and tried to seize him with its sharp claws. But Cadmus leaped quickly aside and struck it in the neck with his long sword.

---

3 sword [sɔːrd] (n.) a cutting or thrusting weapon with a long blade 劍；刀
4 bush [buʃ] (n.) a thick clump of bushes 灌木叢

A great stream of black blood gushed[5] out, and the dragon soon fell to the ground dead. Cadmus had seen many fearful sights, but never anything so dreadful as this

beast. He had never been in so great danger before. He sat down on the ground and trembled; and, all the time, he was weeping for his two friends. How now was he to build a city, with no one to help him?

5 gush [gʌʃ] (v.) to flow or send out quickly and in large amounts
湧出

Remains of the Cadmeia

5 Sowing Dragon's Teeth And the City of Thebes

While Cadmus was still weeping he was surprised to hear some one calling him. He stood up and looked around. On the hillside before him was a tall woman who had a helmet[1] on her head and a shield[2] in her hand. Her eyes were gray, and her face, though not beautiful, was very noble. Cadmus knew at once that she was Athena, the queen of the air—she who gives wisdom to men.

1 helmet ['hɛlmɪt] (n.) a strong hard hat that covers and protects the head 頭盔
2 shield [ʃiːld] (n.) piece of armor carried on arm 盾

Athena told Cadmus that he must take out the teeth of the dragon and sow them in the ground. He thought that would be a queer kind of seed. But she said that if he would do this, he would soon have men enough to help him build his city; and, before he could say a word, she had gone out of his sight.

The dragon had a great many teeth—so many that when Cadmus had taken them out they filled his helmet heaping full. The next thing was to find a good place to sow them. Just as he turned away from the stream, he saw a yoke[3] of oxen standing a little way off. He went to them and found that they were hitched[4] to a plow. What more could he want?

The ground in the meadow was soft and black, and he drove the plow[5] up and down, making long furrows[6] as he went. Then he dropped the teeth, one by one, into the furrows and covered them over with the rich soil. When he had sown all of them in this way, he sat down on the hillside and watched to see what would happen.

---

3 yoke [joʊk] (n.) a wooden bar which is fastened over the necks of two animals 牛軛
4 hitch [hɪtʃ] (v.) join something to something else 拴住
5 plow [plaʊ] (n.) a heavy farming tool with a sharp blade 犁
6 furrow ['fɜːroʊ] (n.) a narrow trench in soil made by a plow 犁溝

In a little while the soil in the furrows began to stir[7]. Then, at every place that a tooth had been dropped, something bright grew up.

It was a brass[8] helmet. The helmets pushed their way up, and soon the faces of men were seen underneath, then their shoulders, then their arms, then their bodies; and then, before Cadmus could think, a thousand warriors leaped out of the furrows and shook off the black earth which was clinging to them.

Every man was clothed in a suit of brass armor; and every one had a long spear in his right hand and a shield in his left.

Cadmus was frightened when he saw the strange crop[9] which had grown up from the dragon's teeth. The men looked so fierce that he feared they would kill him if they saw him. He hid himself behind his plow and then began to throw stones at them.

---

7   stir [stɜːr] (v.) to cause something to move slightly 攪動
8   brass [bræs] (a.) a bright yellow metal made from copper and zinc 黃銅製的
9   crop [krɑːp] (n.) plants grown for use 作物

The warriors did not know where the stones came from, but each thought that his neighbor had struck him. Soon they began to fight among themselves. Man after man was killed, and in a little while only five were left alive.

Then Cadmus ran towards them and called out: "Hold! Stop fighting! You are my men, and you must come with me. We will build a city here."

The men obeyed him. They followed Cadmus to the top of the hill; and they were such good workmen that in a few days they had built a house on the spot where the cow had lain down.

After that they built other houses, and people came to live in them. They called the town Cadmeia, after Cadmus who was its first king. But when the place had grown to be a large city, it was known by the name of Thebes.

6 Alphabet and Europe

(092) Cadmus was a wise king. The Mighty Folk who lived with Jupiter amid the clouds were well pleased with him and helped him in more ways than one.

After a while he married Harmonia, the beautiful daughter of Mars. All the Mighty Ones were at the wedding; and Athena gave the bride a wonderful necklace about which you may learn something more at another time.

But the greatest thing that Cadmus did is yet to be told. He was the first schoolmaster of the Greeks, and taught them the letters which were used in his own country across the sea.

They called the first of these letters alpha and the second beta, and that is why men speak of the alphabet to this day. And when the Greeks had learned the alphabet from Cadmus, they soon began to read and write, and to make beautiful and useful books.

As for the maiden Europa, she was carried safe over the sea to a distant shore. She may have been happy in the new, strange land to which she was taken—I cannot tell; but she never heard of friends or home again.

Whether it was really Jupiter in the form of a bull that carried her away, nobody knows. It all happened so long ago that there may have been some mistake about the story; and I should not think it strange if it were a sea robber who stole her from her home, and a swift ship with white sails that bore her away.

Of one thing I am very sure: she was loved so well by all who knew her that the great unknown country to which she was taken has been called after her name ever since— Europe.

9 The Story of Perseus

Danae and
The Golden Shower

094 There was a king of Argos who had but one child, and that child was a girl. If he had had a son, he would have trained him up to be a brave man and great king; but he did not know what to do with this fair-haired daughter.

When he saw her growing up to be tall and slender and wise, he wondered if, after all, he would have to die some time and leave his lands and his gold and his kingdom to her.

So he sent to Delphi and asked the Pythia about it. The Pythia told him that he would not only have to die some time, but that the son of his daughter would cause his death.

This frightened the king very much, and he tried to think of some plan by which he could keep the Pythia's words from coming true. At last he made up his mind that he would build a prison for his daughter and keep her in it all her life.

So he called his workmen and had them dig a deep round hole in the ground, and in this hole they built a house of brass which had but one room and no door at all, but only a small window at the top.

When it was finished, the king put the maiden, whose name was Danae, into it; and with her he put her nurse and her toys and her pretty dresses and everything that he thought she would need to make her happy.

"Now we shall see that the Pythia does not always tell the truth," he said.

So Danae was kept shut up in the prison of brass. She had no one to talk to but her old nurse; and she never saw the land or the sea, but only the blue sky above the open window and now and then a white cloud sailing across.

Danae and the Brazen Tower

I do not know how many years passed by, but Danae grew fairer every day, and by and by she was no longer a child, but a tall and beautiful woman; and Jupiter amid the clouds looked down and saw her and loved her.

One day it seemed to her that the sky opened and a shower of gold fell through the window into the room; and when the blinding shower had ceased, a noble young man stood smiling before her.

Danae

She did not know that it was mighty Jupiter who had thus come down in the rain; but she thought that he was a brave prince who had come from over the sea to take her out of her prison-house.

After that he came often, but always as a tall and handsome youth; and by and by they were married, with only the nurse at the wedding feast, and Danae was so happy that she was no longer lonesome even when he was away.

But one day when he climbed out through the narrow window there was a great flash of light, and she never saw him again.

2 The Wooden Chest And Exile

097 Not long afterwards a babe was born to Danae a smiling boy whom she named Perseus.

For four years she and the nurse kept him hidden, and not even the women who brought their food to the window knew about him. But one day the king chanced to be passing by and heard the child's prattle[1].

When he learned the truth, he was very much alarmed, for he thought that now, in spite of all that he had done, the words of the Pythia might come true.

The only sure way to save himself would be to put the child to death before he was old enough to do any harm. But when he had taken the little Perseus and his mother out of the prison and had seen how helpless the child was, he could not bear the thought of having him killed outright.

---

1 prattle ['prætl] (n.) idle or childish talk 小孩的咿咿呀呀聲

For the king, although a great coward, was really a kind-hearted man and did not like to see anything suffer pain. Yet something must be done.

So he bade his servants make a wooden chest[2] that was roomy and watertight[3] and strong; and when it was done, he put Danae and the child into it and had it taken far out to sea and left there to be tossed[4] about by the waves.

He thought that in this way he would rid himself of both daughter and grandson without seeing them die; for surely the chest would sink after a while, or else the winds would cause it to drift to some strange shore so far away that they could never come back to Argos again.

All day and all night and then another day, fair Danae and her child drifted over the sea. The waves rippled and played before and around the floating chest, the west wind whistled cheerily, and the sea birds circled in the air above; and the child was not afraid, but dipped[5] his hands in the curling waves and laughed at the merry breeze and shouted back at the screaming birds.

2　chest [tʃest] (n.) a large strong box 箱子
3　watertight [ˈwɑːtərtaɪt] (a.) not allowing water to pass in, out, or through 防水的
4　toss [tɔːs] (v.) to be thrown repeatedly up and down or to and fro 使上下搖動
5　dip [dɪp] (v.) to put something briefly into a liquid 浸入

But on the second night all was changed. A storm arose, the sky was black, the billows were mountain high, and the winds roared fearfully; yet through it all the child slept soundly in his mother's arms. And Danae sang over him this song:

Sleep, sleep, dear child, and take your rest
Upon your troubled mother's breast;
For you can lie without one fear
Of dreadful danger lurking near.

Wrapped in soft robes and warmly sleeping,
You do not hear your mother weeping;
You do not see the mad waves leaping,
Nor heed[6] the winds their vigils[7] keeping.

The stars are hid, the night is drear,
The waves beat high, the storm is here;
But you can sleep, my darling child,
And know naught[8] of the uproar[9] wild.

🎧100 At last the morning of the third day came, and the chest was tossed upon the sandy shore of a strange island where there were green fields and, beyond them, a little town.

A man who happened to be walking near the shore saw it and dragged[10] it far up on the beach. Then he looked inside, and there he saw the beautiful lady and the little boy. He helped them out and led them just as they were to his own house, where he cared for them very kindly.

And when Danae had told him her story, he bade her feel no more fear; for they might have a home with him as long as they should choose to stay, and he would be a true friend to them both.

---

6 heed [hiːd] (v.) to give serious attention to a warning or advice 注意

7 vigil ['vɪdʒɪl] (n.) a period spent in doing something through the night 警戒

8 naught [nɔːt] (n.) nothing 不存在

9 uproar ['ʌprɔːr] (n.) a state of violent and noisy disturbance 騷亂

10 drag [dræg] (v.) to move something by pulling it along a surface, usually the ground 拖行

3 The Quest of Medusa's Head

So Danae and her son stayed in the house of the kind man who had saved them from the sea. Years passed by, and Perseus grew up to be a tall young man, handsome, and brave, and strong.

The king of the island, when he saw Danae was so pleased with her beauty that he wanted her to become his wife. But he was a dark, cruel man, and she did not like him at all; so she told him that she would not marry him.

The king thought that Perseus was to blame for this, and that if he could find some excuse to send the young man on a far journey, he might force Danae to have him whether she wished or not.

One day he called all the young men of his country together and told them that he was soon to be wedded to the queen of a certain land beyond the sea. Would not each of them bring him a present to be given to her father?

102 For in those times it was the rule, that when any man was about to be married, he must offer[1] costly gifts to the father of the bride.

Medusa

"What kind of presents do you want?" said the young men.

"Horses," he answered; for he knew that Perseus had no horse.

"Why don't you ask for something worth the having?" said Perseus; for he was vexed[2] at the way in which the king was treating him. "Why don't you ask for Medusa's head, for example?"

"Medusa's head it shall be!" cried the king. "These young men may give me horses, but you shall bring Medusa's head."

"I will bring it," said Perseus; and he went away in anger, while his young friends laughed at him because of his foolish words.

---

1 offer ['ɑːfər] (v.) give something as worship 給予
2 vexed [vɛkst] (a.) confused 困惑的

103 What was this Medusa's head which he had so rashly promised to bring? His mother had often told him about Medusa. Far, far away, on the very edge of the world, there lived three strange monsters, sisters, called Gorgons. They had the bodies and faces of women, but they had wings of gold, and terrible claws of brass, and hair that was full of living serpents.

They were so awful to look upon, that no man could bear the sight of them, but whoever saw their faces was turned to stone. Two of these monsters had charmed lives, and no weapon could ever do them harm; but the youngest, whose name was Medusa, might be killed, if indeed anybody could find her and could give the fatal[3] stroke[4].

When Perseus went away from the king's palace, he began to feel sorry that he had spoken so rashly. For how should he ever make good his promise and do the king's bidding[5]?

---

3 fatal ['feɪtl] (a.) very serious and having an important bad effect 致命的
4 stroke [stroʊk] (n.) a hit or blow made by the hand 一擊
5 bidding ['bɪdɪŋ] (n.) somebody's orders or instructions 命令

4 Mercury's Winged Slippers

He did not know which way to go to find the Gorgons, and he had no weapon with which to slay the terrible Medusa. But at any rate he would never show his face to the king again, unless he could bring the head of terror with him.

He went down to the shore and stood looking out over the sea towards Argos, his native land; and while he looked, the sun went down, and the moon arose, and a soft wind came blowing from the west. Then, all at once, two persons, a man and a woman, stood before him.

Both were tall and noble. The man looked like a prince; and there were wings on his cap and on his feet, and he carried a winged staff, around which two golden serpents were twined.

He asked Perseus what was the matter; and the young man told him how the king had treated him, and all about the rash words which he had spoken.

Then the lady spoke to him very kindly; and he noticed that, although she was not beautiful, she had most wonderful gray eyes, and a stern but lovable face and a queenly form.

Athena

Mercury

And she told him not to fear, but to go out boldly in quest of the Gorgons; for she would help him obtain[1] the terrible head of Medusa.

"But I have no ship, and how shall I go?" said Perseus.

"You shall don my winged slippers," said the strange prince, "and they will bear you over sea and land."

"Shall I go north, or south, or east, or west?" asked Perseus.

---

1 obtain [əbˈteɪn] (v.) to get something 取得

Western Maidens

"I will tell you," said the tall lady. "You must go first to the three Gray Sisters, who live beyond the frozen sea in the far, far north. They have a secret which nobody knows, and you must force them to tell it to you. Ask them where you shall find the three Maidens who guard the golden apples of the West; and when they shall have told you, turn about and go straight thither². The Maidens will give you three things, without which you can never obtain the terrible head; and they will show you how to wing your way across the western ocean to the edge of the world where lies the home of the Gorgons."

Then the man took off his winged slippers, and put them on the feet of Perseus; and the woman whispered to him to be off at once, and to fear nothing, but be bold and true. And Perseus knew that she was none other than Athena, the queen of the air, and that her companion was Mercury, the lord of the summer clouds. But before he could thank them for their kindness, they had vanished³ in the dusky twilight⁴.

Then he leaped into the air to try the Magic Slippers.

---

2   thither ['θɪðər] (adv.) to that place, in that direction
    那邊（古老用法）
3   vanish ['vænɪʃ] (v.) disappear suddenly 消失
4   twilight ['twaɪlaɪt] (n.) the soft, diffused light from the sky when
    the sun is below the horizon 黃昏

5 The Gray Sisters: With One Eye and One Tooth

106　　Swifter than an eagle, Perseus flew up towards the sky.
On and on he went, and soon the sea was passed. And
then there were frozen marshes[1] and a wilderness[2] of
snow, and after all the sea again,—but a sea of ice.

　　On and on he winged his way, among toppling[3]
icebergs and over frozen billows[4] and through air which
the sun never warmed, and at last he came to the cavern[5]
where the three Gray Sisters dwelt.

1　marsh [mɑːrʃ] (n.) soft wet ground 沼澤；濕地
2　wilderness ['wɪldərnɪs] (n.) natural uncultivated land 荒野
3　topple ['tɑːpəl] (v.) lose balance and fall down 倒塌

These three creatures were so old that they had forgotten their own age, and nobody could count the years which they had lived. The long hair which covered their heads had been gray since they were born; and they had among them only a single eye and a single tooth which they passed back and forth from one to another.

"We know a secret which even the Great Folk who live on the mountain top can never learn; don't we, sisters?" said one.

"Ha! ha! That we do, that we do!" chattered the others.

"Give me the tooth, sister, that I may feel young and handsome again," said the one nearest to Perseus.

"And give me the eye that I may look out and see what is going on in the busy world," said the sister who sat next to her.

"Ah, yes, yes, yes, yes!" mumbled the third, as she took the tooth and the eye and reached them blindly towards the others.

Then, quick as thought, Perseus leaped forward and snatched[6] both of the precious things from her hand.

---

4 billow ['bɪloʊ] (n.) a great wave or surge of the sea 巨浪；波濤
5 cavern ['kævərn] (n.) large cave 巨大的洞穴
6 snatch [snætʃ] (v.) to take hold of something suddenly and
   roughly 奪走

"Where is the tooth? Where is the eye?" screamed the two, reaching out their long arms and groping[7] here and there. "Have you dropped them, sister? Have you lost them?"

Perseus laughed as he stood in the door of their cavern and saw their distress and terror.

"I have your tooth and your eye," he said, "and you shall never touch them again until you tell me your secret. Where are the Maidens who keep the golden apples of the Western Land? Which way shall I go to find them?"

"You are young, and we are old," said the Gray Sisters; "pray, do not deal so cruelly with us. Pity us, and give us our eye."

Then they wept and pleaded and coaxed[8] and threatened. But Perseus stood a little way off and taunted[9] them.

"Sisters, we must tell him," at last said one.

"Ah, yes, we must tell him," said the others. "We must part with the secret to save our eye."

---

7 grope [ɡroʊp] (v.) to search blindly or uncertainly 摸索
8 coax [koʊks] (v.) persuade gently 哄騙
9 taunt [tɔːnt] (v.) to intentionally annoy and upset someone by making unkind remarks to them 奚落；嘲弄

And then they told him how he should go to reach the Western Land, and what road he should follow to find the Maidens who kept the golden apples. When they had made everything plain to him Perseus gave them back their eye and their tooth.

"Ha! ha!" they laughed; "now the golden days of youth have come again!"

And, from that day to this, no man has ever seen the three Gray Sisters, nor does any one know what became of them. But the winds still whistle through their cheerless cave, and the cold waves murmur on the shore of the wintry sea, and the ice mountains topple and crash, and no sound of living creature is heard in all that desolate[10] land.

---

10 desolate ['desələt] (a.) barren or laid waste 荒蕪的

6 The Western Maidens and The Tree of Golden Apples

🎧 109 As for Perseus, he leaped again into the air, and the Magic Slippers bore him southward with the speed of the wind. Very soon he left the frozen sea behind him and came to a sunny land, where there were green forests and flowery meadows and hills and valleys, and at last a pleasant garden where were all kinds of blossoms and fruits.

He knew that this was the famous Western Land, for the Gray Sisters had told him what he should see there. There he saw the three Maidens of the West dancing around a tree which was full of golden apples, and singing as they danced. For the wonderful tree with its precious fruit belonged to Juno; it had been given to her as a wedding gift, and it was the duty of the Maidens to care for it and see that no one touched the golden apples. Perseus stopped and listened to their song:

We sing of the old, we sing of the new,—
Our joys are many, our sorrows are few;
Singing, dancing,
All hearts entrancing[1],
We wait to welcome the good and the true.

The daylight is waning[2], the evening is here,
The sun will soon set, the stars will appear.
Singing, dancing,
All hearts entrancing,
We wait for the dawn of a glad new year.

The tree shall wither, the apples shall fall,
Sorrow shall come, and death shall call,
Alarming, grieving,
All hearts deceiving[3],—
But hope shall abide[4] to comfort us all.

Soon the tale shall be told, the song shall be sung,

The bow shall be broken, the harp[5] unstrung[6],

Alarming, grieving,

All hearts deceiving,

Till every joy to the winds shall be flung[7].

But a new tree shall spring from the roots of the old,

And many a blossom its leaves shall unfold[8],

Cheering, gladdening,

With joy maddening,—

For its boughs[9] shall be laden[10] with apples of gold.

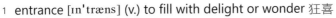

1 entrance [ɪnˈtræns] (v.) to fill with delight or wonder 狂喜
2 wane [weɪn] (v.) to decrease in strength, intensity, etc 轉弱
3 deceive [dɪˈsiːv] (v.) to persuade someone that something false is the truth 欺騙
4 abide [əˈbaɪd] (v.) to remain or continue 繼續
5 harp [hɑːrp] (n.) a large, wooden musical instrument with many strings that you play with the fingers 豎琴
6 unstring [ʌnˈstrɪŋ] (v.) to deprive of strings 解開弦
7 fling [flɪŋ] (v.) to throw, cast, or hurl with force or violence 丟擲
8 unfold [ʌnˈfoʊld] (v.) to open or spread out 展開
9 bough [baʊ] (n.) a branch of a tree 大樹枝
10 laden [ˈleɪdən] (a.) carrying or holding a lot of something 裝滿的

Then Perseus went forward and spoke to the Maidens. They stopped singing, and stood still as if in alarm. But when they saw the Magic Slippers on his feet, they ran to him, and welcomed him to the Western Land and to their garden.

"We knew that you were coming," they said, "for the winds told us. But why do you come?"

Perseus told them of all that had happened to him since he was a child, and of his quest of Medusa's head; and he said that he had come to ask them to give him three things to help him in his fight with the Gorgons.

The Maidens answered that they would give him not three things, but four. Then one of them gave him a sharp sword, which was crooked[11] like a sickle[12], and which she fastened to the belt at his waist; and another gave him a shield, which was brighter than any looking-glass you ever saw; and the third gave him a magic pouch[13], which she hung by a long strap[14] over his shoulder.

---

11 crooked [krʊkɪd] (a.) bent 彎曲的
12 sickle ['sɪkəl] (n.) a tool with a short handle and a curved blade, used for cutting grass and grain crops 鐮刀
13 pouch [paʊtʃ] (n.) a bag for a small object 小袋子
14 strap [stræp] (n.) a narrow strip of flexible material 帶子

The Arming of Perseus

"These are three things which you must have in order to obtain Medusa's head; and now here is a fourth, for without it your quest must be in vain."

And they gave him a magic cap, the Cap of Darkness; and when they had put it upon his head, there was no creature on the earth or in the sky—no, not even the Maidens themselves—that could see him.

And Perseus donned[15] the Cap of Darkness, and sped away and away towards the farthermost edge of the earth; and the three Maidens went back to their tree to sing and to dance and to guard the golden apples until the old world should become young again.

15 don [dɑːn] (v.) to put on a piece of clothing 穿上

7 The Dreadful Gorgons

With the sharp sword at his side and the bright shield upon his arm, Perseus flew bravely onward in search of the dreadful Gorgons; but he had the Cap of Darkness upon his head, and you could no more have seen him than you can see the wind.

He flew so swiftly that it was not long until he had crossed the mighty ocean which encircles[1] the earth, and had come to the sunless land which lies beyond; and then he knew, from what the Maidens had told him, that the lair of the Gorgons could not be far away.

He heard a sound as of some one breathing heavily, and he looked around sharply to see where it came from. Among the foul[2] weeds which grew close to the bank of a muddy river there was something which glittered[3] in the pale light.

---

1 encircle [ɪnˈsɜːrkəl] (v.) surround 圍繞
2 foul [faʊl] (a.) filthy or dirty 骯髒的
3 glitter [ˈglɪtər] (v.) to reflect light with a brilliant, sparkling luster 閃爍

114 He flew a little nearer; but he did not dare to look straight forward, lest he should all at once meet the gaze[4] of a Gorgon, and be changed into stone.

So he turned around, and held the shining shield before him in such a way that by looking into it he could see objects behind him as in a mirror.

Ah, what a dreadful sight it was! Half hidden among the weeds lay the three monsters, fast asleep, with their golden wings folded about them.

Their brazen[5] claws were stretched out as though ready to seize their prey; and their shoulders were covered with sleeping snakes.

The two largest of the Gorgons lay with their heads tucked[6] under their wings as birds hide their heads when they go to sleep. But the third, who lay between them, slept with her face turned up towards the sky; and Perseus knew that she was Medusa.

Very stealthily he went nearer and nearer, always with his back towards the monsters and always looking into his bright shield to see where to go.

---

4 gaze [geɪz] (n.) a steady or intent look 凝視
5 brazen ['breɪzən] (a.) made of brass 黃銅的
6 tuck [tʌk] (v.) to put into a small, close, or concealing place 塞進

🎧 115   Then he drew his sharp sword and, dashing[7] quickly downward, struck a back blow, so sure, so swift, that the head of Medusa was cut from her shoulders and the black blood gushed[8] like a river from her neck.

7   dash [dæʃ] (v.) to go somewhere quickly 急衝
8   gush [gʌʃ] (v.) to flow out suddenly 噴湧出

Quick as thought he thrust the terrible head into his magic pouch and leaped again into the air, and flew away with the speed of the wind.

Then the two older Gorgons awoke, and rose with dreadful screams, and spread their great wings, and dashed after him. They could not see him, for the Cap of Darkness hid him from even their eyes; but they scented[9] the blood of the head which he carried in the pouch, and like hounds[10] in the chase, they followed him, sniffing[11] the air.

But the Magic Slippers were faster than any wings, and in a little while the monsters were left far behind, and their cries were heard no more; and Perseus flew on alone.

---

9 scent [sɛnt] (v.) to perceive or recognize by or as if by the sense of smell 嗅出
10 hound [haʊnd] (n.) a dog used for hunting 獵犬
11 sniff [snɪf] (v.) to smell by short inhalations 嗅

8 Andromeda and the Sea Beast

Straight east Perseus flew over the great sea, and after a time he came to a country where there were palm trees and pyramids and a great river flowing from the south.

Here, as he looked down, a strange sight met his eyes: he saw a beautiful girl chained to a rock by the seashore, and far away a huge sea beast swimming towards her to devour[1] her.

Quick as thought, he flew down and spoke to her; but, as she could not see him for the Cap of Darkness which he wore, his voice only frightened her.

Then Perseus took off his cap, and stood upon the rock; and when the girl saw him with his long hair and wonderful eyes and laughing face, she thought him the handsomest young man in the world.

---

1 devour [dɪˈvaʊr] (v.) to eat something eagerly and in large amounts so that nothing is left 吞噬

"Oh, save me! save me!" she cried as she reached out her arms towards him.

Perseus drew his sharp sword and cut the chain which held her, and then lifted her high up upon the rock. But by this time the sea monster was close at hand, lashing[2] the water with his tail and opening his wide jaws as though he would swallow not only Perseus and the young girl, but even the rock on which they were standing.

He was a terrible fellow, and yet not half so terrible as the Gorgon.

"Oh, save me! save me!"

2 lash [læʃ] (v.) to strike vigorously at someone or something
猛烈打擊

Perseus on Pegasus Hastening to the Rescue of Andromeda

118 As he came roaring towards the shore, Perseus lifted the head of Medusa from his pouch and held it up; and when the beast saw the dreadful face he stopped short and was turned into stone; and men say that the stone beast may be seen in that selfsame[3] spot to this day.

3 selfsame ['self'seɪm] (a.) being the very same 相同的

Delivering Angelica

Then Perseus slipped[4] the Gorgon's head back into
the pouch and hastened to speak with the young girl
whom he had saved. She told him that her name was
Andromeda, and that she was the daughter of the king of
that land.

She said that her mother, the queen, was very beautiful
and very proud of her beauty; and every day she went
down to the seashore to look at her face as it was pictured
in the quiet water; and she had boasted that not even the
nymphs who live in the sea were as handsome as she.

4 slip [slɪp] (v.) to put, place, pass, insert, or withdraw quickly
   快速放入

When the sea nymphs heard about this, they were very angry and asked great Neptune, the king of the sea, to punish the queen for her pride. So Neptune sent a sea monster to crush the king's ships and kill the cattle along the shore and break down all the fishermen's huts[5].

The people were so much distressed[6] that they sent at last to ask the Pythia what they should do; and the Pythia said that there was only one way to save the land from destruction[7],—that they must give the king's daughter, Andromeda, to the monster to be devoured.

The king and the queen loved their daughter very dearly, for she was their only child; and for a long time they refused to do as the Pythia had told them.

But day after day the monster laid waste the land, and threatened to destroy not only the farms, but the towns; and so they were forced in the end to give up Andromeda to save their country.

---

5 hut [hʌt] (n.) a small dwelling of simple construction 小屋
6 distressed [dɪ'strest] (a.) affected with or suffering from distress 痛苦的
7 destruction [dɪ'strʌkʃən] (n.) the condition of being destroyed 毀壞

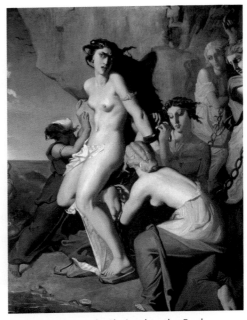

This, then, was why she had been chained to the rock by the shore and left there to perish[8] in the jaws of the beast.

While Perseus was yet talking with Andromeda, the king and the queen and a great company of people came down the shore, weeping and tearing their hair; for they were sure that by this time the monster had devoured his prey.

Andromeda Chained to the Rock
by the Nereids

But when they saw her alive and well, and learned that she had been saved by the handsome young man who stood beside her, they could hardly hold themselves for joy.

---

8 perish ['perɪʃ] (v.) to die, especially in an accident or by being killed 死去

121 And Perseus was so delighted with Andromeda's beauty that he almost forgot his quest which was not yet finished; and when the king asked him what he should give him as a reward for saving Andromeda's life, he said:

"Give her to me for my wife."

This pleased the king very much; and so, on the seventh day, Perseus and Andromeda were married, and there was a great feast in the king's palace, and everybody was merry and glad.

And the two young people lived happily for some time in the land of palms and pyramids; and, from the sea to the mountains, nothing was talked about but the courage of Perseus and the beauty of Andromeda.

9 Medusa's Head and Turning Into Stone

But Perseus had not forgotten his mother; and so, one fine summer day, he and Andromeda sailed in a beautiful ship to his own home.

Now, the wicked king of that land had never ceased trying to persuade Danae to become his wife. At last when he found that she could not be made to have him, he declared that he would kill her.

So, as Perseus and Andromeda came into the town, whom should they meet but his mother fleeing to the altar of Jupiter, and the king following after, intent on killing her?

Danae was so frightened that she did not see Perseus, but ran right on towards the only place of safety. For it was a law of that land that not even the king should be allowed to harm any one who took refuge on the altar of Jupiter.

When Perseus saw the king rushing like a madman after his mother, he threw himself before him and bade him stop. But the king struck at him furiously with his sword.

Perseus caught the blow on his shield, and at the same moment took the head of Medusa from his magic pouch.

"I promised to bring you a present, and here it is!" he cried.

Perseus Fighting King Phineus and His Companions

123 The king saw it, and was turned into stone, just as he stood, with his sword uplifted and that terrible look of anger and passion in his face.

The people of the island were glad when they learned what had happened, for no one loved the wicked king. They were glad, too, because Perseus had come home again, and had brought with him his beautiful wife, Andromeda.

On the morrow[1] therefore, he gave the kingdom to the kind man who had saved his mother and himself from the sea; and then he went on board his ship, with Andromeda and Danae and sailed away across the sea towards Argos.

1　morrow ['mɔːroʊ] (n.) the next day, or tomorrow
　　次日（古老用法）

10 The Death of Grandfather

When Danae's old father, the king of Argos, heard that a strange ship was coming over the sea with his daughter and her son on board, he was in great distress; for he remembered what the Pythia had foretold[1] about his death. So, without waiting to see the vessel, he left his palace in great haste and fled out of the country.

The people of Argos welcomed Danae to her old home; and they were very proud of her handsome son, and begged that he would stay in their city, so that he might some time become their king.

It happened soon afterwards that the king of a certain country not far away was holding games and giving prizes to the best runners and leapers and quoit throwers. And Perseus went thither[2] to try his strength with the other young men of the land; for if he should be able to gain a prize, his name would become known all over the world.

One day, as he was showing what he could do, he threw a heavy quoit a great deal farther than any had been thrown before.

---

1 foretell [fɔːrˈtel] (v.) to state what is going to happen in the future 預言
2 thither [ˈθɪðər] (adv.) to that place 那邊

The Death of Grandfather 155

The Death of King Acrisius

It fell in the crowd of lookers-on[3], and struck a stranger who was standing there. The stranger threw up his hands and sank upon the ground; and when Perseus ran to help him, he saw that he was dead.

Now this man was none other than Danae's father, the old king of Argos. He had fled from his kingdom to save his life, and in doing so had only met his death.

Perseus was overcome with grief, and tried in every way to pay honor to the memory of the unhappy king. The kingdom of Argos was now rightfully his own, but he could not bear to take it after having killed his grandfather.

So he was glad to exchange with another king who ruled over two rich cities, not far away, called Mycenae and Tiryns. And he and Andromeda lived happily in Mycenae for many years.

3　looker-on ['lʊkər'ɑːn] (n.) a person who looks on 旁觀者

10 The Origins of Athens

King of Athens: Cecrops

On a steep stony hill in Greece there lived in early times a few very poor people who had not yet learned to build houses. They made their homes in little caves which they dug in the earth or hollowed out among the rocks; and their food was the flesh of wild animals, which they hunted in the woods, with now and then a few berries or nuts.

They did not even know how to make bows and arrows, but used slings[1] and clubs[2] and sharp sticks for weapons; and the little clothing which they had was made of skins.

They lived on the top of the hill, because they were safe there from the savage beasts of the great forest around them, and safe also from the wild men who sometimes roamed through the land.

The hill was so steep on every side that there was no way of climbing it save by a single narrow footpath³ which was always guarded by some one at the top.

One day when the men were hunting in the woods, they found a strange youth whose face was so fair and who was dressed so beautifully that they could hardly believe him to be a man like themselves. His body was so slender and lithe⁴, and he moved so nimbly⁵ among the trees, that they fancied him to be a serpent in the guise of a human being; and they stood still in wonder and alarm.

The young man spoke to them, but they could not understand a word that he said; then he made signs to them that he was hungry, and they gave him something to eat and were no longer afraid.

Had they been like the wild men of the woods, they might have killed him at once. But they wanted their women and children to see the serpent man, as they called him, and hear him talk; and so they took him home with them to the top of the hill.

---

1 sling [slɪŋ] (n.) a device for hurling stones or other missiles 彈弓
2 club [klʌb] (n.) a heavy stick 棍棒
3 footpath ['fʊtpæθ] (n.) a path, especially in the countryside, for walking on 鄉間小路
4 lithe [laɪð] (a.) able to move and bend gracefully 柔軟的；輕盈的
5 nimbly ['nɪmbli] (adv.) fast and light in movement 敏捷地

They thought that after they had made a show of him for a few days, they would kill him and offer his body as a sacrifice to the unknown being whom they dimly[6] fancied to have some sort of control over their lives.

But the young man was so fair and gentle that, after they had all taken a look at him, they began to think it would be a great pity to harm him. So they gave him food and treated him kindly; and he sang songs to them and played with their children, and made them happier than they had been for many a day.

In a short time he learned to talk in their language; and he told them that his name was Cecrops, and that he had been shipwrecked[7] on the seacoast not far away; and then he told them many strange things about the land from which he had come and to which he would never be able to return.

The poor people listened and wondered; and it was not long until they began to love him and to look up to him as one wiser than themselves. Then they came to ask him about everything that was to be done, and there was not one of them who refused to do his bidding.

---

6 dimly ['dɪmli] (adv.) not clear to mind 模糊地
7 shipwreck ['ʃɪprek] (v.) an accident in which a ship is destroyed or sunk at sea 遭受海難

So Cecrops—the serpent man, as they still called him—became the king of the poor people on the hill.

Ktcrops (Bafenbild in Balermo).

Cecrops

He taught them how to make bows and arrows, and how to set nets for birds, and how to take fish with hooks.

He led them against the savage wild men of the woods, and helped them kill the fierce beasts that had been so great a terror to them. He showed them how to build houses of wood and to thatch[8] them with the reeds which grew in the marshes. He taught them how to live in families instead of herding[9] together like senseless beasts as they had always done before.

And he told them about great Jupiter and the Mighty Folk who lived amid the clouds on the mountain top.

---

8 thatch [θætʃ] (v.) to make a roof for a building with straw or reeds 用茅草蓋屋頂

9 herd [hɜːrd] (v.) to gather together or go somewhere as a group 群居

2 Athena Named Her City: Athens

 By and by, instead of the wretched[1] caves among the rocks, there was a little town on the top of the hill, with neat[2] houses and a market place; and around it was a strong wall with a single narrow gate just where the footpath began to descend[3] to the plain. But as yet the place had no name.

One morning while the king and his wise men were sitting together in the market place and planning how to make the town become a rich, strong city, two strangers were seen in the street. Nobody could tell how they came there. The guard at the gate had not seen them; and no man had ever dared to climb the narrow footway[4] without his leave.

🎧 **131** But there the two strangers stood. One was a man, the other a woman; and they were so tall, and their faces were so grand and noble, that those who saw them stood still and wondered and said not a word.

The man had a robe of purple and green wrapped round his body, and he bore in one hand a strong staff with three sharp spear points at one end. The woman was not beautiful, but she had wonderful gray eyes; and in one hand she carried a spear and in the other a shield of curious[5] workmanship[6].

"What is the name of this town?" asked the man.

The people stared at him in wonder, and hardly understood his meaning.

Then an old man answered and said, "It has no name. We who live on this hill used to be called Cranae; but since King Cecrops came, we have been so busy that we have had no time to think of names."

---

1 wretched ['rɛtʃɪd] (a.) inadequate or of low quality 簡陋的
2 neat [niːt] (a.) clean or orderly 整潔的
3 descend [dɪˈsɛnd] (v.) move downward and lower 沿……而下
4 footway ['fʊtˌweɪ] (n.) footpath 小徑
5 curious ['kjʊriəs] (a.) different from the usual 新奇的
6 workmanship ['wɜːrkmənʃɪp] (n.) the skill with which something was made or done 工藝

"Where is this King Cecrops?" asked the woman.

"He is in the market place with the wise men," was the answer.

"Lead us to him at once," said the man.

When Cecrops saw the two strangers coming into the market place, he stood up and waited for them to speak.

The man spoke first: "I am Neptune," said he, "and I rule the sea."

Neptune

"And I am Athena," said the woman, "and I give wisdom to men."

"I hear that you are planning to make your town become a great city," said Neptune, "and I have come to help you. Give my name to the place, and let me be your protector and patron[7], and the wealth of the whole world shall be yours. Ships from every land shall bring you merchandise[8] and gold and silver; and you shall be the masters of the sea."

---

7 patron ['peɪtrən] (n.) guardian or supporter 守護神
8 merchandise ['mɜːrtʃəndaɪz] (n.) goods; commodities 商品；貨物

Athena

"My uncle makes you fair promises," said Athena; "but listen to me. Give my name to your city, and let me be your patron, and I will give you that which gold cannot buy: I will teach you how to do a thousand things of which you now know nothing. I will make your city my favorite home, and I will give you wisdom that you shall sway the minds and hearts of all men until the end of time."

The king bowed, and turned to the people, who had all crowded into the market place. "Which of these mighty ones shall we elect[9] to be the protector and patron of our city?" he asked. "Neptune offers us wealth; Athena promises us wisdom. Which shall we choose?"

"Neptune and wealth!" cried many.

"Athena and wisdom!" cried as many others

---

9 elect [ɪˈlɛkt] (v.) to decide on or choose 推選

At last when it was plain that the people could not agree, an old man whose advice was always heeded stood up and said:

"These mighty ones have only given us promises, and they have promised things of which we are ignorant[10]. For who among us knows what wealth is or what wisdom is? Now, if they would only give us some real gift, right now and right here, which we can see and handle, we should know better how to choose."

"That is true! that is true!" cried the people.

"Very well, then," said the strangers, "we will each give you a gift, right now and right here, and then you may choose between us."

Neptune gave the first gift. He stood on the highest point of the hill where the rock was bare, and bade the people see his power. He raised his three-pointed spear high in the air, and then brought it down with great force.

Lightning flashed, the earth shook, and the rock was split half way down to the bottom of the hill. Then out of the yawning crevice[11] there sprang a wonderful creature, white as milk, with long slender legs, an arching neck, and a mane and tail of silk.

---

10 ignorant ['ɪgnərənt] (a.) not having enough knowledge or understanding about something 無知的
11 crevice ['krɛvɪs] (n.) a narrow crack or opening 裂縫

The people had never seen anything like it before, and they thought it a new kind of bear or wolf or wild boar that had come out of the rock to devour them.

Some of them ran and hid in their houses, while others climbed upon the wall, and still others grasped their weapons in alarm. But when they saw the creature stand quietly by the side of Neptune, they lost their fear and came closer to see and admire its beauty.

"This is my gift," said Neptune. "This animal will carry your burdens for you; he will draw your chariots; he will pull your wagons[12] and your plows; he will let you sit on his back and will run with you faster than the wind."

"What is his name?" asked the king.

"His name is Horse," answered Neptune.

Then Athena came forward. She stood a moment on a green grassy plot where the children of the town liked to play in the evening. Then she drove the point of her spear deep down in the soil. At once the air was filled with music, and out of the earth there sprang a tree with slender branches and dark green leaves and white flowers and violet[13] green fruit.

---

12 wagon ['wægən] (n.) wheeled vehicle for carrying loads 運貨馬車
13 violet ['vaɪəlɪt] (a.) having a bluish purple color 紫蘿蘭色的

"This is my gift," said Athena. "This tree will give you food when you are hungry; it will shelter you from the sun when you are faint[14]; it will beautify your city; and the oil from its fruit will be sought by all the world."

"What is it called?" asked the king.

"It is called Olive[15]," answered Athena.

Then the king and his wise men began to talk about the two gifts.

"I do not see that Horse will be of much use to us," said the old man who had spoken before. "For, as to the chariots and wagons and plows, we have none of them, and indeed do not know what they are; and who among us will ever want to sit on this creature's back and be borne faster than the wind? But Olive will be a thing of beauty and a joy for us and our children forever."

"Which shall we choose?" asked the king, turning to the people.

"Athena has given us the best gift," they all cried, "and we choose Athena and wisdom!"

"Be it so," said the king, "and the name of our city shall be Athens."

---

14 faint [feɪnt] (a.) to feel weak, as if you are about to lose consciousness 頭暈的

15 olive ['ɑːlɪv] (n.) a small bitter green or black fruit that is eaten or used to produce oil 橄欖

▲ Parthenon: the Temple for Athena   ▼ Temple of Poseidon

From that day the town grew and spread, and soon there was not room on the hilltop for all the people. Then houses were built in the plain around the foot of the hill, and a great road was built to the sea, three miles away; and in all the world there was no city more fair than Athens.

In the old market place on the top of the hill the people built a temple to Athena, the ruins[16] of which may still be seen. The olive tree grew and nourished; and, when you visit Athens, people will show you the very spot where it stood. Many other trees sprang from it, and in time became a blessing both to Greece and to all the other countries round the great sea.

As for the horse, he wandered away across the plains towards the north and found a home at last in distant Thessaly beyond the River Peneus. And I have heard it said that all the horses in the world have descended from that one which Neptune brought out of the rock; but of the truth of this story there may be some doubts.

---

16 ruins ['ruːɪnz] (n.) (pl.) the broken parts that are left from an old building or town 廢墟；遺跡

11 The Adventures of Theseus (I)

Unstable Athens

🎧 138 There was once a king of Athens whose name was Aegeus. He had no son; but he had fifty nephews, and they were waiting for him to die, so that one of them might be king in his stead. They were wild, worthless fellows, and the people of Athens looked forward with dread to the day when the city should be in their power.

It so happened one summer that Aegeus left his kingdom in the care of the elders of the city and went on a voyage across the Saronic Sea to the old and famous city of Troezen, which lay nestled at the foot of the mountains on the opposite shore.

King Pittheus of Troezen was right glad to see Aegeus, for they had been boys together, and he welcomed him to his city and did all that he could to make his visit a pleasant one.

So, day after day, there was feasting and merriment[1] and music in the marble halls of old Troezen, and the two kings spent many a happy hour in talking of the deeds of their youth and of the mighty heroes whom both had known.

---

1 merriment ['merɪmənt] (n.) when people laugh or have an enjoyable time together 歡樂；歡笑

And when the time came for the ship to sail back to Athens, Aegeus was not ready to go. But Aegeus tarried[2], not so much for the rest and enjoyment which he was having in the home of his old friend, as for the sake of Aethra, his old friend's daughter.

For Aethra was as fair as a summer morning, and she was the joy and pride of Troezen; and Aegeus was never so happy as when in her presence.

So it happened that some time after the ship had sailed, there was a wedding in the halls of King Pittheus; which it was kept a secret, for Aegeus feared that his nephews, if they heard of it, would be very angry and would send men to Troezen to do him harm.

Then one morning, when the gardens of Troezen were full of roses and the heather[3] was green on the hills, a babe was born to Aethra—a boy with a fair face and strong arms and eyes as sharp and as bright as the mountain eagle's.

And now Aegeus was more loth[4] to return home than he had been before, and he went up on the mountain which overlooks Troezen, and prayed to Athena, the queen of the air, to give him wisdom and show him what to do.

Even while he prayed there came a ship into the harbor, bringing a letter to Aegeus and alarming news from Athens.

"Come home without delay"—these were words of the letter which the elders had sent—"come home quickly, or Athens will be lost. A great king from beyond the sea, Minos of Crete, is on the way with ships and a host of fighting men; and he declares that he will carry sword and fire within our walls, and will slay our young men and make our children his slaves. Come and save us!"

2 tarry ['tæri] (v.) to stay somewhere for longer than expected and delay leaving 逗留
3 heather ['heðər] (n.) a low spreading bush 石南屬植物
4 loth [louθ] (a.) loath; unwilling to do something 不願意的

"It is the call of duty," said Aegeus.

"Best of wives," he said, when the hour for parting had come, "listen to me, for I shall never see your own fair face, again. Do you remember the old plane tree[5] which stands on the mountain side, and the great flat stone which lies a little way beyond it, and which no man but myself has ever been able to lift? Under that stone, I have hidden my sword and the sandals which I brought from Athens. There they shall lie until our child is strong enough to lift the stone and take them for his own. Care for him, Aethra, until that time; and then, and not till then, you may tell him of his father, and bid him seek me in Athens."

Then Aegeus kissed his wife and the babe, and went on board the ship; the sailors shouted; the oars[6] were dipped into the waves; the white sail was spread to the breeze; and Aethra from her palace window saw the vessel[7] speed away over the blue waters towards Aegina and the distant Attic shore.

5 plane tree: a perennial woody plant 懸鈴木
6 oar [ɔːr] (n.) a long pole with a wide flat part at one end which is used for rowing a boat 槳
7 vessel ['vesəl] (n.) a large boat or a ship（大型）船

2 Theseus Lifting the Stone

Year after year went by, and yet no word reached Aethra from her husband on the other side of the sea.

Then it was rumored that King Minos had seized upon all the ships of Athens, and had burned a part of the city, and had forced the people to pay him a most grievous[1] tribute[2]. But further than this there was no news.

In the meanwhile Aethra's babe had grown to be a tall, ruddy[3]-cheeked lad, strong as a mountain lion; and she had named him Theseus. On the day that he was fifteen years old he went with her up to the top of the mountain, and with her looked out over the sea.

---

1 grievous ['griːvəs] (a.) having very serious effects 極重大的
2 tribute ['trɪbjuːt] (n.) payment by one ruler to another 貢物
3 ruddy ['rʌdi] (a.) with a healthy reddish glow 氣色紅潤的

🎧143 "Ah, if only your father would come!" she sighed.

"My father?" said Theseus. "Who is my father, and why are you always watching and waiting and wishing that he would come? Tell me about him."

And she answered: "My child, do you see the great flat stone which lies there, half buried in the ground, and covered with moss and trailing[4] ivy? Do you think you can lift it?"

"I will try, mother," said Theseus. And he dug his fingers into the ground beside it, and grasped its uneven[5] edges, and tugged[6] and lifted and strained until his breath came hard and his arms ached and his body was covered with sweat; but the stone was moved not at all.

At last he said, "The task is too hard for me until I have grown stronger. But why do you wish me to lift it?"

"When you are strong enough to lift it," answered Aethra, "I will tell you about your father."

After that the boy went out every day and practiced at running and leaping and throwing and lifting; and every day he rolled some stone out of its place.

---

4 trailing ['treɪlɪŋ] (a.) creeping 蔓延的
5 uneven [ʌn'iːvən] (a.) having a surface that is not level or smooth 不平整的
6 tug [tʌg] (v.) to pull something quickly and usually with a lot of force 用力拉（或拖）

And little by little he grew stronger, and his muscles became like iron bands, and his limbs[7] were like mighty levers[8] for strength. Then on his next birthday he went up on the mountain with his mother, and again tried to lift the great stone. But it remained fast in its place and was not moved.

"I am not yet strong enough, mother," he said.

"Have patience, my son," said Aethra.

So he went on again with his running and leaping and throwing and lifting; and he practiced wrestling, also, and tamed the wild horses of the plain, and hunted the lions among the mountains; and his strength and swiftness and skill were the wonder of all men, and old Troezen was filled with tales of the deeds of the boy Theseus.

Yet when he tried again on his seventeenth birthday, he could not move the great flat stone that lay near the plane tree on the mountain side.

"Have patience, my son," again said Aethra; but this time the tears were standing in her eyes.

So he went back again to his exercising. And men said that since the days of Hercules there was never so great strength in one body.

---

7 limb [lɪm] (n.) an arm or leg of a person or animal 四肢
8 lever ['lɛvər] (n.) rigid bar used for leverage 槓桿

Theseus and Aethra

Then, when he was a year older, he climbed the mountain yet another time with his mother, and he stooped[9] and took hold of the stone, and it yielded to his touch; and, lo[10], when he had lifted it quite out of the ground, he found underneath it a sword of bronze and sandals of gold, and these he gave to his mother.

9 stoop [stu:p] (v.) to bend the top half of the body forward and down 屈身；彎腰
10 lo [loʊ] (int.) look (used to draw attention to something) 瞧！

Theseus Lifting the Stone

"Tell me now about my father," he said.

Aethra knew that the time had come for which she had waited so long, and she buckled[11] the sword to his belt and fastened the sandals upon his feet. Then she told him who his father was, and why he had left them in Troezen.

Theseus was glad when he heard this, and his proud eyes flashed with eagerness as he said: "I am ready, mother; and I will set out for Athens this very day."

But the old man shook his head sadly and tried to dissuade Theseus from going.

"How can you go to Athens in these lawless times?" he said. "

---

11 buckle ['bʌkəl] (v.) to fasten or be fastened with a buckle 扣緊

"Which is the most perilous[12] way?" asked Theseus—"to go by ship or to make the journey on foot round the great bend of land?"

"The seaway is full enough of perils, but the landway is beset[13] with dangers tenfold[14] greater." said his grandfather.

"Well," said Theseus, "if there are more perils by land than by sea, then I shall go by land, and I go at once."

"But you will at least take fifty young men, your companions, with you?" said King Pittheus.

"Not one shall go with me," said Theseus; and he stood up and played with his sword hilt[15], and laughed at the thought of fear.

Then when there was nothing more to say, he kissed his mother and bade his grandfather good-by. And with blessings and tears the king and Aethra followed him to the city gates, and watched him until his tall form was lost to sight among the trees which bordered[16] the shore of the sea.

---

12 perilous ['perɪləs] (a.) extremely dangerous 極危險的
13 beset [bɪ'set] (v.) to attack somebody or something from all sides包圍
14 tenfold ['tenfoʊld] (a.) multiplied by ten 十倍的
15 hilt [hɪlt] (n.) sword handle 劍柄
16 border ['bɔːrdər] (v.) run along edge of something 與……接壤

3 The Robber Giant: Club-Carrier

With a brave heart Theseus walked on, keeping the sea always upon his right. Then he climbed one slope after another, until at last he stood on the summit of a gray peak from which he could see the whole country spread out around him.

Then downward and onward he went again, until he came to a dreary wood where the trees grew tall and close together and the light of the sun was seldom seen.

In that forest there dwelt a robber giant, called Club-carrier, who was the terror of all the country. For oftentimes he would go down into the valleys where the shepherds fed their flocks, and would carry off not only sheep and lambs, but sometimes children and the men themselves.

When he saw Theseus coming through the woods, he thought that he would have a rich prize, for he knew from the youth's dress and manner that he must be a prince.

He lay on the ground, where leaves of ivy and tall grass screened[1] him from view, and held his great iron club ready to strike.

But Theseus had sharp eyes and quick ears, and neither beast nor robber giant could have taken him by surprise. When Club-carrier leaped out of his hiding place to strike him down, the young man dodged[2] aside so quickly that the heavy club struck the ground behind him; and then, before the robber giant could raise it for a second stroke, Theseus seized the fellow's legs and tripped[3] him up.

Club-carrier roared loudly, and tried to strike again; but Theseus wrenched[4] the club out of his hands, and then dealt him such a blow on the head that he never again harmed travelers passing through the forest.

Then the youth went on his way, carrying the huge club on his shoulder, and singing a song of victory, and looking sharply around him for any other foes that might be lurking among the trees.

1 screen [skriːn] (v.) to conceal something 遮住
2 dodge [dɑːdʒ] (v.) to avoid something by moving quickly aside 躲開
3 trip [trɪp] (v.) cause somebody to stumble 使絆倒
4 wrench ['rentʃ] (v.) to take by force 搶；攫取

4 Pine-Bender: Sinis

149   Just over the ridge[1] of the next mountain he met an old man who warned him not to go any farther. He said that close by a grove of pine trees, which he would soon pass on his way down the slope, there dwelt a robber named Sinis, who was very cruel to strangers.

"He is called Pine-bender," said the old man; "for when he has caught a traveler, he bends two tall, lithe pine trees to the ground and binds his captive to them—a hand and a foot to the top of one, and a hand and a foot to the top of the other. Then he lets the trees fly up, and he roars with laughter when he sees the traveler's body torn in sunder[2]."

"It seems to me," said Theseus, "that it is full time to rid the world of such a monster."

---

1   ridge [rɪdʒ] (n.) a long narrow hilltop or range of hills 山脈
2   in sunder: a separation into parts 斷裂

Soon he came in sight of the robber's house, built near the foot of a jutting[3] cliff. Behind it was a rocky gorge[4] and a roaring mountain stream; and in front of it was a garden. But the tops of the pine trees below it were laden with the bones of unlucky travelers, which hung bleaching[5] white in the sun and wind.

On a stone by the roadside sat Sinis himself; and when he saw Theseus coming, he ran to meet him, twirling[6] a long rope in his hands and crying out: "Welcome, welcome, dear prince! Welcome to our inn—the true Traveler's Rest!"

"What kind of entertainment have you?" asked Theseus. "Have you a pine tree bent down to the ground and ready for me?"

"Ay; two of them!" said the robber. "I knew that you were coming, and I bent two of them for you."

As he spoke he threw his rope towards Theseus and tried to entangle[7] him in its coils[8].

---

3 jut ['dʒʌt] (v.) to stick out 突出
4 gorge [gɔːrdʒ] (n.) a deep narrow valley 峽谷
5 bleaching ['bliːtʃɪŋ] (a.) be lightened in color 漂白的
6 twirl ['twɜːrl] (v.) to give a sudden quick turn or set of turns in a circle 快速旋轉
7 entangle [ɪn'tæŋgəl] (v.) to cause something to become caught in something such as a net or ropes 使糾結在一起
8 coil [kɔɪl] (n.) something that curls or is curled into a spiral shape 盤繞

Theseus Against Sinis and Sciron

Then the two wrestled together among the trees, but not long, Theseus knelt upon the robber's back as he lay prone[9] among the leaves, and tied him with his own cord[10] to the two pine trees which were already bent down. "As you would have done unto me, so will I do unto you," he said.

Then Pine-bender wept and prayed and made many a fair promise; but Theseus would not hear him. He turned away, the trees sprang up, and the robber's body was left dangling[11] from their branches.

---

9 prone [proʊn] (a.) lying face or front downward 伏地的
10 cord [kɔːrd] (n.) a length of rope or string made of twisted threads 繩索
11 dangle ['dæŋgəl] (v.) to hang loosely 懸蕩；吊掛

5 Perigune and Asparagus

Now this old Pine-bender had a daughter named Perigune, who was no more like him than a fair and tender violet is like the gnarled[1] old oak at whose feet it nestles; and it was she who cared for the flowers and the rare plants which grew in the garden by the robber's house.

When she saw how Theseus had dealt with her father, she was afraid and ran to hide herself from him.

"Oh, save me, dear plants!" she cried, for she often talked to the flowers as though they could understand her. "Dear plants, save me; and I will never pluck[2] your leaves nor harm you in any way so long as I live."

There was one of the plants which up to that time had had no leaves, but came up out of the ground looking like a mere club or stick. This plant took pity on the maiden. It began at once to send out long feathery branches with delicate green leaves, which grew so fast that Perigune was soon hidden from sight beneath them.

---

1 gnarled ['nɑːrld] (a.) twisted and full of knots 多節的
2 pluck [plʌk] (v.) to take something away swiftly 摘採

So he called to her: "Perigune," he said, "you need not fear me; for I know that you are gentle and good, and it is only against things dark and cruel that I lift up my hand."

The maiden peeped from her hiding-place, and when she saw the fair face of the youth and heard his kind voice, she came out, trembling, and talked with him.

And Theseus rested that evening in her house, and she picked some of her choicest flowers for him and gave him food. But when in the morning the dawn began to appear in the east, and the stars grew dim[3] above the mountain peaks, he bade her farewell and journeyed onward over the hills.

And Perigune tended her plants and watched her flowers in the lone garden in the midst of the piny grove; but she never plucked the stalks of asparagus[4] nor used them for food, and when she afterwards became the wife of a hero and had children and grandchildren and great-grandchildren, she taught them all to spare the plant which had taken pity upon her in her need.

---

3 dim [dɪm] (a.) not giving or having much light 微暗的
4 asparagus [əˈspærəgəs] (n.) spear-shaped young plant shoots, eaten cooked as a vegetable 蘆筍

6 Vile Sciron

154 Theseus went on fearlessly and came at last to a place where a spring of clear water bubbled out from a cleft [1] in the rock; and there the path was narrower still, and the low doorway of a cavern opened out upon it.

Close by the spring sat a red-faced giant, with a huge club across his knees, guarding the road so that no one could pass; and in the sea at the foot of the cliff basked a huge turtle, its leaden [2] eyes looking always upward for its food.

Theseus knew—for Perigune had told him—that this was the dwelling-place of a robber named Sciron, who was the terror of all the coast, and whose custom it was to make strangers wash his feet, so that while they were doing so, he might kick them over the cliff to be eaten, by his pet turtle below.

---

1 cleft [klɛft] (n.) an opening or crack, especially in a rock or the ground 裂縫
2 leaden ['lɛdn] (a.) without energy or feeling 沈悶的；無活力的

When Theseus came up, the robber raised his club, and said fiercely: "No man can pass here until he has washed my feet! Come, set to work!"

Then Theseus smiled, and said: "Is your turtle hungry today? and do you want me to feed him?"

The robber's eyes flashed fire, and he said, "You shall feed him, but you shall wash my feet first;" and with that he brandished[3] his club in the air and rushed forward to strike.

But Theseus was ready for him. With the iron club which he had taken from Club-carrier in the forest he met the blow midway, and the robber's weapon was knocked out of his hands and sent spinning away over the edge of the cliff. Then Sciron, black with rage, tried to grapple[4] with him; but Theseus was too quick for that.

He dropped his club and seized Sciron by the throat; he pushed him back against the ledge on which he had been sitting; he threw him sprawling[5] upon the sharp rocks, and held him there, hanging half way over the cliff.

"You must wash my feet now. Come, set to work!" said Theseus.

---

3 brandish ['brændɪʃ] (v.) to wave something about 揮舞
4 grapple ['græpəl] (v.) to fight, especially in order to gain something 抓住
5 sprawl [sprɔːl] (v.) to sit or lie with the arms and legs spread awkwardly in different directions 伸開四肢躺著

Then Sciron, white with fear, washed his feet.

"And now," said Theseus, when the task was ended, "as you have done unto others, so will I do unto you."

There was a scream in mid air which the mountain eagles answered from above; there was a great splashing[6] in the water below, and the turtle fled in terror from its lurking place.

Then the sea cried out: "I will have naught to do with so vile[7] a wretch[8]!

---

6 splash ['splæʃ] (v.) scattering a liquid in large drops or amounts
  濺潑;激起水花
7 vile [vaɪl] (a.) unpleasant, immoral and unacceptable 邪惡的
8 wretch [retʃ] (n.) someone who is unpleasant or annoying
  卑鄙的傢伙

And a great wave cast the body of Sciron out upon the shore. But it had no sooner touched the ground than the land cried out: "I will have naught to do with so vile a wretch!"

And there was a sudden earthquake, and the body of Sciron was thrown back into the sea. Then the sea waxed[9] furious, a raging storm arose, the waters were lashed[10] into foam, and the waves with one mighty effort threw the detested[11] body high into the air; and there it would have hung unto this day had not the air itself disdained to give it lodging[12] and changed it into a huge black rock.

And this rock, which men say is the body of Sciron, may still be seen, grim[13], ugly, and desolate; and one third of it lies in the sea, one third is embedded in the sandy shore, and one third is exposed to the air.

---

9 wax [wæks] (v.) to increase in size, power, or intensity 加劇
10 lash [læʃ] (v.) a strong or powerful, often continuous, impact of something 猛烈衝擊
11 detested [dɪ'testɪd] (a.) to be disliked very much 被厭惡的
12 lodging ['lɑːdʒɪŋ] (n.) somewhere to stay temporarily 住宿
13 grim [grɪm] (a.) extremely unpleasant, distressing, or sinister 陰森的；可怕的

7 Wrestler of Wrong-Doer

Theseus came down into the valleys and into a pleasant plain. The fame of his deeds had gone before him, and men and women came crowding to the roadside to see the hero who had slain Club-carrier and Pine-bender and grim old Sciron of the cliff.

"Now we shall live in peace," they cried; "for the robbers who devoured our flocks and our children are no more."

"Do not go into Eleusis, but take the road which leads round it through the hills," whispered a poor man who was carrying a sheep to market.

"Why shall I do that?" asked Theseus.

"Listen, and I will tell you," was the answer. "There is a king in Eleusis whose name is Cercyon, and he is a great wrestler. He makes every stranger who comes into the city wrestle with him; and such is the strength of his arms that when he has overcome a man he crushes the life out of his body. Many travelers come to Eleusis, but no one ever goes away."

"But I will both come and go away," said Theseus; and with his club upon his shoulder, he strode[1] onward into the sacred city.

"Where is Cercyon, the wrestler?" he asked of the warden at the gate.

"The king is dining in his marble palace," was the answer. "If you wish to save yourself, turn now and flee before he has heard of your coming."

"Why should I flee?" asked Theseus. "I am not afraid;" and he walked on through the narrow street to old Cercyon's palace.

Theseus went up boldly to the door, and cried out: "Cercyon, come out and wrestle with me!"

"Ah!" said the king, "here comes another young fool whose days are numbered. Fetch[2] him in and let him dine with me; and after that he shall have his fill of wrestling."

So Theseus was given a place at the table of the king, and the two sat there and ate and stared at each other, but spoke not a word.

When they had finished, Theseus arose and: "Come now, Cercyon, if you are not afraid; come, and wrestle with me."

---

1 stride [straɪd] (v.) to walk somewhere quickly with long steps
邁大步走
2 fetch [fetʃ] (v.) to go after and bring back somebody or something 去拿⋯⋯給⋯⋯

160 Then the two went out into the courtyard where many
a young man had met his fate, and there they wrestled
until the sun went down, and neither could gain aught³ of
advantage over the other.

But it was plain that the trained skill of Theseus would,
in the end, win against the brute⁴ strength of Cercyon.
Then the men of Eleusis who stood watching the contest,
saw the youth lift the giant king bodily into the air
and hurl him headlong⁵ over his shoulder to the hard
pavement beyond.

3 aught [ɑːt] (n.) anything whatever 任何事物
4 brute [bruːt] (a.) a man who is cruel, violent, and not sensitive
   殘忍的
5 headlong ['hedlɔːŋ] (adv.) with the head in front of the rest of
   the body 頭向前地

Wrestler of Wrong-Doer 197

"As you have done to others, so will I do unto you!" cried Theseus.

But grim old Cercyon neither moved nor spoke; and when the youth turned his body over and looked into his cruel face, he saw that the life had quite gone out of him.

Then the people of Eleusis came to Theseus and wanted to make him their king.

"Some day," said Theseus, "I will be your king, but not now; for there are other deeds for me to do."

And with that he donned[6] his sword and his sandals and his princely cloak, and threw his great iron club upon his shoulder, and went out of Eleusis; and all the people ran after him for quite a little way, shouting, "May good fortune be with you, O king, and may Athena bless and guide you!"

6 don [dɑːn] (v.) to put on 穿戴

8 The Stretcher: Procrustes

Athens was now not more than twenty miles away. The sun was almost down when he came to a broad green valley; and on a hillside close by, half hidden among the trees, there was a great stone house with vines running over its walls and roof.

While Theseus was wondering who it could be that lived in this pretty but lonely place, a man came out of the house and hurried down to the road to meet him.

"This is a lonely place," the man said, "and it is not often that travelers pass this way. Come up, and sup[1] with me, and lodge[2] under my roof; and you shall sleep on a wonderful bed which I have—a bed which fits every guest and cures him of every ill. Now I will go in and make the bed ready for you, and you can lie down upon it and rest."

When he had gone into the house, Theseus looked around him to see what sort of a place it was.

---

1 sup [sʌp] (v.) to drink or to eat 啜飲
2 lodge [lɑːdʒ] (v.) to live in somebody's house 投宿

163 He was filled with
surprise at the richness of
it—at the gold and silver
and beautiful things with
which every room seemed
to be adorned—for it was
indeed a place fit for a
prince.

While he was looking
and wondering, the vines
before him were parted and the fair face of a young girl
peeped out.

"Noble stranger," she whispered, "do not lie down on
my master's bed, for those who do so never rise again. Fly
down the glen and hide yourself in the deep woods ere he
returns, or else there will be no escape for you."

"Who is your master, fair maiden, that I should be afraid
of him?" asked Theseus.

"Men call him Procrustes, or the Stretcher," said the girl,
Did he not tell you that it fits all guests? and most truly it
does fit them. For if a traveler is too long, Procrustes hews[3]
off his legs until he is of the right length; but if he is too
short, as is the case with most guests, then he stretches his
limbs and body with ropes until he is long enough. It is for
this reason that men call him the Stretcher."

3 hew [hjuː] (v.) to cut down 砍

"Hark[4]! hark!" whispered the girl. "I hear him coming!" And the vine leaves closed over her hiding-place.

The very next moment Procrustes stood in the door, bowing and smiling as though he had never done any harm to his fellow men.

"My dear young friend," he said, "the bed is ready, and I will show you the way. Just take a pleasant little nap."

They had come into an inner chamber[5], there, surely enough, was the bedstead[6], of iron, very curiously wrought, and upon it a soft couch.

But Theseus, peering about, saw the ax and the ropes with cunning pulleys[7] lying hidden behind the curtains; and he saw, too, that the floor was covered with stains[8] of blood.

"Is this your wonderful bed?" asked Theseus.

"It is," answered Procrustes, "and you need but to lie down upon it, and it will fit you perfectly."

4 hark [hɑːrk] (v.) to listen to somebody or something 聽
5 chamber ['tʃeɪmbər] (n.) a room used for a particular purpose 房間
6 bedstead ['bedsted] (n.) the structural framework of a bed 床架
7 pulley ['pʊli] (n.) wheel with grooved rim 滑輪
8 stain [steɪn] (n.) a discolored mark made by something such as blood, wine, or ink 汙跡

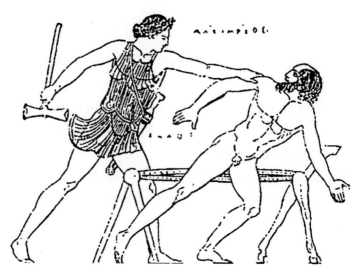

Theseus and Procrustes

"But you must lie upon it first," said Theseus, "and let me see how it will fit itself to your stature[9]."

"Ah, no," said Procrustes, "for then the spell would be broken," and as he spoke his cheeks grew ashy pale.

"But I tell you, you must lie upon it," said Theseus; and he seized the trembling man around the waist and threw him by force upon the bed.

And no sooner was he prone upon the couch than curious iron arms reached out and clasped his body in their embrace[10] and held him down so that he could not move hand or foot. The wretched man shrieked and cried for mercy. "Is this the kind of bed on which you have your guests lie down?" Theseus asked.

---

9 stature ['stætʃər] (n.) the standing height of somebody 身高
10 embrace [ɪm'breɪs] (n.) to hold someone tightly with both arms 擁抱

166 But Procrustes answered not a word. Then Theseus brought out the ax and the ropes and the pulleys, and asked him what they were for, and why they were hidden in the chamber. He was still silent, and could do nothing now but tremble and weep.

"Is it true," said Theseus, "that you have lured hundreds of travelers into your den only to rob them? Is it true that it is your wont to fasten them in this bed, and then chop[11] off their legs or stretch them out until they fit the iron frame? Tell me, is this true?"

"It is true! it is true!" sobbed Procrustes; "and now kindly touch the spring[12] above my head and let me go, and you shall have everything that I possess."

But Theseus turned away. "You are caught," he said, "in the trap which you set for others and for me. There is no mercy for the man who shows no mercy;" and he went out of the room, and left the wretch to perish by his own cruel device[13].

---

11 chop [tʃɑːp] (v.) cut something off 砍
12 spring [sprɪŋ] (n.) coil of metal 彈簧
13 device [dɪˈvaɪs] (n.) an object or machine which has been invented to fulfil a particular purpose 裝置

Theseus looked through the house. Then the girl whose fair face Theseus had seen among the vines, came running into the house; and she seized the young hero's hands and blessed him and thanked him because he had rid the world of the cruel Procrustes.

"Only a month ago," she said, "my father, a rich merchant[14] of Athens, was traveling towards Eleusis, and I was with him. This robber lured us into his den, for we had much gold with us. My father, he stretched upon his iron bed; but me, he made his slave."

Then Theseus called together all the inmates[15] of the house, poor wretches whom Procrustes had forced to serve him; and he parted the robber's spoils[16] among them and told them that they were free to go wheresoever they wished.

---

14 merchant ['mɜːrtʃənt] (n.) a person whose job is to buy and sell products in large amounts, especially by trading with other countries 商人
15 inmate ['ɪnmeɪt] (n.) somebody in an institution 同居住者
16 spoil [spɔɪl] (n.) valuables or property seized by the victor in a conflict 掠奪物；贓物

9 Returning Home

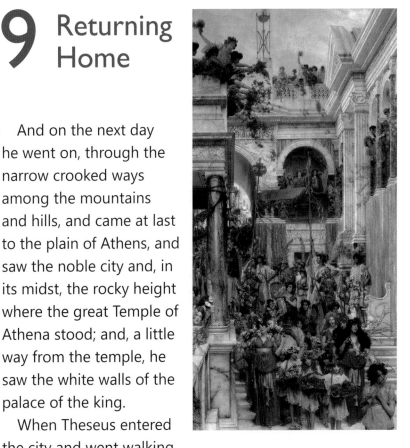

168   And on the next day he went on, through the narrow crooked ways among the mountains and hills, and came at last to the plain of Athens, and saw the noble city and, in its midst, the rocky height where the great Temple of Athena stood; and, a little way from the temple, he saw the white walls of the palace of the king.

When Theseus entered the city and went walking up the street everybody wondered who the tall, fair youth could be. But the fame of his deeds had gone before him, and soon it was whispered that this was the hero who had slain the robbers in the mountains and had wrestled with Cercyon at Eleusis and had caught Procrustes in his own cunning trap.

Theseus Went Up Through Athens

"Tell us no such thing!" said some butchers who were driving their loaded carts[1] to market. "The lad[2] is better suited to sing sweet songs to the ladies than to fight robbers and wrestle with giants."

"See his silken black hair!" said one.

"And his girlish face!" said another.

"And his long coat dangling about his legs!" said a third.

"And his golden sandals!" said a fourth.

---

1 cart [kɑːrt] (n.) a light vehicle pushed by hand 手推車
2 lad [læd] (n.) a boy or young man 小伙子

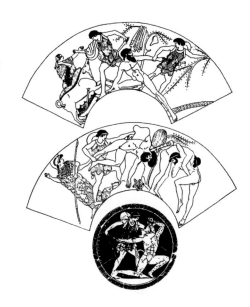

"Ha! ha!" laughed the first; "I wager that he never lifted a ten-pound weight in his life. Think of such a fellow as he hurling old Sciron from the cliffs! Nonsense!"

Theseus heard all this talk as he strode along, and it angered him not a little; but he had not come to Athens to quarrel with butchers.

Without speaking a word he walked straight up to the foremost cart, and, before its driver had time to think, took hold of the slaughtered[3] ox that was being hauled[4] to market, and hurled it high over the tops of the houses into the garden beyond.

Then he did likewise with the oxen in the second, the third, and the fourth wagons, and, turning about, went on his way, and left the wonder-stricken butchers staring after him, speechless, in the street.

He climbed the stairway which led to the top of the steep, rocky hill, and his heart beat fast in his bosom as he stood on the threshold[5] of his father's palace.

---

3 slaughtered ['slɔːtərd] (a.) animals killed for meat 宰殺的
4 haul [hɔːl] (v.) to pull something heavy slowly and with difficulty 拖拉；搬運
5 threshold ['θreʃoʊld] (n.) the floor of entrance to a building or room 門檻

"Where is the king?" he asked of the guard.

"You cannot see the king," was the answer; "but I will take you to his nephews."

The man led the way into the feast hall, and there Theseus saw his fifty cousins sitting about the table, and eating and drinking and making merry; and there was a great noise of revelry[6] in the hall, the minstrels[7] singing and playing, and the slave girls dancing, and the half-drunken princes shouting and cursing.

As Theseus stood in the doorway, knitting his eyebrows and clinching[8] his teeth for the anger which he felt, one of the feasters saw him, and cried out:

"See the tall fellow in the doorway! What does he want here?"

"Yes, girl-faced stranger," said another, "what do you want here?"

"I am here," said Theseus, "to ask that hospitality which men of our race never refuse to give."

"Nor do we refuse," cried they. "Come in, and eat and drink and be our guest."

---

6 revelry ['revəlri] (n.) to dance, drink, sing, etc. at a party, especially in a noisy way 喧鬧的歡宴

7 minstrel ['mɪnstrəl] (n.) entertainer in variety show 表演藝人

8 clinch [klɪntʃ] (v.) hold in a tight grasp 咬緊

"I will come in," said Theseus, "but I will be the guest of the king. Where is he?"

"Never mind the king," said one of his cousins. "He is taking his ease, and we reign in his stead[9]."

But Theseus strode boldly through the feast hall and went about the palace asking for the king.

At last he found Aegeus, lonely and sorrowful, sitting in an inner chamber. The heart of Theseus was very sad as he saw the lines of care upon the old man's face, and marked his trembling, halting ways.

"Great king," he said, "I am a stranger in Athens, and I have come to you to ask food and shelter and friendship such as I know you never deny to those of noble rank and of your own race."

"And who are you, young man?" said the king.

"I am Theseus," was the answer.

"What? the Theseus who has rid the world of the mountain robbers, and of Cercyon the wrestler, and of Procrustes, the pitiless Stretcher?"

"I am he," said Theseus.

The king started and turned very pale. "Troezen! Troezen!" he cried. Then checking himself, he said, "Yes! yes! You are welcome, brave stranger, to such shelter and food and friendship as the King of Athens can give."

---

9 stead [sted] (n.) in place of someone 代替

10 The Wicked Witch: Medea

Now it so happened that there was with the king a fair but wicked witch named Medea, who had so much power over him that he never dared to do anything without asking her leave.

So he turned to her, and said: "Am I not right, Medea, in bidding this young hero welcome?"

"You are right, King Aegeus," she said; "and let him be shown at once to your guest chamber, that he may rest himself and afterwards dine with us at your own table."

Medea had learned by her magic arts who Theseus was, and she was not at all pleased to have him in Athens; for she feared that when he should make himself known to the king, her own power would be at an end.

So, while Theseus was resting himself in the guest chamber, she told Aegeus that the young stranger was no hero at all, but a man whom his nephews had hired to kill him, for they had grown tired of waiting for him to die.

173 The poor old king was filled with fear, for he believed her words; and he asked her what he should do to save his life.

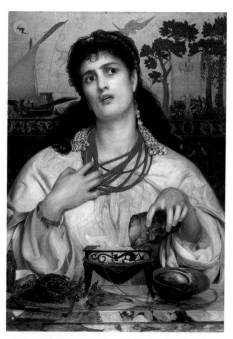

Medea

"Let me manage it," she said. "The young man will soon come down to dine with us. I will drop poison into a glass of wine, and at the end of the meal I will give it to him. Nothing can be easier."

So, when the hour came, Theseus sat down to dine with the king and Medea; and while he ate he told of his deeds and of how he had overcome the robber giants, and Cercyon the wrestler, and Procrustes the pitiless; and as the king listened, his heart yearned strangely towards the young man, and he longed to save him from Medea's poisoned cup.

Then Theseus paused in his talk to help himself to a piece of the roasted meat, and, as was the custom of the time, drew his sword to carve[1] it.

---

1 carve [kɑːrv] (v.) engrave 雕刻

As the sword flashed from its scabbard[2], Aegeus saw the letters that were engraved[3] upon it—the initials[4] of his own name.

He knew at once that it was the sword which he had hidden so many years before under the stone on the mountain side above Troezen.

"My son! my son!" he cried; and he sprang up and dashed the cup of poisoned wine from the table, and flung[5] his arms around Theseus. It was indeed a glad meeting for both father and son, and they had many things to ask and to tell.

As for the wicked Medea, she knew that her day of rule was past. She ran out of the palace, and whistled a loud, shrill[6] call; and men say that a chariot drawn by dragons came rushing through the air, and that she leaped into it and was carried away, and no one ever saw her again.

2 scabbard ['skæbərd] (n.) a long thin cover for the blade of a sword 鞘
3 engrave [ɪn'ɡreɪv] (v.) to cut words, pictures or patterns into the surface of metal, stone 刻
4 initial [ɪ'nɪʃəl] (n.) the first letter of a name 起首字母

The very next morning, Aegeus sent out his heralds[7], to make it known through all the city that Theseus was his son, and that he would in time be king in his stead. When the fifty nephews heard this, they were angry and alarmed.

"Shall this upstart[8] cheat us out of our heritage[9]?" they cried; and they made a plot[10] to waylay[11] and kill Theseus in a grove close by the city gate.

---

5 fling [flɪŋ] (v.) to move quickly 急伸（手臂）
6 shrill [ʃrɪl] (a.) having a loud and high sound 尖聲的
7 herald ['herəld] (n.) a person who delivered important messages and made announcements 傳令官
8 upstart ['ʌpstɑːrt] (n.) an arrogant person 傲慢自負的人
9 heritage ['herɪtɪdʒ] (n.) any attribute or immaterial possession that is inherited from ancestors 世襲財產
10 plot [plɑːt] (n.) to make a secret plan to do something wrong, harmful or illegal 密謀
11 waylay [weɪ'leɪ] (v.) to wait for and then stop someone, especially either to attack them or talk to them 伏擊

Right cunningly did the wicked fellows lay their trap to catch the young hero; and one morning, as he was passing that way alone, several of them fell suddenly upon him, with swords and lances[12], and tried to slay him outright. They were thirty to one, but he faced them boldly and held them at bay, while he shouted for help.

The men of Athens, who had borne so many wrongs from the hands of the nephews, came running out from the streets; and in the fight which followed, every one of the plotters, who had lain in ambush[13] was slain; and the other nephews, when they heard about it, fled from the city in haste and never came back again.

---

12 lance [læns] (n.) a long thin pole with a sharp point used as a weapon 長矛
13 ambush ['æmbʊʃ] (n.) an unexpected attack from a concealed position 埋伏；伏擊

12 The Wonderful Artisan

Perdix and Partridge

While Athens was still only a small city there lived within its walls a man named Daedalus who was the most skillful worker in wood and stone and metal that had ever been known.

It was he who taught the people how to build better houses and how to hang their doors on hinges[1] and how to support the roofs with pillars and posts. He was the first to fasten things together with glue; he invented the plumb[2]-line and the auger[3]; and he showed seamen how to put up masts[4] in their ships and how to rig[5] the sails to them with ropes.

He built a stone palace for Aegeus, the young king of Athens, and beautified the Temple of Athena which stood on the great rocky hill in the middle of the city.

Daedalus had a nephew named Perdix whom he had taken when a boy to teach the trade of builder. But Perdix was a very apt[6] learner, and soon surpassed[7] his master in the knowledge of many things.

1 hinge [hɪndʒ] (n.) a movable joint of metal or plastic used to fasten two things 鉸鏈
2 plumb [plʌm] (n.) a weight, usually made of lead, attached to a line and used to verify a true vertical alignment 鉛錘；測鉛
3 auger ['ɔːgər] (n.) a tool consisting of a twisted rod of metal fixed to a handle, used for making large holes in wood or in the ground 螺旋鑽
4 mast [mæst] (n.) a tall pole on a boat or ship that supports its sails 桅杆
5 rig [rɪg] (v.) to fit out a boat or its mast with sails and rigging 給船隻桅杆裝配帆及索具
6 apt [æpt] (a.) having a natural ability or skill 聰明的
7 surpass [sər'pæs] (v.) to do or be better than 勝過

His eyes were ever open to see what was going on about him, and he learned the lore[8] of the fields and the woods.

Walking one day by the sea, he picked up the backbone of a great fish, and from it he invented the saw[9]. Seeing how a certain bird carved holes in the trunks of trees, he learned how to make and use the chisel[10]. Then he invented the wheel which potters[11] use in molding clay; and he made of a forked stick the first pair of compasses[12] for drawing circles; and he studied out many other curious and useful things.

Daedalus was not pleased when he saw that the lad was so apt and wise, so ready to learn, and so eager to do.

"If he keeps on in this way," he murmured, "he will be a greater man than I; his name will be remembered, and mine will be forgotten."

8 lore [lɔːr] (n.) traditional knowledge and stories about a subject 某門知識
9 saw [sɔː] (n.) hand tool having a toothed blade for cutting 鋸子
10 chisel ['tʃɪzəl] (n.) an edge tool with a flat steel blade with a cutting edge 鑿子
11 potter ['pɑːtər] (n.) a maker of pottery 陶工
12 compass ['kʌmpəs] (n.) a device for finding directions 羅盤；指南針

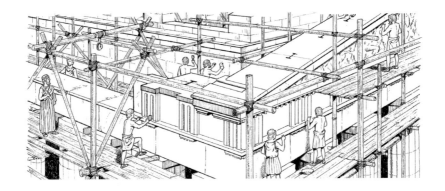

Day after day, while at his work, Daedalus pondered[13] over this matter, and soon his heart was filled with hatred towards young Perdix.

One morning when the two were putting up an ornament[14] on the outer wall of Athena's temple, Daedalus bade his nephew go out on a narrow scaffold[15] which hung high over the edge of the rocky cliff whereon the temple stood. Then, when the lad obeyed, it was easy enough, with a blow of a hammer, to knock the scaffold from its fastenings.

Poor Perdix fell headlong through the air, and he would have been dashed in pieces upon the stones at the foot of the cliff had not kind Athena seen him and taken pity upon him.

13 ponder ['pɑːndər] (v.) to think carefully about something
    仔細考慮
14 ornament ['ɔːrnəmənt] (n.) an object which is beautiful rather
    than useful 裝飾品
15 scaffold ['skæfoʊld] (n.) framework to support workers 鷹架

Partridges

🎧 179 While he was yet whirling through mid-air she changed him into a partridge[16], and he flitted away to the hills to live forever in the woods and fields which he loved so well.

And to this day, when summer breezes blow and the wild flowers bloom in meadow and glade, the voice of Perdix may still sometimes be heard, calling to his mate from among the grass and reeds or amid the leafy underwoods[17].

16 partridge ['pɑːrtrɪdʒ] (n.) a bird with a round body and a short tail which is sometimes hunted for food 鷓鴣
17 underwood ['ʌndərwʊd] (n.) the brush growing beneath taller trees in a wood or forest 林下灌叢

2 The King of Crete: Minos

As for Daedalus, when the people of Athens heard of his dastardly[1] deed, they were filled with grief and rage—grief for young Perdix, whom all had learned to love; rage towards the wicked uncle, who loved only himself.

At first they were for punishing Daedalus with the death which he so richly deserved, but when they remembered what he had done to make their homes pleasanter and their lives easier, they allowed him to live; and yet they drove him out of Athens and bade him never return.

There was a ship in the harbor just ready to start on a voyage across the sea, and in it Daedalus embarked[2] with all his precious tools and his young son Icarus.

Day after day the little vessel sailed slowly southward, keeping the shore of the mainland always upon the right. It passed Troezen and the rocky coast of Argos, and then struck boldly out across the sea.

1　dastardly [ˈdæstərdli] (a.) evil and cruel 卑鄙的
2　embark [ɪmˈbɑːrk] (v.) to go onto a ship 上船

The King of Crete: Minos　221

At last the famous Island of Crete was reached, and there Daedalus landed and made himself known; and the King of Crete, who had already heard of his wondrous skill, welcomed him to his kingdom, and gave him a home in his palace, and promised that he should be rewarded with great riches and honor if he would but stay and practice his craft there as he had done in Athens.

Now the name of the King of Crete was Minos. His grandfather, whose name was also Minos, was the son of Europa. This elder Minos had been accounted the wisest of men—so wise, indeed, that Jupiter chose him to be one of the judges of the Lower World.

The younger Minos was almost as wise as his grandfather; and he was brave and farseeing[3] and skilled as a ruler of men. He had made all the islands subject to his kingdom, and his ships sailed into every part of the world and brought back to Crete the riches of foreign lands. So it was not hard for him to persuade Daedalus to make his home with him and be the chief of his artisans[4].

---

3 farseeing ['fɑːˈsiːɪŋ] (a.) wise and able to anticipate the future 有先見之明的

4 artisan ['ɑːrtɪzən] (n.) person who does skilled work with his or her hands 工匠

And Daedalus built for King Minos a most wonderful palace with floors of marble and pillars of granite[5]; and in the palace he set up golden statues which had tongues and could talk; and for splendor[6] and beauty there was no other building in all the wide earth that could be compared with it.

---

5 granite ['grænɪt] (n.) a very hard, grey, pink and black rock, which is used for building 花崗石
6 splendor ['splɛdər] (n.) great beauty which attracts admiration and attention 壯觀

3 Minotaur and Labyrinth

There lived in those days among the hills of Crete a terrible monster called the Minotaur, the like of which has never been seen from that time until now. This creature, it was said, had the body of a man, but the face and head of a wild bull and the fierce nature of a mountain lion.

The people of Crete would not have killed him if they could; for they thought that the Mighty Folk who lived with Jupiter on the mountain top had sent him among them, and that these beings would be angry if any one should take his life.

He was the pest[1] and terror of all the land. Where he was least expected, there he was sure to be; and almost every day some man, woman, or child was caught and devoured by him.

---

1 pest [pest] (n.) an insect or small animal which is harmful
   有害的動物

"You have done so many wonderful things," said the king to Daedalus, "can you not do something to rid the land of this Minotaur?"

"Shall I kill him?" asked Daedalus.

"Ah, no!" said the king. "That would only bring greater misfortunes upon us."

"I will build a house for him then," said Daedalus, "and you can keep him in it as a prisoner."

"But he may pine[2] away and die if he is penned[3] up in prison," said the king.

"He shall have plenty of room to roam about," said Daedalus; "and if you will only now and then feed one of your enemies to him, I promise you that he shall live and thrive[4]."

So the wonderful artisan brought together his workmen, and they built a marvelous house with so many rooms in it and so many winding ways that no one who went far into it could ever find his way out again; and Daedalus called it the Labyrinth, and cunningly persuaded the Minotaur to go inside of it.

2 pine [paɪn] (v.) to become weak and lose vitality as a result of grief or longing 消瘦；憔悴
3 pen [pen] (v.) confine somebody or something 囚禁
4 thrive [θraɪv] (v.) to grow, develop or be successful 繁榮

Minotaur and Labyrinth

The monster soon lost his way among the winding[5] passages[6], but the sound of his terrible bellowings[7] could be heard day and night as he wandered back and forth vainly[8] trying to find some place to escape.

5 winding [ˈwaɪdɪŋ] (a.) made up of many consecutive curves or twists 迂迴的
6 passage [ˈpæsɪdʒ] (n.) a path enclosed on both sides 通道
7 bellowing [ˈbeloʊɪŋ] (n.) to shout something in a loud deep voice 吼叫
8 vainly [ˈveɪnli] (adv.) unsuccessfully 徒勞地

4 Daedalus Wings

Not long after this it happened that Daedalus was guilty of a deed which angered the king very greatly.

"Hitherto[1]," said the king, "I have honored you for your skill and rewarded you for your labor. But now you shall be my slave and shall serve me without hire and without any word of praise."

Then he gave orders to the guards at the city gates that they should not let Daedalus pass out at any time, and he set soldiers to watch the ships that were in port so that he could not escape by sea.

---

1 hitherto [ˌhɪðərˈtuː] (adv.) until now 迄今

Daedalus and Icarus

But although the wonderful artisan was thus held as a prisoner, he did not build any more buildings for King Minos; he spent his time in planning how he might regain his freedom.

"All my inventions," he said to his son Icarus, "have hitherto been made to please other people; now I will invent something to please myself."

So, all through the day he pretended to be planning some great work for the king, but every night he locked himself up in his chamber and wrought secretly by candle light.

By and by he had made for himself a pair of strong wings, and for Icarus another pair of smaller ones; and then, one midnight, when everybody was asleep, the two went out to see if they could fly.

They fastened the wings to their shoulders with wax, and then sprang up into the air. They could not fly very far at first, but they did so well that they felt sure of doing much better in time.

The next night Daedalus made some changes in the wings; and then he and Icarus went out in the moonlight to try them again. They did finely this time. But they were not ready to undertake a long journey yet; and so, just before daybreak, they flew back home.

Every fair night after that they practiced with their wings, and at the end of a month they felt as safe in the air as on the ground, and could skim² over the hilltops like birds.

---

2 skim [skɪm] (v.) to move quickly just above a surface without touching it 掠過

The Fall of Icarus

5 The Fall of Icarus and Icarian Sea

Early one morning; before King Minos had risen from his bed, they fastened on their wings, sprang into the air, and flew out of the city.

Once fairly away from the island, they turned towards the west, for Daedalus had heard of an island named Sicily, which lay hundreds of miles away, and he had made up his mind to seek a new home there.

All went well for a time, and the two bold flyers sped swiftly over the sea, skimming along only a little above the waves, and helped on their way by the brisk[1] east wind.

Towards noon the sun shone very warm, and Daedalus called out to the boy who was a little behind and told him to keep his wings cool and not fly too high. But the boy was proud of his skill in flying, and as he looked up at the sun he thought how nice it would be to soar like it high above the clouds in the blue depths of the sky.

"At any rate," said he to himself, "I will go up a little higher. Perhaps I can see the horses which draw the sun car, and perhaps I shall catch sight of their driver, the mighty sun master himself."

So he flew up higher and higher, but his father who was in front did not see him. Pretty soon, however, the heat of the sun began to melt the wax with which the boy's wings were fastened. He felt himself sinking through the air; the wings had become loosened from his shoulders. He screamed to his father, but it was too late.

Daedalus turned just in time to see Icarus fall headlong into the waves. The water was very deep there, and the skill of the wonderful artisan could not save his child. He could only look with sorrowing eyes at the unpitying[2] sea, and fly on alone to distant Sicily.

There, men say, he lived for many years, but he never did any great work, nor built anything half so marvelous as the Labyrinth of Crete.

And the sea in which poor Icarus was drowned was called forever afterward by his name, the Icarian Sea.

---

1 brisk [brɪsk] (a.) refreshingly cool 沁涼的
2 unpitying [ʌnˈpɪtiɪŋ] (a.) without mercy or pity 不仁慈的

Mourning for Icarus

13 The Adventures of Theseus (II)

The Cruel Tribute

Minos, king of Crete, had made war upon Athens. He had come with a great fleet[1] of ships and an army, and had burned the merchant vessels in the harbor, and had overrun[2] all the country and the coast even to Megara, which lies to the west.

Then Aegeus, the king of Athens, with the twelve elders who were his helpers, went out to see King Minos and to treat with him.

"O mighty king," they said, "what have we done that you should wish thus to destroy us from the earth?"

"O cowardly and shameless men," answered King Minos, "why do you ask this foolish question, since you can but know the cause of my wrath? I had an only son, Androgeos by name. Three years ago he came hither to take part in the games which you held in honor of Athena. You know how he overcame all your young men in the sports, and how your people honored him with song and dance and laurel crown. But when your king, this same Aegeus who stands before me now, saw how everybody ran after him and praised his valor, he was filled with envy and laid plans to kill him."

---

1 fleet [fliːt] (n.) a group of ships 船隊
2 overrun [ˌoʊvəˈrʌn] (v.) run beyond or past 橫行

"But we do deny it—we do deny it!" cried the elders. "For at that very time our king was sojourning[3] at Troezen on the other side of the Saronic Sea, and he knew nothing of the young prince's death. Androgeos was slain, not through the king's orders but by the king's nephews, who hoped to rouse your anger against Aegeus so that you would drive him from Athens and leave the kingdom to one of them."

"Will you swear that what you tell me is true?" said Minos.

"We will swear it," they said.

"Now then," said Minos, "you shall hear my decree[4]. Athens has robbed me of my dearest treasure, a treasure that can never be restored to me; so, in return, I require from Athens, as tribute, that possession which is the dearest and most precious to her people; and it shall be destroyed cruelly as my son was destroyed."

---

3 sojourn ['soʊdʒɜːrn] (v.) to stay at a place for a time 逗留
4 decree [dɪ'kriː] (n.) an official statement that something must happen 政令

"The condition[5] is hard," said the elders, "but it is just. What is the tribute which you require?"

"Has the king a son?" asked Minos.

The face of King Aegeus lost all its color and he trembled as he thought of a little child then with its mother at Troezen, on the other side of the Saronic Sea. But the elders knew nothing about that child, and they answered:

"Alas, no! he has no son, but he has fifty nephews."

"I have naught to do with those fellows," said Minos; "you may deal with them as you like. But you ask what is the tribute that I require, and I will tell you. Every year when the springtime comes and the roses begin to bloom, you shall choose seven of your noblest youths and seven of your fairest maidens, and shall send them to me in a ship which your king shall provide. This is the tribute which you shall pay to me, Minos, king of Crete."

"We agree to all this, O King," said the elders; "for it is the least of two evils. But tell us now, what shall be the fate of the seven youths and the seven maidens?"

5 condition [kənˈdɪʃən] (n.) something that must exist for something else to happen 條件

"In Crete," answered Minos, "there is a house called the Labyrinth, the like of which you have never seen. In it there are a thousand chambers and winding ways, and whosoever goes even a little way into them can never find his way out again. Into this house the seven youths and the seven maidens shall be thrust[6], and they shall be left there—"

"To perish[7] with hunger?" cried the elders.

"To be devoured by a monster whom men call the Minotaur," said Minos.

Then King Aegeus and the elders covered their faces and wept and went slowly back into the city to tell their people of the sad and terrible conditions upon which Athens could alone be saved.

"It is better that a few should perish than that the whole city should be destroyed," they said.

6 thrust [θrʌst] (v.) to push suddenly and strongly 用力推
7 perish ['perɪʃ] (v.) to die or to be destroyed 死去

2 Bound for Crete

Years passed by. Every spring when the roses began to bloom seven youths and seven maidens were put on board of a black-sailed ship and sent to Crete to pay the tribute which King Minos required.

In the meanwhile the little child at Troezen on the other side of the sea had grown to be a man; and at last he had come to Athens to find his father, King Aegeus, who had never heard whether he was alive or dead; and when the youth had made himself known, the king had welcomed him to his home and all the people were glad because so noble a prince had come to dwell among them and, in time, to rule over their city.

The springtime came again. The black-sailed ship was rigged for another voyage. The rude Cretan soldiers paraded the streets; and the herald of King Minos stood at the gates and shouted: "Yet three days, O Athenians, and your tribute will be due and must be paid!"

Then in every street the doors of the houses were shut and no man went in or out, but every one sat silent with pale cheeks, and wondered whose lot it would be to be chosen this year.

192 "What is the meaning of all this?" the young prince, Theseus cried. "What right has a Cretan to demand tribute in Athens? and what is this tribute of which he speaks?"

Then Aegeus led him aside and with tears told him of the sad war with King Minos, and of the dreadful terms of peace.

"Athens shall not pay tribute to Crete. I myself will go with these youths and maidens, and I will slay the monster Minotaur, and defy[1] King Minos himself upon his throne," cried Theseus.

On the third day all the youths and maidens of the city were brought together in the market place, so that lots[2] might be cast for those who were to be taken. Then two vessels of brass were brought and set before King Aegeus and the herald who had come from Crete; and all the balls were white save only seven in each vessel, and those were black as ebony[3].

1 defy [dɪˈfaɪ] (v.) openly resist 公然反抗
2 lot [lɑːt] (n.) anything taken or chosen at random 籤
3 ebony [ˈebəni] (n.) a hard blackish wood 黑檀

Then every maiden, without looking, reached her hand into one of the vessels and drew forth a ball, and those who took the black balls were borne away to the black ship, which lay in waiting by the shore.

The young men also drew lots in like manner, but when six black balls had been drawn Theseus came quickly forward and said: "Hold! Let no more balls be drawn. I will be the seventh youth to pay this tribute. Now let us go aboard the black ship and be off."

Then the people, and King Aegeus himself, went down to the shore to take leave of the young men and maidens, whom they had no hope of seeing again; and all but Theseus wept and were brokenhearted.

"I will come again, father," he said.

"I will hope that you may," said the old king. "If when this ship returns, I see a white sail spread above the black one, then I shall know that you are alive and well; but if I see only the black one, it will tell me that you have perished."

And now the vessel was loosed from its moorings, the north wind filled the sail, and the seven youths and seven maidens were borne away over the sea, towards the dreadful death which awaited them in far distant Crete.

3 The Princess: Ariadne

194   At last the black ship reached the end of its voyage. The young people were set ashore, and a party of soldiers led them through the streets towards the prison, where they were to stay until the morrow.

They did not weep nor cry out now, for they had outgrown their fears. But with paler faces and firm-set lips, they walked between the rows of Cretan houses. The windows and doors were full of people who were eager to see them.

"What a pity that such brave young men should be food for the Minotaur," said some.

"Ah, that maidens so beautiful should meet a fate so sad!" said others.

And now they passed close by the palace gate, and in it stood King Minos himself, and his daughter Ariadne, the fairest of the women of Crete.

"Indeed, those are noble young fellows!" said the king.

"Yes, too noble to feed the vile Minotaur," said Ariadne.

"The nobler, the better," said the king; "and yet none of them can compare with your lost brother Androgeos."

195 Ariadne said no more; and yet she thought that she had never seen any one who looked so much like a hero as young Theseus.

How tall he was, and how handsome! How proud his eye, and how firm his step! Surely there had never been his like in Crete.

All through that night Ariadne lay awake and thought of the matchless hero, and grieved that he should be doomed to perish; and then she began to lay plans for setting him free.

At the earliest peep of day she arose, and while everybody else was asleep, she ran out of the palace and hurried to the prison. As she was the king's daughter, the jailer opened the door at her bidding and allowed her to go in. There sat the seven youths and the seven maidens on the ground, but they had not lost hope.

She took Theseus aside and whispered to him. She told him of a plan which she had made to save him; and Theseus promised her that, when he had slain the Minotaur, he would carry her away with him to Athens where she should live with him always.

196 Then she gave him a sharp sword, and hid it underneath his cloak, telling him that with it alone could he hope to slay the Minotaur.

"And here is a ball of silken thread," she said. "As soon as you go into the Labyrinth where the monster is kept, fasten one end of the thread to the stone doorpost[1], and then unwind it as you go along. When you have slain the Minotaur, you have only to follow the thread and it will lead you back to the door. In the meanwhile I will see that your ship, is ready to sail, and then I will wait for you at the door of the Labyrinth."

Theseus thanked the beautiful princess and promised her again that if he should live to go back to Athens she should go with him and be his wife. Then with a prayer[2] to Athena, Ariadne hastened away.

---

1 doorpost ['dɔːrpoʊst] (n.) either of the vertical side pieces of a doorframe 門柱
2 prayer [prer] (n.) address to God 祈禱

4 The Labyrinth and the Aegean Sea

〔197〕 As soon as the sun was up the guards came to lead the young prisoners to the Labyrinth. They did not see the sword which Theseus had under his cloak, nor the tiny ball of silk which he held in his closed hand.

They led the youths and maidens a long way into the Labyrinth, turning here and there, back and forth, a thousand different times, until it seemed certain that they could never find their way out again. Then the guards, by a secret passage which they alone knew, went out and left them, as they had left many others before, to wander about until they should be found by the terrible Minotaur.

"Stay close by me," said Theseus to his companions, "and with the help of Athena who dwells in her temple home in our own fair city, I will save you."

Then he drew his sword and stood in the narrow way before them; and they all lifted up their hands and prayed to Athena.

For hours they stood there, hearing no sound, and seeing nothing but the smooth, high walls on either side of the passage and the calm blue sky so high above them.

Theseus in the Labyrinth

Then the maidens sat down upon the ground and covered their faces and sobbed, and said: "Oh, that he would come and put an end to our misery and our lives."

At last, late in the day, they heard a bellowing, low and faint[1] as though far away. They listened and soon heard it again, a little louder and very fierce and dreadful.

"It is he! it is he!" cried Theseus; "and now for the fight!"

Then he shouted, so loudly that the walls of the Labyrinth answered back, and the sound was carried upward to the sky and outward to the rocks and cliffs of the mountains. The Minotaur heard him, and his bellowings grew louder and fiercer every moment.

---

1 faint [feɪnt] (a.) not strong or clear 微弱的

"He is coming!" cried Theseus, and he ran forward to meet the beast.

The seven maidens shrieked[2], but tried to stand up bravely and face their fate; and the six young men stood together with firm-set teeth and clinched[3] fists, ready to fight to the last.

Soon the Minotaur came into view, rushing down the passage towards Theseus, and roaring most terribly.

He was twice as tall as a man, and his head was like that of a bull with huge sharp horns and fiery[4] eyes and a mouth as large as a lion's; but the young men could not see the lower part of his body for the cloud of dust which he raised in running.

When he saw Theseus with the sword in his hand coming to meet him, he paused, for no one had ever faced him in that way before. Then he put his head down, and rushed forward, bellowing. But Theseus leaped quickly aside, and made a sharp thrust with his sword as he passed, and hewed off one of the monster's legs above the knee.

The Minotaur fell upon the ground, roaring and groaning and beating wildly about with his horned head and his hoof-like fists; but Theseus nimbly ran up to him and thrust the sword into his heart, and was away again before the beast could harm him. A great stream of blood gushed from the wound, and soon the Minotaur turned his face towards the sky and was dead.

2 shriek [ʃriːk] (v.) to make a loud high-pitched piercing sound
   尖叫
3 clinch [klɪntʃ] (v.) hold in a tight grasp 捏緊
4 fiery ['faɪəri] (a.) bright red, like fire 火一般的

Then the youths and maidens ran to Theseus and kissed his hands and feet, and thanked him for his great deed; and, as it was already growing dark, Theseus bade them follow him while he wound up the silken thread which was to lead them out of the Labyrinth.

Through a thousand rooms and courts and winding ways they went, and at midnight they came to the outer door and saw the city lying in the moonlight before them; and, only a little way off, was the seashore where the black ship was moored[5] which had brought them to Crete.

The door was wide open, and beside it stood Ariadne waiting for them.

"The wind is fair, the sea is smooth, and the sailors are ready," she whispered; and she took the arm of Theseus, and all went together through the silent streets to the ship.

When the morning dawned they were far out to sea, and, looking back from the deck of the little vessel, only the white tops of the Cretan mountains were in sight.

Minos, when he arose from sleep, did not know that the youths and maidens had gotten safe out of the Labyrinth. But when Ariadne could not be found, he thought that robbers had carried her away. He sent soldiers out to search for her among the hills and mountains, never dreaming that she was now well on the way towards distant Athens.

---

5 moor [mʊr] (v.) to tie a boat so that it stays in the same place
使停泊

Many days passed, and at last the searchers returned and said that the princess could nowhere be found.

Then the king covered his head and wept, and said: "Now, indeed, I am bereft[6] of all my treasures!"

In the meanwhile, King Aegeus of Athens had sat day after day on a rock by the shore, looking and watching if by chance he might see a ship coming from the south. At last the vessel with Theseus and his companions hove in sight, but it still carried only the black sail, for in their joy the young men had forgotten to raise the white one.

"Alas! alas! my son has perished!" moaned Aegeus; and he fainted and fell forward into the sea and was drowned.

And that sea, from then until now, has been called by his name, the Aegean Sea.

Thus Theseus became king of Athens.

---

6 bereft [bɪˈrɛft] (a.) lacking something or feeling great loss
失去⋯⋯的

TRANSLATION

前言

　　希臘神話故事恐怕是世人傳述最頻繁、也聽得最津津有味的故事了。幾千年來，這些故事為男女老少、凡夫智者、為所有為神秘、美麗和宏偉事物著迷思索的人們帶來無窮的歡樂。

　　希臘神話故事已經融入我們的語言和思想，與我們的文學緊密交織在一起，成為我們心中無法割捨的一部分。它們是遠古時代遺留下來的文化遺產，在現代知性生活當中所占的重要性恐怕與當時並無二致。

　　我在書裡敘述朱比特與眾神的故事，還有其它希臘英雄的故事，我說的就是故事，僅此而已。我很小心避免暗示任何闡釋意義，因為意圖分析和解釋，最後只會破壞讀者看故事的興致。

　　反覆強調這些故事只不過是以敘事體或詩體描述某些自然現象，只會奪走故事的魅力，就如同把珍貴的黃金變成了實用的鐵，把浪漫的傳奇變成枯燥的科學論文。明智的老師會小心避免這樣的錯誤。

　　本書每篇故事都各自獨立，可以不照順序閱讀，但是篇篇故事之間還是存在一定的連續性，因此也可以把整本書視為一篇完整的故事。

　　為了讓現代的青少年更容易瞭解這些故事，我特意選用簡單的語言，並儘量淡化超自然的成分，不把朱比特和眾神突出為宗教神明。

　　希望這樣的做法，能更增加故事的趣味性。

詹姆斯·鮑丁

1 朱比特與眾神

p. 2 很久很久以前，當這個世界比現在還年輕很多很多的時候，人們相信並訴說著許多美麗的故事，故事裡說的都是美麗的人和事，你和我都沒見過的人和事。

他們常常說著一個威力強大的朱比特，朱比特也叫做宙斯（Zeus），是天上與人間的國王，還說他大多時候都坐在一座雲層環繞的高山山頂上，從那裡他可以看到所有在人間發生的事情。

他喜歡乘著暴風雨雲，左一個右一個丟出熊熊燃燒的閃電，打在地上的樹木和石頭之間。他具有無窮的威力，所以他一點頭，大地就震動，群山顫抖，冒出硝煙，天空變得一片漆黑，太陽也躲藏起來，不敢露面。

朱比特有兩個兄弟，都很可怕，但是不像朱比特威力強大。其中一個叫涅普頓，也叫做波賽頓，他是海神。

他在深深的海底洞穴裡，有一個金光閃閃的黃金宮殿，魚群生活在此，紅色的珊瑚也生長在此。

每次他一生氣，海浪就會升得如山一般高，狂風可怕地咆哮，整個海洋彷彿要把大地都吞沒，所以人們也把他稱為「大地的搖撼者」。

朱比特的另外一個兄弟，是一個神情憂鬱、臉色蒼白的傢伙，他的王國在地底下，永遠照不到太陽，永遠只有黑暗、哭泣和悲傷。他叫做普魯托，也叫做艾東尼亞斯（Aidoneus），他的王國叫做「陰間」，也叫做「陰影國度」，或是「地獄」。

相傳人死亡時，普魯托（Pluto）就會派遣「地獄使者」，把死去的人帶到他陰沈淒涼的王國，這也是為什麼人們都不喜歡普魯托，都把他視為生命的敵人。

有好多神明和朱比特一起住在山頂上的雲層間，多到我在這裡只能列舉其中一些。

維納斯（Venus）是愛神與美神，她比所有你我見過的女子都美麗。

雅典娜也叫做蜜娜娃（Minerva），是空氣女神。她賜給人類智慧，教導人類許多有用的事物。

朱諾（Juno）是人間與天上的皇后，她就坐在朱比特的右手邊，給他各種建議。馬爾斯是偉大的戰士，他就喜歡戰場上的喧囂。

墨丘利（Mercury）是動作敏捷的信使，帽子上和腳上都有翅膀，總是像夏天被風吹動的雲一樣，從一處飛到另一處。

伏爾岡（Vulcan）是技術精良的鐵匠，他在一座燃燒的火山打鐵，並用鐵、銅和黃金製作許多精美的物品。除此之外，還有許多其他的神明，關於他們有許多神奇而美麗的故事流傳著，你馬上就會認識他們了。

他們都住在輝煌燦爛的黃金宮殿裡，在高高的雲層間，高到人眼看不到。但是他們可以往下看，看到人類正在做什麼；相傳他們還會離開高在天際的家，偷偷在大地和海上漫遊。

而在這群威力強大的眾神當中，就屬朱比特的威力最強大。

2 泰坦神族和黃金時代

p. 10 其實，朱比特和眾神並不是一開始就住在山頂上的雲層間。很久很久以前，住在這裡的是叫做泰坦的一家人，他們統治整個世界。他們總共有十二個人——六個兄弟和六個姊妹。他們說，自己的父親是天空，母親是大地。他們的外表就跟人類一樣，但是他們的個子更高大，臉龐也更漂亮。

泰坦一家人裡年紀最小的是薩圖恩（Saturn），但是他也非常非常老了，所以人們把他稱為時間之父。他是泰坦族的國王，所以也是整個世界的國王。

在薩圖恩的治理下，人們過著幸福快樂的生活。那是真正的「黃金時代」。一整年都是春天，樹林和草原總是開著花，時時刻刻都聽得到小鳥悅耳的鳴叫。那時同樣也是夏天和秋天，樹上永遠垂著熟透的蘋果、無花果和柳橙，果藤上永遠結著紫色的葡萄，還有各式各樣的甜瓜和莓果，人們只要伸手一摘，就可以吃了。

在那段快樂的時光，人們當然也不必工作。當時也沒有生病、悲傷和年老這些問題。人們都活上幾百幾千年，而且永保青春美麗，頭髮不會轉灰，臉上不會長出皺紋，腳步也不會變遲緩。

他們不需要房子，因為天氣不會變冷，也不會刮暴風雨，也沒有任何事物令他們害怕。

沒有一個人是窮困的，因為每個人都擁有一樣寶物——陽光，純淨的空氣，健康的泉水，草地就是地毯，藍天就是屋頂，還有樹林裡和草原上的果實與花朵。所以，每個人都是均富的，當時也沒有錢幣、門鎖和門閂。每個人都是朋友，沒有人想比自己的鄰居擁有更多的東西。

　　這些快樂的人們活得夠久了之後，就會睡著，然後他們的身體會消失不見。他們飛到空中，飛越高山，飛越大海，最後到達遙遠西方一個開滿鮮花的國度。有些人說，直到今天，這些人依舊在世界上快樂地漫遊，逗搖籃裡的小嬰兒笑，減輕疲累的人與生病的人的負擔，祝福各地的人類。

　　可惜的是，這樣的黃金時代也有結束的一天！一手導致這個悲劇的，就是朱比特和他的兄弟。

　　雖然聽了令人難以置信，但是相傳朱比特是老泰坦王薩圖恩的兒子，不到一歲就開始策劃發動戰爭推翻父親。

　　他長大後，馬上說服兄弟涅普頓和普魯托，還有姊妹朱諾、希瑞絲（Ceres）和維斯塔（Vesta）參與他的計畫；最後，他們立誓把老泰坦王一家從世界上趕走。

　　接下來，就是一場漫長而可怕的戰爭。但是朱比特有許多威力強大的幫手。一群獨眼巨人，忙著為朱比特在火山的烈焰中鍛造閃電。

　　三個有一百隻手的怪物，被請來對著泰坦王的堡壘丟擲石塊和樹木。朱比特自己則忙著投出銳利的閃電，他投得又密又快，最後樹林都著火了，河水都被煮沸。

　　當然，善良、安靜又年老的薩圖恩和他的兄弟姊妹，無法永遠抵擋這樣的敵手。戰爭打到第十年，他們只能放棄求和。

他們被以世界上最堅硬的石頭製成的鏈子綑綁，丟進陰間的監牢裡。獨眼巨人和百手怪物被派去擔任獄卒，永生永世地看守他們。

接著，人類開始對自己的命運感到不滿。有些人想變富有，擁有世界上所有的寶物。有些人想當國王，統治世上所有的人。有些力量強大的人，則是想奴役力量弱小的人。

有些人把樹林裡的果樹砍倒，就怕別人把樹上的果實吃了。有些人為了好玩，追獵那些一度是人類朋友的膽小動物。有些人甚至殺死那些可憐的動物，吃牠們的肉。

最後，人人不再是朋友，反成了敵人。

所以，存在於世界各地的，是戰爭，而不是和平；是飢餓，而不是富裕；是罪惡，而不是清白；是悲苦，而不是歡樂。

而這就是朱比特使自己強大起來的經過，同時也是黃金時代結束的緣由。

3 普羅米修斯的故事

❶ 人類開始用火的經過

p. 20 在那古老的時代，曾經有兩個兄弟，他們既不是人類，也不是住在山頂上的眾神。他們是泰坦族人。他們的父親當初也參戰對抗朱比特，最後被綁上鍊子，丟進陰間的監牢。

這兩個兄弟當中，哥哥的名字叫做普羅米修斯，也叫做「先見」，因為他總是在思考未來，為明天、下星期、明年，甚至一百年後可能發生的事情做準備。

弟弟的名字叫做艾皮米修斯，他也叫做「後思」，因為他總是忙著回顧昨天、去年，或一百年前的事情，根本無心顧慮待會兒可能會發生的事。

不知什麼緣故，朱比特並沒有把這兩兄弟跟其他泰坦族人一起關進牢裡。

普羅米修斯並不想住在山頂的雲間，他可是非常忙碌的。當眾神們無所事事，只顧著享用神酒、仙饌的時候，他卻一心想要讓這個世界更進步，變得更美好。

於是他來到人間，與人類一起生活，幫助他們。他發現，人類不再像過去薩圖恩當國王那段黃金時代一般快樂，他心裡非常悲傷。

啊，人類多麼可憐不幸啊！他發現人類住在洞穴裡，冷得發抖，因為沒有火，人人都瀕臨餓死，還被野獸和同胞追獵，真的是世界上最悲慘的生物了。

「如果他們有火，」普羅米修斯對自己說：「至少可以取取暖，還可以煮東西吃，不久後他們還可以學習製作各種工具，為自己蓋房子。沒有火，他們的生活連野獸都不如。」

於是他大膽地來到朱比特面前，求他賜給人類火種，讓人類在漫長陰沉的冬月裡，可以得到一點點舒適。

「我一點火星都不會給。」朱比特說：「一點都不給！如果人類得到火，他們就會變得跟我們一樣強壯聰明；過了一段時間，他們就會把我們從王國裡趕出去。讓他們在寒冷裡受凍吧，讓他們活得像野獸一般吧。讓他們這樣貧困無知最好，這樣我們才能繁榮歡樂。」

普羅米修斯沒有回話，但是他已經下定決心要幫助人類，並不會因此放棄。他轉身，永遠地離開了朱比特和眾神。

有一天，他走在海邊，發現一根正在生長的蘆葦（也有人說他看到的是一根長長的茴香）。他把蘆葦折斷，看到裡面乾燥柔軟的芯。這種植物的芯，著火後燃燒得很緩慢，能夠燒上很長一段時間。他拿著這根長長的莖，前往遙遠的東方太陽的居所。

「人類應該得到火，不管那個坐在山頂上的暴君怎麼說。」他說。

清晨，當那團熾熱的金黃火球正從地上升起，準備開始一天橫越天空的旅程時，普羅米修斯剛好到達他的居所。他把長長的蘆葦，伸向太陽的火焰，蘆葦芯著火了，開始慢慢地燃燒。他馬上轉身，趕回人類的世界，將帶著的珍貴火種，藏在身上的蘆葦芯裡。

他把受凍發抖的人類，從洞穴裡叫出來，為他們生起一團火，然後教他們怎麼用火取暖，又怎麼用燃燒的餘燼，另起一團火。不久以後，大地上每個簡陋的家裡，就都有了一團燃燒的火。男人女人聚在火堆旁，溫暖又開心，感謝普羅米修斯為他們從太陽那裡，帶來了這份神奇的禮物。

沒過多久，人類便學會用火烹煮食物，從此開始像「人」一樣地吃飯，不再像野獸一般。他們隨之改掉各種野蠻的習慣，也不再躲在黑暗的洞穴裡。他們走到洞穴外和陽光下，欣喜自己重獲新生。

之後，普羅米修斯又慢慢教導人們許多事情——他教他們怎麼用木頭和石頭蓋房子，怎麼馴養和利用羊群牛隻，怎麼犁田、播種、收割，怎麼保護自己，不受冬天的暴風雨和林間野獸的攻擊。

然後他又教導他們怎麼開採銅礦和鐵礦，怎麼熔化礦石，怎麼把金屬捶打成各種形狀和樣式，製成平時和戰時需要的工具和武器。而當他看到世上的人類變得有多快樂時，他忍不住大喊：

「新的黃金時代要來臨了！比上個黃金時代還要燦爛，還要美好！」

❷ 第一個女人：潘朵拉

p. 26 如果不是因為朱比特，人們很可能就這樣一直幸福快樂地生活著，黃金時代也很可能真的會再度來臨。但是有一天，朱比特剛好低頭往下看，看到一團團的火在燃燒，看到人類都住在房子裡，看到羊群牛隻在山丘上吃草，看到田野裡的穀物正在成熟，他非常生氣。

「這是誰幹的好事？」他問。

一個聲音回答：「普羅米修斯！」

「什麼？那個泰坦家的小夥子？」他大吼：「好，我要好好懲罰他，讓他痛不欲生，讓他寧願當初被我把他跟他的族人一起關進牢裡。至於那些弱小的人類，就讓他們把火留著吧，我會讓他們比得到火種之前還要痛苦十倍。」

要懲罰普羅米修斯，隨時都可以，所以朱比特並不急著懲罰他。他決定先對付人類，想出了一個奇怪又拐彎抹角的方法。

首先，他給鐵匠伏爾岡一塊黏土，命令這個在火山口煉鐵的鐵匠，做個模子，把黏土塑成一個女人。伏爾岡照著做了。完工後，他把塑像帶去找朱比特，這時朱比特正與眾神坐在雲間。那塊塑像，只不過是一個沒有生命的形體，但是偉大的鐵匠伏爾岡把它做得比世界上所有的雕像都完美。

「大家都過來！」朱比特說：「讓我們每個人都送她一份禮。」說著，他帶頭先給了她生命。

接著，眾神也一一送給這個美妙的女子各種禮物。有人送給她美麗的外貌，有人送給她悅耳的聲音，有人送給她優雅的舉止，有人送給她一顆善良的心，還有人送給她藝術天分，最後，一位神明送給了她好奇心。

　　他們將她取名為潘朵拉，意思是「得到所有天賦的」，因為她從每一位神明那裡都得到了一份禮物。

　　潘朵拉漂亮又多才，讓每個人一見就愛。眾神對她稱讚一番後，便把她交給腳步輕快的神使墨丘利。墨丘利把她帶下山，帶到普羅米修斯和弟弟艾皮米修斯的居所；一個他們為人類福祉辛苦工作的地方。

　　他先見到艾皮米修斯，於是對他說：「艾皮米修斯，你看看這個美麗的女子，是朱比特送給你當妻子的。」

　　普羅米修斯常常警告弟弟，不要收下朱比特送的禮物，因為他知道他們不能信任這個強權的暴君，但是艾皮米修斯一見到美麗又聰明的潘朵拉，就忘了哥哥所有的警告，把潘朵拉帶回家娶為妻子了。

❸ 潘朵拉的盒子

p. 31 潘朵拉在新家過得很快樂，就連普羅米修斯見到她，也很高興自己有個美麗動人的弟媳。潘朵拉還帶了一個金盒子來，那是臨行前朱比特送給她的，還告訴她裡面放了許多寶物；但是智慧的空氣女神雅典娜警告她，絕對不能打開這個金盒子，連往裡面瞄一眼也不行。

「裡面一定都是珠寶。」潘朵拉對自己說，她想自己如果能戴上這些珠寶，一定會更加美麗。「如果我不能戴上這些珠寶，甚至連看都不能看一眼，那朱比特為什麼要把這個盒子送給我？」

她越想著這個金盒子，就越發好奇，越想看看裡面到底放了什麼東西。她每天把金盒子從架子上拿下來，撫摸它的蓋子，想從蓋子的接口看到裡面。

「我為什麼要管雅典娜說什麼？」她最後說：「她長得又不漂亮，又不需要這些珠寶。不管怎麼樣，我還是要看一眼，反正雅典娜也不會知道。沒有人會知道的。」

她把蓋子打開一條小縫，想偷看一眼，頓時卻響起一片呼呼沙沙的聲響。她嚇得趕緊把蓋子蓋上，但是盒子裡已經飛出成千上萬個面容枯槁、外形可怕的鬼怪，從來沒有人見過這些恐怖的鬼怪。

他們在潘朵拉的房間裡東飛西竄了一會兒，就飛去人類的家中，尋找棲身之地。這些鬼怪是疾病與憂慮。以前，人類不會生病，沒有憂慮，不必擔心明天會發生什麼災難。

這些鬼怪飛到每家每戶，在沒有人看到的狀況下，在每個男人、女人與小孩的心中，安頓了下來，結束了人類所有的歡樂。

從此以後，他們飛越、爬行於整個人間，沒有人看見，也沒有人聽到，為每個家庭帶來痛苦、悲傷和死亡。

　　如果當初潘朵拉沒有那麼快就把蓋子蓋上，情況還會更糟，還好她及時蓋上蓋子，沒讓最後一個鬼怪跑出來。這最後一個鬼怪叫做「預感」。當時牠已經從盒子裡伸出半個身子，但是潘朵拉硬是把牠推回去，再把蓋子緊緊蓋上，才沒讓牠逃出來。

　　如果當初牠跑出來了，人類從小就會知道他們以後每一天會遇上什麼麻煩與困境，一生都不會有歡樂與希望了。

　　這就是朱比特讓人類更痛苦的做法，情況變得比普羅米修斯開始幫助他們之前更糟。

❹ 普羅米修斯的受罰

`p. 35` 接下來，朱比特就要懲罰普羅米修斯從太陽那裡偷取火種。他命令兩個分別叫做「力氣」與「力量」的僕人，把膽大包天的普羅米修斯，抓到高加索山的最高峰，然後派鐵匠伏爾岡用鐵鍊把普羅米修斯綁在石頭上，讓他動彈不得。

伏爾岡並不願意，因為他是普羅米修斯的朋友，但是他不敢違抗朱比特。於是這個人類的朋友，這個帶給人類火種，把人類從困苦生活中拯救出來，教人類怎麼生活的朋友，就這樣被綁在山頂上。

他吊在那裡，狂風在身邊呼嘯，無情的冰雹打在臉上，兇猛的老鷹在耳邊尖聲鳴叫，用殘酷的爪子撕扯他的身體。但是普羅米修斯默默地承受這一切，不跟朱比特求饒，也不說後悔。

日復一日，年復一年，普羅米修斯就這樣吊在那裡。偶爾，乘駕太陽車的赫利奧斯（Helios）會低頭看看他，對他微笑；偶爾，成群的鳥兒會為他帶來遙遠國度的消息；有一次，海洋仙女來到山上，為他唱起美妙的歌曲；而人類常常一臉不忍地仰頭看他，然後大聲譴責懲罰他的暴君。

❺ 普羅米修斯的獲救

p. 38 然後有一天，一隻白色的母牛走過山下。那隻母牛異常漂亮，有一雙憂鬱的大眼睛，和一張酷似人臉的面龐。牠停下來，抬頭望向寒冷灰暗的山峰，和被綁在山峰上那巨大的身軀。普羅米修斯看到牠，溫柔地對牠說：

「我知道你是誰。」他說：「你是愛兒，以前住在遙遠的阿爾戈斯（Argos），是個美麗快樂的少女。但是現在，因為暴君朱比特和他善妒的皇后，你被困在這個非人的形體裡，四處流浪。但是不要絕望。往南走，然後再往西走，幾天後，你就會到達偉大的尼羅河。到了那裡，你就會變回少女的形態，而且比以前還要漂亮，還要美麗。你會成為埃及國王的皇后，並生下一個兒子，而他的後代，就會是為我打斷鐵鍊、讓我重獲自由的英雄。至於我，我會耐心等待這天的到來，連朱比特也無法提前或延遲這一天。再會！」

可憐的愛兒想說話，但是無法出聲。她用憂傷的雙眼，又看了一次山峰上受苦的英雄，然後便轉身，踏上前往尼羅河漫長艱辛的旅途。

時光流轉，最後終於有一名叫做海格力士（Hercules）的英雄，來到了高加索。儘管朱比特丟出可怕的閃電和雷聲，又吹起嚇人的暴風雪和暴風雨，他還是爬上崎嶇的山峰，殺死長久以來不斷折磨這名無助犯人的兇殘老鷹，然後他猛力一擊，打斷了普羅米修斯的鐵鍊，讓這名古老的英雄重獲自由。

「我就知道你會來。」普羅米修斯說：「十代以前，我跟愛兒提過你，她後來成為尼羅河王國的皇后。」

「而愛兒，」海格力士說：「就是我這一族的母親。」

4 大洪水和人類的創造

❶ 毀滅人類的大洪水

p. 42 那個古老的年代，有一個叫做杜卡隆（Deucalion）的男子，他是普羅米修斯的兒子。他只是個凡人，不像他偉大的父親是泰坦族人，但是他一生的善舉和正直，使他遠近馳名。他的妻子叫做琵拉（Pyrrha），是人類最美麗的女兒之一。

朱比特把普羅米修斯綁在高加索山上，並把疾病和憂慮傳播到人間後，人類就變得非常邪惡。他們不再建屋蓋房，不再照料他們的家禽家畜，也不再和平共處。每個人都跟鄰居起衝突，法律和治安在各地都蕩然無存。

情況比普羅米修斯來到人間之前還要糟，而這就是朱比特想看到的結果。但是隨著世人一天比一天更邪惡，朱比特開始厭倦看到這麼多人流血傷亡，厭倦不斷聽到受欺者和可憐人的呼喊。

「這些人類，根本就是禍患的根源。」他對眾神說：「以前，他們善良快樂的時候，我們擔心他們會變得比我們更強大；現在他們壞到極點，我們的處境卻比以前更危險。如今，對他們只有一件事要做，就是把他們全部消滅。」

於是他在人間掀起一場豪雨，日夜不停，下了好長好長一段時間。海水逼到海岸，淹上陸地，先淹沒了平原，然後淹掉了森林，然後又淹沒了山丘。但是即使大雨不停地下，海水不停地淹上陸地，人類還是不斷地爭鬥搶劫。

只有普羅米修斯的兒子杜卡隆，為這場大雨做好了準備。他從來沒有參與過身邊人們的惡行，甚至還常常跟他們勸說，除非他們改邪歸正，否則最後一定會遭到報應。他每年都會去高加索山找父親談話，當時他父親還被綁在山峰上。

普羅米修斯說：「算總帳的那天，朱比特會興起一場大洪水，把人類從大地上毀滅掉。你千萬要為這場大洪水做好準備，兒子。」

所以開始下大雨的那一天，杜卡隆從棚子拖出一隻小船；這隻小船，就是他為了這一天而建造的。他把美麗的妻子琵拉叫來，然後兩人便坐在船裡，在上漲的水勢中安然地漂浮著。

日日夜夜，不知道有多久，小船四處漂泊。樹梢在洪水中隱沒了，山丘在洪水中隱沒了，最後連高山也在洪水中隱沒了。除了一片片的汪洋大水，杜卡隆和琵拉什麼也看不到；他們知道，大地上的人類都淹死了。

過了一會兒，雨停了。烏雲漸漸飄走，露出藍色的天空與金色的太陽。接著大水開始迅速退去，從陸地一路退回海洋。隔天一早，小船漂到一座叫做帕納索斯（Parnassus）的高山上，杜卡隆和琵拉跨出小船，踏上乾燥的陸地。

接著，只一轉眼的時間，整片陸地就在他們面前展開，樹木在風中抖動枝葉，田野開滿一片綠草鮮花，景色更勝大洪水發生之前。

但是杜卡隆和琵拉心裡很難過，因為他們知道，他們是世界上唯一還倖存的人類。他們往山下去，往平原走，心想如今在這個廣大的世界上，只剩他們孤單兩人，未來將會如何？

❷ 人類的創造

p. 46 正當兩人討論著該怎麼辦，卻聽到身後傳來一個聲音。他們轉身一看，看到一位高雅的王子，站在高聳的石頭上。

　　他個子很高，有著藍色的眼睛和金色的頭髮，鞋子上和帽子上都有翅膀，手裡握著一跟纏著金蛇的手杖。他們立刻明白他是墨丘利，那個動作敏捷的神使，於是便等著聽他要說些什麼。

　　「你們心裡有沒有什麼願望？」他問，「告訴我，我就能夠幫你們達成。」

　　「我們最希望的就是，再次看到這個世界充滿人類。」杜卡隆說：「沒有鄰居，沒有朋友，這個世界真的好孤單。」

　　「往山下走，」墨丘利說：「一邊走，一邊把你母親的骨頭朝肩膀向身後丟。」說完，他往天空一跳，不見了。

　　「他是什麼意思？」琵拉問。

　　「我也不知道呀，我們得好好想一想。」杜卡隆說：「誰是我們的母親？不就是大地嗎？所有的生物，都是從大地滋生出來的。只是，他說『母親的骨頭』，這是指什麼呢？」

　　「也許他指的是土地裡的石頭。」琵拉說：「我們下山吧，然後邊走邊把路上的石頭撿起來，越過肩膀往後面丟。」

　　「這樣做很愚蠢呀，」杜卡隆說：「但是反正也不會有害，我們就試試看，看看會發生什麼事吧。」

269

於是，他們沿著帕納索斯山陡峭的斜坡往下走，邊走邊把地上的石頭撿起來，越過肩膀往後面丟。奇怪的是，杜卡隆丟的石頭立刻變成了一個個男人，個個強壯、英俊、勇敢；而琵拉丟的石頭，立刻變成了一個個的女人，個個美麗動人。

　　最後他們走到山下的平原時，身後早已跟著一群高貴的人類，急於為他們服務。

　　於是杜卡隆成為他們的國王，教他們住在房子裡，教他們耕田，教他們一些實用的事務。大地上又住滿了人類，而且這些人類比大洪水之前的人類都更快樂、更善良。他們取用杜卡隆和琵拉之子「希倫」（Hellen）的名字，把自己的國家稱為希臘（Hellas），而這個國家的人，至今依舊稱為希臘人。不過，我們把這個國家稱為格里斯（Greece，羅馬人對希臘的稱法）。

5 愛兒的故事

❶ 愛兒變身一頭白母牛

p. 50 在阿爾戈斯鎮裡，住著一個叫做愛兒的少女。她既漂亮又善良，每個認識她的人都關愛她，都說這世界上再也沒有像她這樣的少女。待在雲間家中的朱比特聽說她了，就下凡到阿爾戈斯看她。

愛兒很討他喜歡，而且她善良又聰明，使得朱比特忍不住第二天又來找她，第三天也是，第四天也是……。沒多久，他乾脆就一直待在阿爾戈斯，常伴在愛兒的身邊。愛兒並不知道他是誰，以為他是個來自遙遠國度的王子，因為朱比特化身成青年的模樣，看起來一點都不像統治人間與天上的天神。

然而，跟朱比特一起住在雲間又一起分享王位的天后朱諾，一點都不喜歡愛兒。

她得知朱比特一直不回家的原因後，便決定使出所有手段，傷害這個美麗的少女。有一天，她下凡來到阿爾戈斯，看看能怎麼辦。

271

朱比特遠遠就看到朱諾了，也知道朱諾為什麼來。於是，為了保護愛兒，他把愛兒變成一頭白色的母牛。他心想，等朱諾回去了以後，再把愛兒變回原形也不難。

　　然而，天后朱諾一看到母牛，就知道那是愛兒。

　　「噢，好漂亮的牛啊！」她說：「送給我吧！朱比特，行行好，送給我吧！」

　　朱比特不想把牛給她，但是朱諾百般要求，他最後不得不從，把牛送給她。他心想，不用多久時間，他就可以把母牛從天后身邊弄走，然後再把她變回少女的樣子。但是朱諾非常聰明，知道朱比特不可靠。她抓著母牛的角，把牠領出城。

　　「現在，親愛的愛兒，」她說：「我要你當一輩子的牛。」

　　她把母牛交給一個奇怪的守衛看管，這個守衛叫做阿古斯（Argus），他不像你我一樣有兩隻眼睛，而是有一百隻眼睛。阿古斯把母牛帶到一座小樹林，用一根長長的繩子，把牠綁在樹邊。牠只能在那裡站著吃草，從早到晚「哞！哞！」地叫。太陽下山後，夜色昏暗，牠在冷冷的地上躺下，哭喊著「哞！哞！」，一直哭喊到睡著。

➋ 阿古斯和孔雀

p. 53 沒有善心的朋友聽到牠的叫聲，也沒有人過來幫牠，因為除了朱比特和朱諾之外，沒有人知道這隻站在樹林裡的白色母牛，就是全世界都關愛的愛兒。日復一日，長滿眼睛的阿古斯，就坐在旁邊的山丘上看守牠。而且你根本不能說阿古斯會真的睡著，因為他一半的眼睛閉上時，另外一半的眼睛還睜得大大的，兩邊的眼睛就這樣輪流睡覺，輪流看守。

朱比特看到愛兒遭到這樣的厄運，心裡非常難過，決定想辦法救她。

一天，他把聰明狡黠、鞋子上有翅膀的墨丘利叫來，命令他去把母牛帶出樹林。

於是墨丘利來到凡間，站在阿古斯坐著的山丘腳邊，用笛子吹起悅耳的音樂。這種音樂就是這位奇怪的守衛喜歡聽的音樂，於是他呼叫墨丘利，請他上來坐在他身邊，繼續吹奏其他的曲調。

墨丘利答應了，為他吹奏出世界上從來沒有人聽過的美妙旋律。

古怪的老阿古斯在草地上躺下，邊聽邊想著自己這一生還未有過這樣的享受呢。很快地，這些甜美的樂聲，就像是對他下了魔咒，他一下就閉上了所有的眼睛，沉沉地睡著了。

這就是墨丘利的目的。雖然這不是一件很英勇的行為，但他還是從皮帶抽出銳利的長刀，把可憐的阿古斯的頭砍下來，然後跑到山丘下，把母牛的繩子解開，帶牠進城。

但是朱諾看到墨丘利把她的守衛殺死了。她在路上攔住他，對他大喊，要他把母牛放了。她一臉怒容，嚇得墨丘利一看到她就轉身逃走了，留下可憐的愛兒，任由命運擺佈。

朱諾看到死掉的阿古斯躺在山丘草原上，心裡悲痛不已。她把阿古斯的一百隻眼睛，裝在一隻孔雀的尾巴上，而直到今天，你還可以在孔雀的尾巴上看到它們。

❸ 牛虻和博斯普魯斯

p. 57 接著，她找來一隻跟蝙蝠一樣大的大牛虻，把牠放進母牛的耳朵裡，讓牠嗡嗡作響，叮咬愛兒，讓她一刻也得不到安寧。

可憐的愛兒，四處亂跑，想甩掉牛虻，但是牛虻還是不停地嗡嗡叫，不停地叮啊叮。既害怕又痛苦的愛兒，最後都發狂了，寧願自己乾脆死掉算了。

日復一日，她不停地跑，一會兒跑過濃密的樹林，一會兒跑在空曠平原的長草裡，一會兒又跑到海邊。

沒多久，她來到一處海洋特別狹窄之處。因為對岸好像有可以休息的地方，於是她跳進海裡，游到對岸。而這個地方從那時起，便叫做博斯普魯斯（Bosphorus），意思是「母牛之海」，你在學校用的地圖，就是這麼標示的。

❹ 遇見普羅米修斯

p. 58 走了一段時間後，她來到一個地方，那裡矗立著一座座的高山，覆蓋著白雪的山峰，直入雲霄。牠停下來休息，抬頭看著那些寂靜寒冷的峭壁，心裡希望自己也能死在一個這麼壯麗寧靜的地方。

這時，她看到在天與地之間，有一個巨大的身軀貼在岩石上，她立刻就知道那是普羅米修斯，泰坦的後裔；他因為把火種給了人類，而被朱比特綁在那裡。

「我受的苦，還沒有他受的苦多。」她想著，雙眼充滿了淚水。

普羅米修斯低頭對她說話，聲音溫柔祥和。

「我知道你是誰。」他說。他要她不要放棄希望，往南走，再往西走，很快就會找到一個可以安身休息的地方。

如果可以，她很想跟他道謝，但是她一開口說話，就只能「哞！哞！」地叫。

普羅米修斯又告訴她，她終有一天會變回人形，還會成為一個族群的母親，一個代代出英雄的族群。

「至於我，」他說：「我會耐心地等待，因為我知道其中一個英雄，會來打斷我的鐵鍊，讓我重獲自由。再會了！」

⑤ 來到埃及

p. 60 於是愛兒帶著一顆勇敢的心，離開了這位偉大的泰坦巨神，並按照他所說的，先往南走，再往西走。牛虻比以前更囂張了，但是愛兒一點都不害怕，因為她的心中充滿希望。

她走了整整一年，最後來到非洲的埃及。她覺得好疲憊，再也走不動了，便在尼羅河邊躺下。

這麼多年來，要不是因為朱比特這麼怕朱諾，他早就來救愛兒了。而現在，可憐的愛兒在尼羅河邊躺下的這一刻，天后朱諾剛好在雲間高高的家中躺下小睡。

她一進入沉沉的夢鄉，朱比特就如一道閃電般，飛越海洋來到埃及。

他把那隻牛虻殺死，丟到河裡，然後輕輕撫摸母牛的頭。此時母牛不見了，站在那裡的是少女愛兒，她蒼白虛弱，但依舊跟在家鄉阿爾戈斯城時一樣的美麗善良。朱比特什麼話也沒對她說，也沒現身給這個疲倦發抖著的少女看。

他隨即趕回雲間的家，因為他怕朱諾醒來，會發現他做了什麼事。

埃及人對愛兒很好，在他們陽光明媚的國土上，給了她一個家。沒多久，埃及國王就向她求婚，把她娶為皇后。她在尼羅河邊的大理石皇宮裡，度過了長壽而快樂的一生。

好幾個世代以後，愛兒曾孫的曾孫的曾孫，打斷了普羅米修斯的鐵鍊，使這位人類的巨神朋友，重新獲得了自由。

這名英雄就叫做海格力士。

6 神乎其技的織布女

❶ 奧拉克妮：自誇的織布女

p. 64 希臘有一個叫做奧拉克妮（Arachne）的少女，她的臉龐白皙美麗，眼睛又大又藍，長長的頭髮就如黃金一般。從早上到中午，她唯一想做的事，就是坐在陽光下紡紗；從中午到晚上，她唯一想做的事，就是坐在陰影裡織布。

噢，她在織布機上織出來的料子多細緻、多漂亮啊！亞麻、棉花、蠶絲，她都織。而這些原料到了她手裡，都被織成又薄又軟又亮麗的料子，世界各地的人都聞名而來。

他們說，這麼罕見的料子，根本不可能是亞麻、棉花或蠶絲製成的；他們說，這些料子的經線是陽光，緯線是黃金。

有一天，她坐在陽光下紡紗，也或許是坐在陰影裡織布時，她說：「全世界沒有人紡的紗，比我紡的紗更細緻；沒有人織的布，比我織的布更柔軟、更平滑，也沒有人的絲綢，比我的絲綢更亮麗、更稀有。」

「誰把你教得這麼會紡紗織布的？」一個聲音問。

「沒有人教過我。」她說：「我坐在太陽下和陰影裡時就學會了，沒有人教過我。」

「可能是空氣女神雅典娜教會你的，只是你不知道。」

「空氣女神雅典娜？呸！」奧拉克妮說：「她怎麼可能教我紡紗織布？她能紡出這樣的紗嗎？她能織出這樣的料子嗎？我倒想看看她怎麼紡紗織布，我還可以教教她。」

她抬頭，立刻看到一個披著長袍的高大女人站在門口。她的臉孔很漂亮，但是表情好嚴峻，真的好嚴峻！灰色的雙眼銳利明亮，奧拉克妮簡直無法直視。

「奧拉克妮，」那女人說：「我是空氣女神雅典娜，我聽到你怎麼自誇了。你現在還是要說不是我教會你紡紗織布的嗎？」

「沒有人教過我，」奧拉克妮說：「我也不用謝任何人。」她站起來，筆直而驕傲地站在織布機旁。

「你還是認為，你可以紡得跟我一樣好？織得跟我一樣好？」雅典娜說。

奧拉克妮的雙頰轉白了，但她還是說：「對，我可以織得跟你一樣好。」

「那我來告訴你，我們該怎麼做。」雅典娜說：「三天後，我們兩人都來織布，你用你的織布機，我用我的織布機。我們請全世界的人都來看，而坐在雲端的朱比特會當我們的裁判。如果你織得比我好，那只要這世界還存在，我就永遠都不織布。如果我織得比你好，那你永遠都不能再碰織布機，不能再碰紡錘，也不能再碰紡紗桿。同意嗎？」

「我同意。」奧拉克妮說。

「好。」說完，雅典娜就走了。

❷ 織布比賽和蜘蛛

p. 68 織布比賽當天，全世界的人都來了，偉大的朱比特也坐在雲端觀看。

奧拉克妮把織布機擺在桑樹下，樹陰下一整天都有蝴蝶飛舞，蚱蜢唧唧。雅典娜把織布機擺在天上，天空裡微風徐徐，夏陽明媚。她把織布機放在天上，因為她是空氣女神。

奧拉克妮拿出她最好的絲開始織。她織出一張極其美麗的網子，輕盈細薄得可以飄在空中，又強韌地足以網住一頭獅子。縱橫的絲線五彩繽紛，交錯有序，每個人見了心中都不由得充滿欣喜。

「難怪這個女孩敢這樣自誇。」人們說。

朱比特也點點頭。

接著雅典娜開始織。她拿了幾束為山峰鑲了金邊的陽光，幾撮夏日雲朵雪白的毛絮，又拿了一點夏日天空的蔚藍，田野的亮綠，和秋天樹林輝煌的紫──你猜她織了什麼？

她在天上織出來的網子，充滿了迷人的圖畫，有花朵、有花園，有城堡、有城鎮，有高山，有人、有野獸，有巨人、有侏儒，還有跟朱比特一起住在雲間的眾神。每個人看到這張網子，都既驚嘆又喜悅，完全忘了奧拉克妮那張美麗的網。奧拉克妮自己看了，是既愧疚又害怕。她把臉埋在雙手裡，開始哭泣。

「噢，我現在怎麼活下去？」她哭著說：「現在我再也不能碰織布機，不能碰紡錘，也不能碰紡紗桿了。」

她不停地哭，眼淚止不住不停地掉，又不停地說：「我現在怎麼活下去？」

雅典娜看到這個可憐的女孩，若不能夠繼續紡紗織布，心中就再也不會有任何快樂，心裡很不忍，便對她說：

「如果我做得到的話，一定會免了你的懲罰，但是沒人能做到這件事。你只能遵守你的諾言，再也不碰織布機，再也不碰紡錘。但是，既然除非能夠繼續紡紗織布，否則你就再也快樂不起來，那我會教你一個新織法，這樣你就可以繼續紡紗織布，但是不需要紡錘，也不需要織布機。」

　　她用有時帶在身邊的長矛尖端，輕輕碰一下奧拉克妮，奧拉克妮便立刻變成一隻動作敏捷的蜘蛛，鑽進陰暗的草叢，開始快樂地吐絲結網，結出一張漂亮的網。

　　傳說從那時候起，所有存在於世界上的蜘蛛，都是奧拉克妮的孩子，但是我懷疑這樣的說法。不過，說不定奧拉克妮依然活著，依然在吐絲結網，而你下一次看到的蜘蛛，可能就是她了。

7 銀弓之王阿波羅

❶ 蕾托的逃亡和海豚

p. 74 在你我或任何人都無法記憶的遠古，曾有一位溫柔美麗的女子與眾神一起住在山頂上，她的名字是蕾托（Leto）。她是如此溫柔美麗，連朱比特都愛上了她，娶她為妻。

但是天后朱諾聽到這件事時，心裡非常憤怒。她把蕾托趕出山頂，並命令大地上的萬物都不能幫助蕾托。

於是蕾托像隻野鹿，從一地逃到另一地，找不到安身之所。但她不能停下腳步，因為她一停下來，腳下的大地就開始搖動，石頭也大喊：「繼續走啊！繼續走啊！」而鳥兒、野獸、樹木和人們，都會跟著一起大喊；廣闊的大地上，沒有一個人同情她。

一天，她來到海邊。她沿著海邊跑，邊舉起雙手大喊，請求偉大的涅普頓幫助她。

海神涅普頓聽到了，仁慈地回應她的請求。他派了一隻叫做達爾芬（意謂「海豚」）的大魚，把她載離殘酷的大地。達爾芬讓蕾托坐在牠寬闊的背上，一路游到提洛島，提洛島是一座猶如一艘小船漂在水上的小島。

蕾托在這裡找到了休息的地方，也找到了一個家，因為這裡是涅普頓的領地，沒有人會聽從無情朱諾的命令。涅普頓在島下放了四根大理石柱，這樣小島就能固定在上面，又用堅固的鍊子把小島緊緊綁住，鍊子直接固定在海底，這樣小島就不會隨海浪漂走。

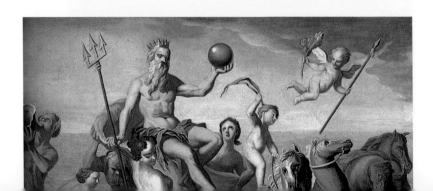

❷ 阿波羅和黛安娜的誕生

p.76 沒過多久，蕾托就在提洛島生下一對雙胞胎。一個是男孩，她取名為阿波羅，一個是女孩，她取名為阿緹米絲（Artemis），阿緹米絲又叫做黛安娜。

雙胞胎出生的消息，傳到山頂上的朱比特和眾神耳裡時，整個世界都為之歡喜。太陽在水上起舞，天鵝歌唱繞著提洛島（Delos）飛了七圈。月亮彎下腰，親吻搖籃中的兩個小寶寶。連朱諾都忘了她的憤怒，命令地上與天上的萬物都要善待蕾托。

兩個小孩長得非常快。阿波羅長得高大挺拔，舉止優雅。他的臉龐就跟陽光一樣明亮，不管走到哪，他都帶著喜悅與歡樂。

朱比特送給他一對天鵝，和一輛雙輪黃金馬車，不管他想去哪裡，上山下海馬車都會帶他去；又送給他一把七弦琴，讓他彈奏出世上最悅耳的旋律；還送給他一把銀色的弓，鋒利的箭從不錯失目標。

阿波羅進入凡間，人們漸漸認識他後，有些人稱他為光之神（Bringer of Light），有些人稱他為音樂大師（Master of Song），還有一些人稱他為銀弓之王（Lord of the Silver Bow）。

黛安娜也長得高挑優雅，而且非常俊美。她喜歡跟她的仙女侍從，在山林裡漫遊；她細心照顧膽小的野鹿，和樹林間無助的動物，還喜歡追獵狼、熊等野獸。她在各地都受到愛慕與敬畏，朱比特把她封為森林女神（queen of the green woods）和狩獵女神（queen of the chase）。

❸ 世界的中心：帕納索斯山

p. 78 「世界的中心在哪裡？」

朱比特坐在他的黃金宮殿裡時，有人這樣問。這麼簡單的問題，當然難不倒掌管大地與天空的天神朱比特，但是他太忙了，一時沒時間回答。

於是他説：「一年後再來，我會讓你看到世界的中心。」

接著，朱比特找來兩隻飛得比狂風還要快的老鷹進行訓練，直到兩隻老鷹飛行的速度一樣快。

一年期限快到時，他對侍從説：「把這隻老鷹帶到地球的最東邊，太陽從海上出來的地方；把另外一隻老鷹，帶到大地的最西邊，海洋在黑暗中隱沒、什麼也不存在的地方。然後看我的手勢，讓兩隻老鷹同時起飛。」

侍從照著做了，把兩隻老鷹帶到世界的最兩邊。

接著朱比特拍拍手，霎時電閃雷鳴，兩隻迅捷的老鷹起飛了。

一隻直直往西飛，一隻直直往東飛；沒有一枝出弓的箭，會比這兩隻離手的鷹飛得更快。

牠們像兩顆流星般衝向彼此，朱比特和眾神坐在雲間，看著牠們飛翔。牠們越靠越近，但是誰也不向右躲，誰也不向左閃。

牠們越飛越近，然後就像兩艘在海上相撞的船，在空中猛一撞，掉到地上都死了。

「是誰在問世界的中心在哪裡？」朱比特説：「兩隻老鷹躺在哪裡，哪裡就是世界的中心。」

兩隻老鷹掉在希臘一座山頂上，這座山此後被人們稱為帕納索斯山。

「如果那就是世界的中心，那我要在那裡住下來。」年輕的阿波羅説：「我要在那個地方蓋一棟房子，這樣全世界的人都可以看到我的光。」

❹ 派森巨蛇和德爾菲城

p. 80 於是阿波羅下凡來到帕納索斯山，尋找合適的地點，為房子打地基。這座山原始蠻荒，山下的山谷淒涼黑暗。山上沒住多少人，而且人們都躲在岩石間，像是怕遇到什麼可怕的危險。

他們告訴阿波羅，在陡峭岩壁一分為二的山腳邊，住著一條叫做派森（Python）的巨蛇。這隻巨蛇常常襲擊羊群牛隻，有時候連男人、女人、小孩也攻擊，再把他們拖到牠可怕的巢穴裡，一口吞掉。

「沒有人殺得了這隻野獸嗎？」阿波羅問。

他們說：「沒有。我們和孩子還有牲畜，都會被牠吃掉。」

阿波羅帶著銀弓，前往派森藏身的地方。牠一見到阿波羅的身影，就展開蜷曲的身子，出來迎戰。

派森一看到他的對手不是普通人，轉身就逃。但此時阿波羅的箭咻地一聲離弓，轉眼派森已死。

「我就要在這裡蓋起我的家。」阿波羅說。

他在陡峭的峭壁腳邊，在朱比特的老鷹落地葬身的地點下方，打下地基。沒過多久，本來是派森巢穴的岩石之間，立起了阿波羅宮殿的白牆。

那些可憐的人類都來到此地，在附近建起他們的家園。阿波羅跟他們一起生活了好幾年，教他們要溫和有智慧，教他們如何快快樂樂過活。帕納索斯山不再原始蠻荒，成了一個充滿音樂與歌聲的地方。

「我們該給我們的城市取什麼名字呢？」人們問。

「就叫做德爾菲（Delphi）吧，或是叫做達爾芬。」阿波羅說：「因為把我的母親載過海的，是一隻達爾芬。」

⑤ 阿波羅對達芙妮的追求和月桂樹

p. 82 在德爾菲城遙遠的北邊，有個滕比山谷（Vale of Tempe），裡面住著一個叫做達芙妮的少女。她是個奇怪的孩子，個性像小鹿一樣狂野害羞，腳步像平原上的野鹿一樣輕盈迅速。但是她就像六月的夏日一樣清新美麗，因此每個人都忍不住關愛她。

達芙妮大部分的時間都待在田野和森林裡，與鳥兒、野花和樹木為伍。她最喜歡漫步在珀紐斯河邊（Peneus）。她常對著珀紐斯河唱歌、說話，彷彿珀紐斯河有生命一樣，能夠聽到她說的話。懂她的好人們會說：「她是珀紐斯河的女兒。」

「對，親愛的河流，」她說：「讓我當你的孩子吧。」

河水對她微笑，用只有她才了解的語言回應她。從此以後，她總是稱呼珀紐斯河為「珀紐斯父親」。

一天，當太陽溫暖地照耀，空氣裡充滿花香時，達芙妮信步走離河邊，往比以前走過更遠的地方前進。

她身後還有層層山丘，以及奧薩（Ossa）這座山綠色的山坡和成林的山峰。唉，如果她能爬到奧薩山的最高峰，她就可以看到海洋，看到附近的高山，還可以看到遠遠南邊帕納索斯山的雙峰！

「再見了，珀紐斯父親，」她說：「我要去爬奧薩山了，但是我很快就會回來了。」

沒過多久，她來到一個樹木成林的山坡下。那裡有一個漂亮的瀑布，地上長滿美麗的野花，於是她決定坐下來休息一會兒。

此時，山坡上的小樹林傳來一陣美妙的音樂，她從來沒有聽過這麼美妙的音樂。她站起來，仔細聆聽。有人正在彈奏七弦琴，歌聲搭配著樂音。

她覺得很害怕，但是這麼迷人的音樂使她捨不得跑走。

接著音樂突然停止了，一個英俊挺拔的青年，臉龐就如早晨的太陽一般明亮，他走下山坡，向她走來。

「達芙妮！」他喊。但是達芙妮沒有繼續聽他說。她像隻受驚的野鹿，轉身就跑，向著滕比山谷跑去。

「達芙妮！」青年又喊。達芙妮不知道那是阿波羅，她只知道有個陌生人在追她，所以拚了命地跑。從來沒有年輕男子跟她說過話，因此阿波羅的聲音讓她害怕極了。

「她是我見過最美麗的女子。」阿波羅對自己說：「如果我能夠再看她一眼，跟她說說話，我會有多快樂啊。」

穿過叢林與荊棘，跳過石頭與倒在地上的樹幹，跑下崎嶇的山坡，越過山中的小溪，達芙妮又飛又跳，喘著氣不停地跑。

她一次也沒回頭，但是她聽到阿波羅輕快的腳步，越靠越近；她聽到掛在他肩上的銀弓，咔咔作響；她聽到他的呼吸聲，已經離她非常近了。

最後，她終於跑回滕比山谷，這裡地面平坦，跑起來更容易，但是她再也沒有力氣了。不過此時珀紐斯河就躺在她面前，泛著白光在陽光下微笑。

她張開雙臂，大喊：「噢，珀紐斯父親，救救我！」

此時河水升起，就像是要迎向她。空氣裡頓時充滿一片白茫茫的霧氣，阿波羅有好一會兒看不到達芙妮的身影。之後，他看到她站在河岸邊，跟他離得好近好近，她身後飄揚的長髮，就輕撫在他的臉頰上。

他以為達芙妮要跳進洶湧怒號的河水中，便伸出手拉住她；然而，他抓在手裡的，並不是美麗羞怯的達芙妮，而是一棵月桂樹的樹幹，枝上的綠葉在微風中抖動著。

「噢，達芙妮！達芙妮！」他喊道：「這就是珀紐斯河救你的方式嗎？珀紐斯父親為了保護你，把你變成一棵樹了嗎？」

我不知道達芙妮是不是真的變成了一棵樹，但是現在也無所謂了，畢竟那已經是那麼久以前的事情了。然而阿波羅相信，達芙妮的確變成了一棵月桂樹，因此他用月桂的樹葉，編成花環，像皇冠般地戴在頭上，並說為了紀念美麗的達芙妮，他會永遠戴著這頂桂冠。

從此以後，月桂一直是阿波羅最喜愛的樹，而直到今天，詩人和音樂家都會以桂冠加冕。

❻ 可羅妮斯和烏鴉

p. 88 阿波羅不喜歡老是一起跟眾神住在山上，他喜歡四處漫步，到處遊歷，看人們為更美好的生活而努力工作著。

人們第一次看到阿波羅清秀稚氣的臉龐，和白皙細嫩的雙手時，都瞧不起他，說他只是個遊手好閒、一無所長的傢伙。然而，當他們一聽他開口說話時，都不禁停下腳步，像中了魔咒般地站在原地聆聽；從此以後，人們就把阿波羅說的話當成法律。

人們都很納悶，為什麼阿波羅這麼有智慧，因為阿波羅整天做的，不過就是到處閒晃，彈彈美妙的七弦琴，看看樹啊、花啊、鳥兒啊、蜜蜂啊。

但是如果有人生病了去找他，他會告訴他們，要去植物、石頭或小溪裡找些什麼，就可以把病治好，讓他們又強壯起來。

人們還注意到，阿波羅不會像他們一樣變老，而是永遠都年輕俊美。

在滕比山谷之外的一個小山村，住著一個叫做可羅妮斯（Coronis）的美麗女子。阿波羅一見到她，就愛上了她，並把她娶為妻子。好長一段時間，兩人一起過著幸福快樂的日子。

他們很快就生下了一個小寶寶，是個男娃娃，擁有一雙全世界最漂亮的眼睛，他們為他取名為艾斯庫拉比（Aesculapius）。

一天，阿波羅要離開可羅妮斯和孩子，前去造訪帕納索斯山中他最喜愛的家園。

「我每天都要聽到你的消息。」跟妻子分開前，他說道：「我的烏鴉每天早晨都會飛去帕納索斯山，告訴我你跟孩子是否都安好，告訴我我不在的時候，你們都做了什麼。」

阿波羅養了一隻烏鴉，這隻烏鴉非常聰明，而且還會講話。牠不像你看到的烏鴉是黑色的，而是雪一般的白。傳說那個時候烏鴉都是白色的，但是我懷疑還有沒有人知道這件事。

　　阿波羅的烏鴉很愛閒扯，而且牠說的話並不一定是真的。牠一看到事情的開端，不等它的後續發展，就會急急忙忙編出一個精彩的故事。

　　連續幾天下來，一切都很安好。每天早上，白烏鴉飛越山丘，飛越平原，飛越河流，飛越森林，最後找到阿波羅，不是在帕納索斯山頂上的樹林裡，就是在他位於德爾菲的家中。牠停在阿波羅的肩上，說：「可羅妮斯很好！可羅妮斯很好！」

　　但是有一天，烏鴉講的話不一樣了。牠比平常到得還要早，而且看起來特別急。

　　「可──可──可！」牠叫著，因為氣喘吁吁，連可羅妮斯的全名都叫不出來。

　　「怎麼了？」阿波羅驚慌地喊道：「可羅妮斯怎麼了？快說！快跟我講！」

　　「她不愛你了！她不愛你了！」烏鴉說：「我看一個男人──我看到一個男人──」然後，牠不停下來喘口氣，也不繼續把故事說完，就振翅飛去，又趕回家了。

　　平常一向很明智的阿波羅，這時候簡直變得和他的烏鴉一樣笨了。他以為，可羅妮斯真的為了另一個男人拋棄了他，心中又悲傷又憤怒。他把銀弓拿在手上，立刻出發回家。

　　走了一段時間後，他終於回到了度過多年快樂日子的村莊，隨即看到自己的家半掩在蒼鬱的橄欖樹林裡。他馬上就會知道，烏鴉說的話是真是假了。

　　樹林裡傳來人跑動的腳步聲。他在樹隙間瞥見一個穿著白色長袍的身影，心裡很確定那就是烏鴉看到的男人，而那男人正想逃走。他迅速在弓上架了一枝箭，拉弓，然後砰地一聲，百無虛發的箭，像一道閃電往前掣去。

　　阿波羅聽到一聲尖銳的慘叫，立刻跑進樹林。性命垂危躺在草地上的，是他親愛的可羅妮斯。她看到阿波羅回來了，高興地跑來迎接他，卻被殘酷地一箭穿心。

　　阿波羅悲痛不已。他把可羅妮斯抱在懷裡，一聲一聲地呼喚她，希望她起死回生，但一切都枉然了。她只是再一次輕輕呼喚他的名字，然後便撒手歸去了。

　　一會兒後，烏鴉飛到旁邊一棵樹上。「可——可——可！」牠又開始叫，想把故事說完。但是阿波羅命令牠立刻離開。

　　「可惡的烏鴉，你以後再也不許說話，」他喊道：「一輩子就只能喊『可——可——可！』，而你引以自豪的羽毛，將像午夜一樣黑，再也不會是白色的了。」

　　從此以後，所有的烏鴉都是黑色的，就跟你現在看到的烏鴉一樣。牠們從一棵死樹飛到另一棵死樹，不停地叫著：「可——可——可！」

❼ 喪子之慟和醫神

p. 94 不久後，阿波羅把年幼的艾斯庫拉比抱在懷裡，帶去給一位年邁而有智慧的老師。這位老師叫做奇戎（Cheiron），住在海邊灰色峭壁下的山洞裡。

「收下這個孩子，」他說：「教會他所有關於山的、森林的、田野的知識，教會他那些他最需要用來造福人類的知識。」

艾斯庫拉比是個聰明的孩子，而且個性溫和體貼又很受教，在所有學生當中，最受奇戎喜愛。他學會關於山的、森林的、田野的知識。他發現藥草、鮮花和沒有感覺的石頭有什麼用處，又研究鳥兒、野獸和人類的習性。

但是最重要的，他成了敷裹傷口和治癒疾病的能手。直到今天，醫生依舊紀念他，尊他為醫界的始祖與模範。艾斯庫拉比成年後，名聲傳遍各地，人們都崇敬他、祝福他，因為他是生命的朋友，死亡的敵人。

時光流轉，艾斯庫拉比治癒了好多好多人，救了好多好多條命，陰間臉色蒼白的普魯托國王，開始不安起來。

「我很快就無事可做了，」他說：「如果這個醫生繼續不讓人類進入我的王國。」

於是他傳話給他的兄弟朱比特，投訴說艾斯庫拉比把他該得到的東西都騙走了。偉大的朱比特聽進了這番抱怨後，站在暴風雨雲上，

對著艾斯庫拉比猛擲閃電。最後,這位偉大的醫師便被無情地劈死了。

全世界都為之悲痛,連野獸、樹木和石頭都落淚哭泣,因為這位生命的朋友不再存在了。

阿波羅得知兒子的死訊時,悲痛又憤怒。他無法報復朱比特和普魯托,因為他們的威力比他強大,於是他來到伏爾岡在火山下煉鐵的地方,把這個製造致命閃電的巨神鐵匠殺死了。

這下子,輪到朱比特為此事發火了。他把阿波羅叫到跟前,為所做的事接受懲罰。

他把他的弓箭拿走,把他美妙的七弦琴拿走,把他身上美好的東西都取走,然後給他穿上乞丐的破舊衣裳,趕出山中,說他得去當別人的奴隸,服侍別人一整年後,才能回來,才能變回原來的樣子。

於是阿波羅孤孤單單、無依無靠地回到凡間。人們看到他,沒有人會想到他曾經是陽光一般明亮的銀弓之王。

8 卡德摩斯與歐羅芭

❶ 歐羅芭和白色公牛

p. 100 在亞洲住著一個國王，他有兩個孩子，一個男孩和一個女孩。男孩叫做卡德摩斯（Cadmus），女孩叫做歐羅芭（Europa）。

這個國王的國家非常小，他只要站在皇宮頂上，就可以看盡整片國土。但是他在自己小小的王國裡過得很快樂，而且他非常疼愛自己的孩子。他有充分的理由以這兩個孩子自豪，因為卡德摩斯長大後成為全國最英勇的青年，而歐羅芭長大後成為眾人見過最美麗的少女。然而，厄運終究還是降臨到他們頭上。

一天早上，歐羅芭走到海邊的草原採花。她父親畜養的牛這時都在草原上，嚼著香甜的三葉草。這些牛很溫馴，而且每隻牛的名字歐羅芭都知道。

這天早上，她注意到牛群中多了一隻她不認識的牛。這隻牛很壯，毛像雪一般白，一雙溫柔的棕色眼睛，讓牠看起來特別溫和善良。

起先牠看都不看歐羅芭一眼，只是在這裡走走，那裡走走，吃著長在三葉草之間的嫩草。但是等歐羅芭的圍裙都裝滿了摘來的雛菊和毛茛後，牠便慢慢地走向她。

牠走近她，用鼻子蹭她的手臂，就像是在說：「早安！」

歐羅芭撫摩牠的頭和頸子，牠看起來一副很享受的樣子。然後歐羅芭用雛菊做了一個花環，掛在牛的脖子上。

接著，歐羅芭又做了一個更小的花環，她爬上牛背，想把花圈掛在牛角上，此時公牛突然跳起來，拔腿就跑，歐羅芭根本來不及反應。

她不敢跳下來，因為公牛跑得很快，她只能緊緊抓著牛脖子，尖聲大叫。

樹下的牧牛人聽到她的尖叫，急得跳起來，看到公牛正載著歐羅芭，往海邊奔去。

他使盡全力追趕，但還是沒有用，公牛跳到海裡，一下就游走了，背上載著可憐的歐羅芭。

幾個人看到了這個景象，立刻跑去稟告國王，沒多久全城就陷入一片驚慌。國王派出最快的船，想追上公牛。水手們把船划出海，遠至未曾航過之處，還是沒看到歐羅芭的蹤影。水手們回來後，大家都覺得沒有希望了。

❷ 尋找歐羅芭

p. 103 每個婦女和小孩，都為失蹤的歐羅芭而哭泣。國王把自己關在家裡，連續三天不吃不喝。然後他把兒子卡德摩斯叫來，命令他乘船去尋找失蹤的妹妹。他對卡德摩斯說，不管在路上會遇到什麼危險，一定要找到妹妹才准回來。

卡德摩斯欣然接受這個命令。他挑了十二個英勇的青年跟他同行，然後第二天就出發了。這是一個偉大的任務，因為他們要穿過未知的海域，而且他們不知道會航行到什麼樣的地方和國家。

其實大家都很擔心他們根本就碰不到陸地，那個時候的人都不敢航行到離海岸太遠的地方，但是卡德摩斯和他的同伴並不害怕，他們已經準備好面對任何危險。

幾天後，他們來到一個叫做塞普勒斯（Cyprus）的大島。卡德摩斯走上岸，試圖跟當地人交談。他們對卡德摩斯很親切，但是他們不懂卡德摩斯的語言。

最後卡德摩斯想辦法用手勢告訴他們他是誰，並問他們有沒有看到他的妹妹歐羅芭，或是那隻把她載走的白色公牛。他們搖搖頭，伸手指向西方。

這群青年乘著他們的小船繼續前進。他們來到許多不同的島嶼，在每個島上都停下來，想找到歐羅芭的蹤跡，但是什麼線索也沒發現。

最後，他們來到我們現在稱為希臘的國家。希臘在那時是一個新國家，沒有多少居民，而卡德摩斯很快就學會他們的語言。接下來好長一段時間，他從一個小鎮走到另一個小鎮，跟人們說著妹妹失蹤的事。

❸ 阿波羅的女祭司皮希雅

p. 106 一天，一個老人告訴卡德摩斯，如果他去德爾菲請教皮希雅，也許皮希雅能夠告訴他歐羅芭的下落。卡德摩斯從來沒有聽過德爾菲，也沒有聽過皮希雅，便向老人問個究竟。

「讓我來告訴你。」老人說：「德爾菲是一座城，它建在帕納索斯山的山腳邊，在世界的正中央。德爾菲是光之神阿波羅的城；那裡有一座神殿，就建在許多年前阿波羅殺死黑色巨蛇的地點旁。這座神殿是世界上最華麗的地方，它的地板中央有一道很寬的裂縫；這條裂縫穿過岩石一直往下，沒有人知道它有多深。裂縫裡會飄出一股怪味，人吸了太多，就會倒地昏過去。」

「那誰又是皮希雅？」卡德摩斯問。

「讓我來告訴你。」老人說：「皮希雅是一個充滿智慧的女人，她住在神殿裡。每次有人問她很難的問題，她就會把一張三腳椅放在裂縫上，坐在上面，吸進怪味。她不會像一般人一樣昏過去，而是會開始跟阿波羅說話，而阿波羅會告訴她問題的答案。世界各地的人有問題，都會去那裡請教皮希雅。神殿裡擺滿了漂亮珍貴的禮物，都是人們為了答謝皮希雅帶來的。她的回答有時候很直接，有時候像在打啞謎，但是不管她說什麼，最後都會成真。」

於是卡德摩斯前往德爾菲，想問出妹妹的消息。有智慧的皮希雅對他非常親切，而卡德摩斯送給她一個漂亮的金杯作為謝禮後，她便坐上三角椅，吸進石頭裂縫飄出的怪味。

　　這時，她的臉色變得慘白，睜圓雙眼，看起來痛苦不堪，但是人們説，她這樣是在跟阿波羅説話。卡德摩斯請她説出歐羅芭的下落。她回答説：是朱比特變成白色的公牛，把歐羅芭帶走了，而沒人能找到她的下落。

　　「那我該怎麼辦？」卡德摩斯説：「父親告訴我，找到妹妹才能回家。」

　　「你的父親已經死了，」皮希雅説：「現在統治你國家的，是一個異族的國王。你必須待在希臘，因為你在這裡還有工作要完成。」

　　「我要做什麼？」卡德摩斯問。

　　「跟著白色的乳牛走，」皮希雅説：「在她躺下的山丘上，你要建立一座城市。」

　　卡德摩斯不明瞭她的意思，但是她停止了談話。

　　「這想必是她打的啞謎。」説完，他便離開神殿了。

❹ 城市地點和惡龍

p. 110 卡德摩斯一走出神殿，就看到一隻雪白色的乳牛，站在門邊不遠處。牠看起來好像是在等卡德摩斯，因為牠棕色的大眼睛一直看著他，接著牠轉身走開。卡德摩斯想到皮希雅剛剛跟他說過的話，便跟著乳牛走。他走了整整一天一夜，走過一片陌生的荒野；而當初跟著他從家鄉出航的青年們，還有兩個跟著他。

第二天早上，太陽升起的時候，他們發現自己站在一片美麗的山丘頂上，一邊是森林，一邊是草原。此時乳牛在地上躺下了。

「我們就在這裡建立我們的城市。」卡德摩斯說。

他們用枯枝升起一團火，然後卡德摩斯把乳牛宰了。

他們心想如果烤些肉，烤肉的香味就會飄上天際，討好住在雲間的朱比特和眾神；他們希望能因此跟朱比特成為朋友，這樣朱比特就不會妨礙他們的工作。

但是他們需要水洗肉洗手，於是其中一個青年下山去找水。他去了好久都沒有回來，另外一個青年擔心起來，便下山去找他了。

卡德摩斯等到火都快燒完了，兩人還是沒回來。他等了又等，等到太陽都已經高掛天際。他又喊又叫，但是沒有人回應。最後，他拿起他的劍，下山去看看到底是怎麼回事。

他沿著兩個朋友走過的小徑往下行，很快來到山腳下一條清澈冰涼的小河邊。他看到樹叢間有什麼東西在動，正要向小河靠近。

原來那是一條兇猛的惡龍，準備要撲向他。草上、樹葉上都有血跡，要猜出兩個青年的下場並不難。

惡龍撲向卡德摩斯，想用尖銳的爪子抓住他。

但是卡德摩斯迅速往旁邊一躍，然後用他長長的劍刺向惡龍的頸子。

頓時黑色的血泉湧而出，沒多久惡龍就倒地而死了。卡德摩斯見識過許多可怕的景象，但都不及這隻惡龍來得嚇人，這是他遇過最危險的處境。

他在地上坐下來，打著顫，為兩個朋友不停地哭泣。沒有他們的幫忙，他怎麼建立一座城市呢？

❺ 種植惡龍牙齒和底比斯城

p. 113 卡德摩斯還在哭泣的時候，突然聽到有人叫他的名字。他站起來，看看四周。他看到山坡上站著一個高大的女子，頭上帶著頭盔，手裡拿著盾牌。她的眼睛是灰色的，臉龐雖然不是很漂亮，但是充滿高貴的氣質。卡德摩斯立刻知道那是空氣女神雅典娜，賜給人類智慧的女神。

雅典娜告訴卡德摩斯，他必須把惡龍的牙齒拔出來，種在土裡。卡德摩斯覺得把龍齒當成種子來種，實在很奇怪，但是雅典娜告訴他，如果他照著做，馬上就會有足夠的人，來幫他建立他的城市。卡德摩斯還沒來得及說話，雅典娜就消失了。

惡龍有好多牙齒，多到把卡德摩斯的頭盔都裝得滿滿的。接下來，就是要找一個合適的地方，把牙齒種下。卡德摩斯才轉身背對小溪，就看到不遠處站著兩隻牛。他走過去，發現牠們已經套好犁了，他求之不得。

草原上的土壤又軟又黑，他來回犁地，犁出一道道的長溝。然後他把龍齒一個一個丟進溝裡，再用肥沃的土壤覆蓋住。所有的龍齒都種完後，他在山坡上坐下，等著看會發生什麼事。

一會兒後，溝裡的土壤動了起來，每個種下龍齒的地方，都開始露出閃亮的東西，那是黃銅頭盔。

頭盔一一鑽出土壤，接著在頭盔下現出一張張人臉，然後是肩膀、手臂、身體。卡德摩斯還來不及反應過來，一千名戰士就已從犁溝裡跳出，抖去身上的黑土。

每個人穿著黃銅盔甲，而且右手都握著一枝長矛，左手拿著一面盾牌。

卡德摩斯看到龍齒長出這麼奇怪的作物，著實嚇壞了。他們每個人看起來都這麼兇猛殘暴，卡德摩斯真怕他們看到他，會把他給殺了。他躲在犁後面，開始朝他們身上丟石頭。

戰士們不知道石頭是從哪來的，但是每個人都以為是旁邊的人丟的。他們很快就開始互相打鬥，結果戰士一個接一個地被殺死，沒多久，就只剩下五個戰士還活著。

這時卡德摩斯跑出來，大喊：「停一停！別打了！你們是我的人，去哪都要跟著我。我們要在這裡建立一座城市。」

戰士們順從他，跟著他走到山丘上。他們是很有效率的工人，短短幾天內，就在乳牛躺下的地方蓋好一棟房子。

之後，他們又蓋了更多房子，人們一一前來居住。他們以建國國王卡德摩斯的名字，把這個小城稱為卡德邁亞，但是後來它發展成大城市後，人們通常把它稱為底比斯。

❻ 字母系統和歐洲

p. 117 卡德摩斯是個有智慧的國王。與朱比特一起住在雲間的眾神，都非常喜歡他，並用各種方式幫助他。

沒過多久，他娶了戰神馬爾斯美麗的女兒哈慕妮亞（Harmonia）。眾神都參加了他們的婚禮，雅典娜還送給新娘一條漂亮的項鍊，關於這條項鍊，你以後可能還會聽到更多故事。

但是我們還沒提到卡德摩斯最偉大的事蹟：他是希臘第一位老師，教會希臘人他在海外家鄉所使用的字母。

其中第一個字母叫做阿法（alpha），第二個字母叫做貝塔（beta），這就是人們到今天一直把整套字母稱為alphabet的原因。希臘人學會這套字母後，很快就開始讀和寫，創作出許多精彩實用的書。

至於少女歐羅芭，她已經越過大海，被安全地載到一個遙遠的海岸。她可能在陌生的新國度，快樂的生活著，但我也不知道那個地方在哪裡，總之她和家鄉親友斷了消息。

朱比特是不是真的化成公牛把她載走，也沒有人知道。畢竟那已經是那麼久以前的事了，說不定故事有誤傳的部分。如果說是海盜把她從家鄉擄走，然後乘著揚著白帆的輕快小船把她帶走，我也不會感到奇怪。

但是有一點我非常確定：每個人認識她的人都很喜愛她，最後連她所到達的未知國度，都以她的名字取名為「歐羅巴洲」。

9 柏修斯的故事

❶ 黛妮和黃金雨

p. 120 阿爾戈斯曾有個國王，他只有一個孩子，而且是個女兒。如果他生的是兒子，一定會把他訓練成一個勇敢的青年和偉大的國王，但是對於這個有著一頭秀髮的女兒，他就不知道該怎麼辦了。

他看著她長成一個高挑聰明的少女，便心想自己是不是終有一天會死去，然後國土、黃金和王國都要繼位給她。

於是他派人前往德爾菲，請教皮希雅。皮希雅告訴他，他不只是終有一天要死去，而且導致他死亡的，還是她女兒的兒子。

這個回答著實嚇壞國王了。他開始想辦法，希望皮希雅的預言無法成真。最後他決定為女兒蓋一座監牢，把女兒一輩子都關在裡面。

他把工人召來，要他們在地上挖出一個又深又圓的大洞，然後在洞裡建一棟黃銅的屋子，裡面只有一個房間，沒有門，只在頂上有一面小窗子。

屋子建好後，國王便把女兒黛妮（Danae）關進去。為了讓女兒在裡面過得開心，他還把女兒的保母、玩具、漂亮衣裳，和所有他覺得她會需要的東西，也一起送進去。

「不久，我們就會看到皮希雅的話並不一定會成真。」他說。

於是黛妮被關在黃銅監牢裡。除了保母外，她沒有說話的對象。她看不到陸地或海洋，只看得到窗外的藍天，和偶爾飄過的白雲。

也不知道中間過了多少年，但是黛妮一天比一天長得更漂亮，沒過多久，她就不再是當初的小女孩，而是出落得亭亭玉立的女子。坐在雲端的朱比特往下看，第一眼就愛上了她。

一天，她看到天上好像開了一個洞，接著一陣黃金雨從窗口落進屋內。閃亮耀眼的黃金雨下完後，一個高貴的青年微笑著站在她面前。

她不知道那就是天神朱比特，利用黃金雨來到凡間，只覺得他一定是個英勇的王子，從海外異國來到這，要把她從監牢裡救出去。

之後朱比特常常來，但是總是化身為英俊挺拔的青年。很快他們兩人就結婚了，但是婚宴上的來賓只有保母一人。黛妮非常快樂，所以即使是王子不在的時候，她也不會感到寂寞。

但是有一天，王子從窄小的窗戶爬出去時，突然出現一道強烈的閃光，從此以後，她就再也沒有見過他了。

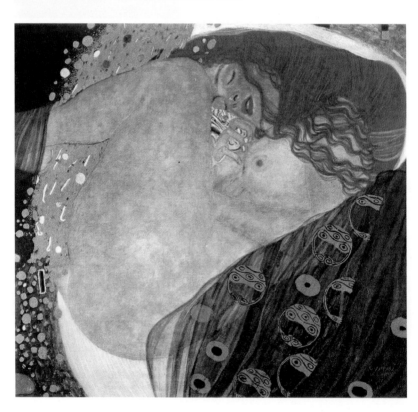

❷ 木箱和流放

p. 123 不久以後，黛妮生下一個孩子，一個微笑的小男娃娃，黛妮為他取名為柏修斯。

整整四年，她和保母把他隱藏得很好，連為他們把食物送到窗口的女僕，都不知道有寶寶的存在。但是有一天，國王剛好經過，聽到寶寶吱吱喳喳的講話聲。

他發現真相後，非常驚慌，因為他發覺儘管他做了這些努力，皮希雅的預言還是可能會成真。

唯一拯救自己的辦法，就是趁孩子還小，不足以傷害他時，就把孩子處死。但是他把幼小的柏修斯和女兒從監牢裡帶出來後，看到小娃娃無助的樣子，實在不忍心立刻把他處死。

這國王雖然是個懦夫，卻是一個心腸很好的人，不願意看到任何人受苦，但是他還是得做些什麼。

於是他命令僕人做一個寬敞、防水、堅固的木箱。木箱做好後，他把黛妮和孩子送進去，然後派人把木箱放到遙遠的海上，任憑海浪衝擊拍打。

他認為這樣可以擺脫掉女兒和孫子，也不用親眼見他們死去，因為木箱過一陣子一定會沉沒，不然也會被風吹到遙遠陌生的海岸上，遠到再也回不了阿爾戈斯。

一天一夜過去了，然後又是一天，美麗的黛妮跟孩子在海上漂流。海浪在木箱四周起伏嬉戲，西風愉快地吹著，海鳥在空中盤旋。柏修斯並不害怕，把手浸入上下起伏的海浪，對著快樂的微風笑，大喊回應海鳥的鳴叫。

但是這天晚上，整個變天了。海上刮起一場暴風雨，天空一片漆黑，波濤如山一般高，狂風不停地呼嘯。柏修斯一直安詳地睡在媽媽的懷抱裡，聽黛妮為他吟唱歌曲：

睡吧，睡吧，親愛的寶寶
在不安的媽媽懷裡安睡吧
躺在媽媽懷裡什麼都不怕
不用擔心會有危險靠近你

裹在柔軟的袍子裡睡好覺
你不會聽到媽媽的哭泣聲
不會看到洶湧海浪捲過來
也不用管大風一直吹不停

星星躲起來，夜裡好陰暗
海浪狂拍打，暴風雨降臨
但你安睡吧，親愛的寶寶
不用管呼嘯嘯的狂風暴雨

第三天早上終於來臨了，木箱被沖到一個陌生島嶼的沙岸上。島上有綠色的田野，再遠處還有一個小鎮。

這時，一個男子剛好走過，他看到木箱，便把木箱拖到沙灘上。然後他往裡面一瞧，看到一位美麗的女子和一個小男孩。他幫忙他們爬出箱子，沒多問什麼就帶兩人到自己家，親切地照料他們。

黛妮把事情原委告訴他後，他請她不要再擔憂，因為只要他們願意留下來，就可以把這裡當作新家，而他會一直是他們最忠誠的朋友。

❸ 尋找梅杜莎的頭

p. 127 於是黛妮跟兒子，就在這個救了他們的好心男人家裡住了下來。好幾年過去了，柏修斯長成一名挺拔的青年，英俊、勇敢又強壯。

有一次，島上的國王看到黛妮，立刻就被她的美貌吸引，想娶她為妻。但是他是個陰險殘酷的人，黛妮一點都不喜歡他，所以她告訴國王，自己不會嫁給他。國王認為，這一切都是柏修斯的錯，如果他能找到藉口把柏修斯送上一趟遙遠的旅程，他可能就可以強迫黛妮嫁給她，不管她是否願意。

一天，他把國內所有的青年都集合起來，宣布說他不久要與海外異國的女王結婚。他問他們是不是都願意帶一份禮物給他，他好送給女王的父親。在那個時代，準備要結婚的男人，都要先送幾份珍貴的禮物給新娘的父親。

「您想要什麼樣的禮物？」青年們問。

「馬。」他說，因為他知道柏修斯沒有馬。

「你為什麼不要些更有價值的東西？」柏修斯說，他很生氣國王這樣刁難他。

「比如說，你為什麼不要梅杜莎（Medusa）的頭？」

「那我就要梅杜莎的頭！」國王喊道：「其他人可以給我馬，但是你要給我梅杜莎的頭。」

「我會把梅杜莎的頭帶回來的。」柏修斯說完，就氣憤地走開了，其他的青年則在一旁笑他說了傻話。

他這麼輕率就答應要帶給國王的「梅杜莎的頭」，到底是什麼東西？他的母親常常跟他說梅杜莎的故事。在遙遠、遙遠的世界的邊緣，住著三個妖怪，叫做蛇髮三女妖（Gorgons）。她們的身體和臉是女人的樣子，但是除此之外，她們還有金色的翅膀，和可怕的黃銅爪子，而且頭髮都是活生生的蛇。

她們實在太可怕了，所以沒有人能忍受看著她們，而且看到她們臉的人，都會變成石頭。其中兩隻妖怪有魔法保護，什麼武器都傷不了她們；但是梅杜莎，也就是最年輕的那隻，要是有人能夠找到她，給她致命的一擊，她就有可能被殺死。

柏修斯離開國王的皇宮後，開始後悔剛剛信口開河。他怎麼可能履行他的諾言，完成國王的命令呢？

❹ 墨丘利的神奇涼鞋

p. 130 他根本不知道要去哪裡找蛇髮三女妖，也沒有武器可以殺死可怕的梅杜莎。但是無論如何，他都不能再出現在國王面前，除非他帶著梅杜莎的頭。

他走到海邊，站在那裡眺望大海，望向他的家鄉阿爾戈斯。他看著看著，太陽下山，月亮升起，一陣和風從西方吹來。然後，霎時便有兩個人，一男一女，站在他面前。

兩個人都身材高挑，氣質高貴。男的看起來像個王子，帽子上和腳上有著翅膀，手上的木杖除了翅膀，還纏著兩條金蛇。

他問柏修斯怎麼了，柏修斯便把國王怎麼對待他，以及他信口說話的事，都告訴了他。

接著，女子開始親切地對他說話。他注意到她雖然不是非常漂亮，卻有一雙全世界最美麗的灰眼睛，而且神情嚴峻而迷人，體態如女王般尊貴。

　　她要柏修斯不要害怕，勇敢地去尋找蛇髮三女妖，因為她會幫助他取得梅杜莎可怕的頭。

　　「但是我沒有船，我要怎麼去？」柏修斯問。

　　「穿上我這雙有翅膀的涼鞋，」那陌生的王子說：「它們會帶你飛越海洋和大地。」

　　「那我該往北、往南、往東還是往西走？」柏修斯問。

　　「讓我來告訴你，」那高挑的女子說：「你先去找格雷三姊妹（Gray Sisters），她們住在遙遠的、遙遠的北邊，在冰凍海洋的另一邊。她們有一個祕密，沒有人知道的祕密，你去把這祕密問出來。詢問她們，要怎麼找到看守西方金蘋果的三少女，得到答案後，馬上就去找她們。三少女會給你三樣東西，少了這三樣東西，你就取不了梅杜莎的頭。她們另外還會告訴你怎麼飛過西邊的海洋，到達蛇髮三女妖在世界邊緣的巢穴。」

　　接著，男子把他那雙有翅膀的涼鞋脫下來，穿在柏修斯的腳上；女子輕聲對他說：立刻出發，畏懼無物，保持一顆勇敢真誠的心。柏修斯知道，她就是空氣女神雅典娜，而她的同伴是墨丘利，夏日雲朵之神。但是他還沒來得及感謝他們的好心，他們就已經消失在朦朧的暮色之中了。

　　然後柏修斯往空中一跳，試試那雙神奇的涼鞋。

❺ 單眼獨牙的格雷三姊妹

p. 133 柏修斯一跳,就飛上了天,飛得比老鷹還要快。他飛啊飛,很快就飛過了那片大海。接著經過冰凍的沼澤和荒涼的雪原,之後又是一片海,一整片的冰海。

他繼續飛著,躲開倒塌的冰山,飛過冰冷的波濤,穿越長久缺乏陽光溫暖的空氣,最後來到格雷三姊妹居住的洞穴。

這三姊妹,已經老得連自己的年紀都忘了,也沒有人數得出來她們到底活了多少年。她們頭上的長髮,從出生起就是灰色的,而且她們三個人總共只有一隻眼睛和一顆牙齒,只能互相遞來遞去輪流使用。

柏修斯聽到她們在淒涼的穴中,又咕噥又哼唱的,於是他站定不動,仔細聆聽。

「我們知道一個祕密,連住在山頂上的眾神都無法得知的祕密,是不是啊,姊妹們?」

「哈!哈!沒錯,沒錯!」另外兩姊妹嘰嘰喳喳地附和。

「把牙齒給我,好姊妹,讓我再享受一次年輕美麗的感覺。」離柏修斯最近的姊妹說。

「把眼睛給我,讓我看看外面忙碌的世界,有什麼新鮮事。」坐在她隔壁的姊妹說。

「唉,好,好,好,好!」第三個姊妹咕噥道,手上拿著牙齒和眼睛，盲目地伸向兩個姊妹。

此時柏修斯往前一跳，一下就把那兩個珍貴的東西從她手裡抓過來。

「我們的牙齒在哪裡？我們的眼睛在哪裡？」另外兩個姊妹大喊，伸出長長的手臂，四處摸索。「你是不是掉了？你是不是把它們弄丟了？」

柏修斯站在洞口，看到她們那副驚慌失措的樣子，忍不住笑了出來。

「你們的牙齒和眼睛，都在我這裡。」他說：「除非你們把你們的祕密告訴我，否則就別想再拿到它們。看守西方世界金蘋果的三少女在哪裡？我要怎麼走，才能找到她們？」

「你還年輕，我們已經老了，」格雷三姊妹說：「求求你，別這樣殘酷地對待我們。可憐可憐我們，把我們的眼睛還給我們吧。」

她們又哭又求，又哄又威脅。但是柏修斯只是站在一邊嘲笑她們。

「姊妹們，我們得告訴他。」最後其中一人說。

「唉，對，我們得告訴他。」另外兩個姊妹說：「為了救我們的眼睛，我們得把祕密告訴他。」

於是她們告訴柏修斯，該怎麼走，才能到達西方世界，該選哪條路，才能找到看守金蘋果的三少女。她們把一切都說清楚後，柏修斯便把眼睛和牙齒還給她們。

「哈！哈！」她們大笑，「年輕少女的黃金時代又來臨了！」

從那天起，就再也沒有人看過格雷三姊妹，也沒有人知道她們最後到底怎麼樣了。但是寒風依舊吹進她們淒涼的洞穴，冰冷的海浪依舊在冰海岸邊呢喃，冰山依舊倒塌碎裂，而在那片荒涼的大地上，再也沒有人聽過任何生物的聲息。

❻ 西方三少女和金蘋果樹

p. 137 柏修斯又往空中一跳,神奇的涼鞋便以風的速度,帶著他往南飛。他很快就飛離那片冰凍的海洋,來到一片陽光普照的大地,那兒有綠色的森林、開滿鮮花的草原、山崗和山谷,還有一座長滿各種鮮花與果實的美麗花園。

他知道這就是著名的西方世界,因為格雷三姊妹跟他描述過西方世界的模樣。他看到西方世界的三少女,正圍著一棵結滿金蘋果的樹在跳舞,還邊唱著歌。這棵結著珍貴果實的美妙果樹,是天后朱諾的果樹,它是一份結婚禮物,而三少女的職責,就是照顧這棵果樹,不讓任何人碰到金蘋果。柏修斯停下來,聽她們唱:

我們為過去而唱,我們為未來而唱,
我們的快樂很多,我們的憂傷很淡;
唱歌,跳舞,
每一顆心都歡喜,
我們等待迎接真與善。

陽光漸弱,傍晚漸臨,
太陽下山,星兒現身,
唱歌,跳舞,
每一顆心都歡喜,
我們等待快樂新年的清晨。

樹木枯萎,蘋果凋零,
憂愁來臨,死亡召喚,
驚慌,悲痛,
每一顆心都虛假,
但是希望永存,我們並不孤單。

故事流傳，歌曲傳唱，

弦弓將斷，琴弦也死，

驚慌，悲痛，

每一顆心都虛假，

直到所有歡樂都隨風而逝。

但是新樹將從老樹根裡冒出，

葉上開出鮮花無數，

歡愉，喜悅

快樂似瘋狂

金色的蘋果在枝上累累結出。

　　柏修斯走上前，想與三位少女說話。三少女立刻停下歌聲，害怕得楞在原地。然而，當她們一看到柏修斯腳上那雙神奇的涼鞋，就都跑向他，歡迎他來到西方世界，來到她們的花園。

　　「我們知道你會來，風告訴過我們了。」她們說：「但是，你是為了什麼而來呢？」

　　於是柏修斯把自幼以來發生的事情，一五一十地告訴她們，還有為什麼他要尋找梅杜莎的頭。他表示來這裡，是要請她們給他三樣東西，幫助他對付蛇髮三女妖。

　　三少女回答說，她們不會給他三樣東西，而是四樣東西。說完，其中一位少女便交給他一把利劍，彎彎的就跟鐮刀一樣，並為他綁在腰帶上；接著，第二位少女送給他一面盾牌，盾面比所有的鏡子都還光亮；最後，第三位少女送給他一個神奇的皮囊，並用一條長長的帶子，為他掛在肩膀上。

　　「你要取下梅杜莎的頭，這三樣東西缺一不可。現在要給你的是第四樣東西，沒有這第四樣東西，你就找不到梅杜莎。」

　　說完，她們便給他一頂神奇的頭盔：「隱形頭盔」。她們為他戴上頭盔，不管是地上或天上，將沒有人可以看到他了，連三少女也看不到。

　於是，柏修斯戴上隱形頭盔，越飛越遠，飛向世界最遠的邊緣。三少女則走回果樹，又開始唱歌跳舞，看守樹上的金蘋果，直到古老的世界再次變年輕的那一天。

❼ 可怕的蛇髮三女妖

p. 142 柏修斯腰間綁著利劍，手上握著盾牌，勇敢地飛去尋找可怕的蛇髮三女妖了。但是他頭上戴著隱形頭盔，所以你根本看不到他，就跟你看不見風一樣。

他飛得好快，一下就飛過環繞陸地的大海，來到大海外圍陰暗無光的大地。根據三少女的描述，他知道蛇髮三女妖的巢穴不遠了。

他聽到一股沉重的呼吸聲，他迅速地掃視一周。泥濘河邊的汙濁野草中，有什麼東西閃著白光。

他飛近一些，但是他不敢直視，以免看到蛇髮三女妖的眼睛，變成石頭。

他轉個身，把閃亮的盾牌舉在面前，像看鏡子一樣，從盾牌上的反射，看到身後的東西。

唉，多可怕的景象啊！野草當中，半隱半露地躺著那三個妖怪，睡得正熟，金色的翅膀收在身邊。

黃銅一般的爪子，已經伸出，就好像準備好隨時要攫取獵物；肩膀上覆滿了沉睡的蛇。

兩隻比較大的妖女，把頭藏在翅膀下，就跟鳥類睡覺時一樣。但是睡在她們倆中間的第三個妖女，卻把頭仰向天空，柏修斯知道她就是梅杜莎。

他悄悄地靠近，一直背對妖怪，利用盾牌看路。

他把利劍抽出，迅速往下一揮，揮得又快又準，一下就把梅杜莎的頭斬下，頓時，黑色的血，像條河流從她的頸子湧出。

他把那可怕的頭顱，朝神奇的皮囊裡一塞，往空中一跳，就像風一樣飛走了。

兩個大妖女隨後醒了過來，她們發出淒厲的叫聲，坐了起來，然後展開巨大的翅膀，追起柏修斯。她們看不到他，因為她們也無法看到戴著隱形頭盔的柏修斯，然而，她們聞得到皮囊裡頭顱的血腥味，所以她們像獵犬一樣邊嗅邊追。

但是神奇的涼鞋比任何一雙翅膀都飛得快，所以兩隻妖怪一下就被拋在後面，淒厲的叫聲也聽不到了，只剩柏修斯獨自一人繼續往前飛。

❽ 安德柔美妲和海怪

p. 146 柏修斯直直往東飛，飛在大海上。一段時間後，他便來到一個有著棕櫚樹與金字塔的國家，還有一條大河由南向北流。

他往下看，看到一幅奇怪的景象。他看到一位美麗的少女，被綁在海邊一塊大石頭上，而遠遠的海上，有一隻大海怪正游過來要吃掉她。

柏修斯立刻飛下去跟少女說話，但是因為他還戴著隱形頭盔，少女看不到他，所以他的聲音只讓她更害怕。

於是柏修斯脫下頭盔，站在大石頭上。少女一看到他長長的頭髮、迷人的雙眼和燦爛的笑臉，心想這真是世界上最英俊的男子了。

「噢，救救我！救救我！」她邊喊，邊把手臂伸向柏修斯。

柏修斯抽出利劍，把綁住少女的鍊子打斷，然後把少女抱到大石頭的最頂上。此時海怪已經很接近他們了，牠用尾巴拍打海水，張開巨大的嘴巴，就像是除了要吞掉柏修斯和少女外，連大石頭也要一併吞掉。

雖然這隻海怪很可怕，但是還不及蛇髮三女妖可怕。

牠咆哮著游到海邊，此時柏修斯立刻從皮囊裡抓出梅杜莎的頭，對著海怪一舉，而海怪一看到那張可怕的臉，就停住變成了石頭。聽說直至現在，你還是可以在那個地方，看到那隻變成石頭的海怪。

柏修斯把梅杜莎的頭收回皮囊裡，跟少女說起話來。少女告訴他，她叫做安德柔美妲（Andromeda），是當地國王的女兒。

她說，她的皇后母親非常美麗，為自己的美貌感到非常自豪。

她每天都會來海邊，看著自己在平靜海中的倒影，甚至自誇說，連海裡的仙女都沒有她美麗。

海裡的仙女聽到這句話後，非常生氣，便請求海神涅普頓懲罰這個驕傲的皇后。於是涅普頓派來一隻海怪，搗毀國王的船隻，殺死海邊的牛群，打壞漁人的小屋。

人民都痛苦不堪，最後不得不派人去問皮希雅他們到底該怎麼辦。皮希雅告訴他們，要拯救這個國家，只有一個辦法，就是把國王的女兒安德柔美妲送給海怪吃掉。

國王與皇后都很愛他們的女兒，因為她是他們唯一的孩子，所以有好長一段時間，他們都不願意照著皮希雅的話去做。

但是海怪日復一日地作亂，最後甚至威脅，除了農地之外，連城鎮也不會放過。於是他們不得不為了國家的福祉，犧牲安德柔美妲。這就是為什麼她會被綁在海邊的大石頭上，等著死在海怪的嘴裡。

柏修斯跟安德柔美妲說話的這時，國王、皇后及一大群人正哭哭啼啼、憂心忡忡地來到海邊，他們以為海怪想必已經把牠的獵物吃掉了。

但是當他們看到安德柔美妲完好無恙，並得知是站在她身旁的英俊青年救了她時，都忍不住內心的喜悅。

柏修斯深深被安德柔美妲的美貌給迷住，都忘了自己還有任務沒有完成。當國王問他，他該怎麼感謝他救了安德柔美妲的性命時，他說：

「請讓我娶她為妻。」

國王非常高興。於是在第七天的時候，柏修斯和安德柔美妲結婚了。國王的宮殿裡，舉辦了一場盛大的宴會，每個人都開心不已。

柏修斯和安德柔美妲在這個充滿棕櫚樹與金字塔的國家，快快樂樂地住了一段時間。而從海邊到山上，每個人都在傳述著柏修斯的英勇和安德柔美妲的美麗。

❾ 看到梅杜莎的頭，變成石頭

p. 153 但是柏修斯沒有忘記他的母親。於是，在一個美好的夏日，他和安德柔美妲乘著一艘美麗的船出發回家了。

邪惡的國王從來沒有停止嘗試說服黛妮嫁給她，但是黛妮就是不願意。最後，國王發現強迫不了她，便宣布要將她處死。

所以柏修斯和安德柔美妲來到城裡時，除了他那逃往朱比特神殿的母親，和追殺在後的國王，他們還會遇見誰呢？

驚恐的黛妮根本沒看到柏修斯，只是逕自跑向這島上唯一安全的地方：朱比特神殿。因為這個國家的法律規定，連國王都不能傷害在朱比特神殿尋求庇護的人。

柏修斯看到國王像個瘋子追殺他的母親，立刻擋在他面前，要他站住。但是國王只是氣憤地把劍往他身上一揮。柏修斯用盾牌擋住那一劍，同時從皮囊抽出梅杜莎的頭。

「我說過要給你帶個禮物的，這就是了！」柏修斯大喊。

國王一看到梅杜莎的頭，就變成了石頭，還是站著的姿勢，劍高高地舉著，臉上一副憤怒猙獰的表情。

島上的人聽到這件事都很高興，因為沒有人喜歡那個邪惡的國王。他們也很高興柏修斯回來了，而且還帶回來一位美麗的妻子安德柔美妲。

隔天早上，他把王國交給那個曾在海邊救了母親和他的善心人。然後他登上船，跟著安德柔美妲和母親黛妮，一起駛向大海，航向阿爾戈斯了。

⑩ 誤殺祖父

p. 155 黛妮的老父親，也就是阿爾戈斯的國王，聽說有艘來自異國的船，載著他的女兒和孫子漂洋過海回來時，心裡非常苦惱。因為他還記得，皮希雅預言他會死在孫子的手上。於是他不等看到那艘船，就匆匆忙忙離開皇宮，逃出國了。

阿爾戈斯的人民，都很歡迎黛妮回到家鄉，同時也為他英俊的兒子感到驕傲。他們都懇求他留下來，這樣有一天，他就可以成為他們的國王。

不久之後，有個鄰國的國王舉辦一場競賽，跑步、跳遠和丟鐵環最優秀的人，都會得到獎項。柏修斯和阿爾戈斯其他的青年也前往參加，因為如果他能夠奪得獎項，就能名傳千里。

這天，他在展示自己丟鐵環的能力。他把一只沉重的鐵環，丟得好遠好遠，超過以前所有人的距離。

結果鐵環落在旁觀的群眾裡，擊中一名站在那裡的陌生人。那人雙手一舉，就倒在地上了。柏修斯跑過去想幫忙，卻看到那人已經死了。

而這人不是別人，就是黛妮的父親，阿爾戈斯的老國王。他逃到國外想逃過一劫，反而讓自己更加在劫難逃。

柏修斯非常悲痛，用各種方式想對這位不快樂的國王表示敬意。阿爾戈斯現在名正言順是他的王國了，但是他實在無法在殺死外公後，接下王位。

於是他跟另一位國王交換，這個國王在不遠處統治兩個富裕的城市，邁錫尼（Mycenae）和梯林斯（Tiryns）。最後，他和安德柔美妲在邁錫尼過了好多年幸福快樂的日子。

10 雅典城由來

❶ 雅典的國王凱克羅普斯

p. 158 很久很久以前，在希臘一座陡峭多石的山丘上，住著一群非常窮困的人。他們還沒學會怎麼蓋房子，所以都住在地上掘出的坑洞，或是岩石間挖出來的小洞裡。他們吃的是動物的肉，動物是他們在森林裡打獵得來的，有時候也配上一點莓果或堅果。

他們甚至連弓箭都沒有，都是以彈弓、棍棒和尖銳的樹枝作為武器。他們身上僅有的衣服，是動物的毛皮。

他們住在山頂上，因為在那裡就不會受到周圍森林裡野獸的攻擊，也不怕有時候會過來找麻煩的野人。

這座山丘每一邊都很陡峭，除了一條窄小的步道外，就沒有別的路可以上來，而步道頂端，總是有人守衛。

一天，他們在森林裡打獵時，看到一個陌生的青年。這個青年臉龐俊美，衣著華麗，他們簡直無法相信他跟他們一樣也是人。青年的體態修長優美，跑在樹林間動作靈活敏捷，看得他們開始相信他是一條化為人形的蛇，一個個著迷又驚慌地站在原地。

青年跟他們說話，但是他們一個字都聽不懂，於是他用手勢表示他餓了，他們便給他一點東西吃，也不再害怕了。

如果這些人跟森林裡的野人一樣，可能立刻就把青年殺了。但是他們想讓家裡的婦女和孩子，也看看這個他們稱為「蛇人」的青年，聽他講講話，所以就把他帶回山丘頂上的家。

他們心想，等他們把蛇人給大家看個幾天後，就可以把他殺了，獻給他們認為掌控性命的未知神明。

但是這個青年實在太俊美太溫柔了，所以等所有人都看過他後，都覺得把他殺了實在很可惜。於是他們給他吃的，友善地對待他，而青年會唱歌給他們聽，陪他們的孩子玩，使他們的生活比以前還快樂。

　　沒過多久，青年就學會了他們的語言。他告訴他們，他的名字是凱克羅普斯（Cecrops），在不遠處的海岸發生船難後，才來到這裡的。他又告訴他們許多家鄉的奇聞軼事，而現在他再也回不了家鄉了。

　　這些人邊聽邊驚嘆，沒過多久，他們開始敬愛他，認為他比他們都更有智慧。然後他們問他可以為他做什麼，而沒有一個人會不聽從他的吩咐。

　　於是凱克羅普斯，這位「蛇人」，他們依舊這樣叫他，就成為山丘上這群人的國王。

　　他教他們製造弓箭，設網捕鳥，用魚鉤釣魚。

　　他帶領他們反抗森林裡的野人，幫助他們殺死一直讓他們生活在恐懼之中的野獸；並教他們怎麼用木頭蓋房子，再用長在沼澤裡的蘆葦鋪成屋頂；他教他們一家人一家人生活在一起，不要再跟以前一樣，像野獸似地窩在一起。

　　他還跟他們講起，住在山頂雲間的偉大朱比特與眾神。

❷ 雅典娜為雅典城命名

p. 162 不久以後，山丘頂上就不再是一個個簡陋的石洞，而是一座小鎮，有整潔的房屋和一個市場。小城周圍，是一整道堅固的圍牆，只有一個狹窄的大門，連接著通往山下平原的小徑。只不過，這個地方到現在一直沒有個名字。

一天早上，國王和他的謀臣一起坐在市場邊，計畫怎麼讓小鎮成為富有強大的城市時，兩個陌生人出現在街上。沒有人知道他們怎麼進來的，大門的守衛沒有看到他們，而從來沒有人膽敢在有守衛守門時，爬上那條狹窄的小徑。

但是兩個陌生人此時就站在那裡，一男一女，兩人都個子高大，神情高貴，每個人看到他們，都忍不住停下來，驚奇得什麼話也說不出來。

男的披著一件紫綠相間的長袍，手裡拿著一根堅固的長棍，其中一端伸出三個尖銳的矛頭。女的並不漂亮，但是她有一雙美麗的灰眼睛。她一隻手裡拿著長矛，一隻手裡握著一面工藝奇特的盾牌。

「這座小城叫什麼名字？」男的問。

人們都驚奇地瞪著他看，不了解他的意思。

此時一個老人回答他：「這座小城沒有名字，以前大家都把我們這些住在山上的人，叫做克瑞納人（Cranae），但是自從凱克羅普斯國王來了以後，我們就忙得沒時間想名字。」

「凱克羅普斯國王在哪裡？」女的問。

「他正跟他的謀臣坐在市場邊。」

「現在馬上帶我們去找他。」男的說。

凱克羅普斯看到那兩個陌生人向市場這邊走來，便站起來，等著他們開口說話。

男的先說話了：「我是涅普頓，」他說：「我掌管海洋。」

「我是雅典娜，」女的說：「我把智慧賜給人類。」

「我聽說，你們在計畫把你們的小鎮變成一個偉大的城市，」涅普頓說：「我就是來幫你們的。用我的名字為你們的小鎮取名吧，讓我成為你們的守護神，全世界的財富就都會屬於你們。世界各地的船隻，都會過來帶給你們商品貨物、金銀珠寶，你們會成為海上的霸王。」

「我叔叔提出的條件是很好，」雅典娜說：「但是請聽我說。還是用我的名字為你們的小鎮取名吧，讓我成為你們的守護神，我就會給你們黃金也買不到的東西：我會教會你們成千上萬件你們一無所知的事情。我會把你們的城市，當作我最喜歡的家，我會送給你們智慧，而你們的智慧，將會永遠地影響所有人類的思想與心靈。」

國王向他們一鞠躬，然後轉向聚集在市場上的人民。「我們該選哪位神明，作為我們城市的守護神？」他問，「涅普頓願意給我們財富，雅典娜承諾給我們智慧。我們該選誰？」

「涅普頓和財富！」許多人喊。

「雅典娜和智慧！」其他人喊。

最後，大家顯然無法做出一致的決定，一位德高望重的老人站起來，說：

「這兩位神明都只給了我們承諾，而他們承諾的東西，我們都一無所知。我們當中，有誰知道財富是什麼？又有誰知道智慧是什麼？如果他們能夠給我們具體一點的東西，就在此時此地，給我們一點看得到、摸得到的東西，我們就比較知道要選誰了。」

「沒錯！沒錯！」大家喊。

「好，那麼，」兩個陌生人說：「我們就在此時此地，各送你們一樣東西，然後你們再做決定。」

涅普頓先送出他的禮物。他站在山丘上裸岩的最高處，要大家看他施展神力。他把三叉長矛高高舉在空中，然後用力往下一頂，頓時閃電大作，大地搖撼，他腳下的岩石裂成兩半，一路裂到山腳。然後從這個大裂縫中，跳出一隻美妙的動物，牛奶一般的白，有修長的腿和弓形的頸，還有絲一般的鬃毛與尾巴。

這些人從來沒有看過這樣的動物，還以為牠是一種新種類的熊、狼或野豬，從岩石裡跳出來要把他們吃掉。

於是有些人跑回家躲起來，有些人爬到圍牆上，還有些人驚慌地抓起武器。但是當他們看到那隻動物安靜地站在涅普頓身邊時，就不再害怕，並走近讚賞牠的美。

「這就是我送給你們的禮物。」涅普頓說：「這隻動物會為你們負重擔，拉馬車，托車拉犁。牠會讓你們騎在牠的背上，載著你奔馳得比風還要快。」

「牠叫什麼名字？」國王問。

「牠叫做馬。」涅普頓回答。

接著，雅典娜走向前。她在一塊綠色的草地上站了一會兒，鎮裡的小孩很喜歡傍晚的時候在這塊草地上玩耍。然後她把長矛的尖端，深深插進土裡，頓時空中充滿了音樂，土裡則開始長出一棵樹，有纖細的枝條，深綠色的樹葉，白色的花，和紫綠色的果實。

「這就是我送給你們的禮物。」雅典娜說：「你們餓了，它會給你們食物。你們被太陽曬昏了，它會給你庇蔭。它會美化你們的城市，而從它的果實所得到的油，會成為世界各地爭相尋找的珍品。」

「它叫什麼名字？」國王問。

「它叫做橄欖樹。」雅典娜回答。

接著，國王和謀臣們開始討論這兩樣禮物。

「我覺得馬對我們的用處不大。」之前說話的老人說：「因為馬車、貨車和犁，我們都沒有，而且我們也不知道它們是什麼東西。再來，我們當中有誰會想坐在牠的背上，奔馳得比風還要快？而橄欖樹，卻永遠都會為我們和我們的子孫帶來美和喜悅。」

「我們要選誰？」國王轉向人民問。

「雅典娜的禮物最好，」大家喊，「我們就選雅典娜和智慧！」

「好，就這麼辦，」國王說：「我們的城市，就取名為雅典。」

從這天起，小鎮不斷成長擴大，沒多久，山丘上就容不下所有的人了。於是他們在山腳下的平原建起房屋，還闢了一條大路，直通三英里外的大海，而世界上沒有一個城市比雅典還要漂亮。

他們在山丘頂上原來是市場的地方，建起一座神殿紀念雅典娜，到今天我們還看得到這座神殿的遺跡。那棵橄欖樹，後來也不斷成長滋養，如果你去雅典玩，當地人還會把它當初站立的地點指給你看。它生出許多小樹苗，一段時間後，它們便成為希臘與大海周圍所有國家都珍惜的恩典。

至於那匹馬，牠跑過一片片的平原，一路流浪到北方，最後終於在珀紐斯河（Peneus）岸外遙遠的色薩利（Thessaly）找到一個家。我聽說世界上所有的馬，都是這隻涅普頓從岩石間所變出的馬的後代，但是這個說法的真實性，也許還有值得懷疑的地方。

11 鐵修斯的歷險記（I）

❶ 政局不安的雅典城

p. 172 雅典曾經有個國王叫做愛琴斯（Aegeus）。他沒有兒子，但是有五十個姪子，他們都等著他過世，這樣他們其中一人就可以當上國王。他們每個都是放蕩不羈、一事無成的傢伙，雅典人民都很擔憂雅典落入他們手中的那天。

一年夏天，愛琴斯代表城裡的長老離開雅典，坐船穿越薩羅尼加灣（Saronic Sea），前往出名的特洛伊西納城（Troezen）。特洛伊西納就坐落在對岸的山腳下。

特洛伊西納的國王皮特修斯（Pittheus）很高興看到愛琴斯，因為他們小的時候就經常玩在一塊兒。他歡迎愛琴斯來到他的城市，熱情地招待他。

於是日復一日，特洛伊西納的大理石宮殿裡，充滿了饗宴、歡樂和音樂，兩位國王開心地聊著年輕時的經歷，和世間英雄的事蹟。

等到該坐船回雅典的時候，愛琴斯一點都不想離開。但是愛琴斯留下來，並不只是為了在老朋友家中，得到休息和歡樂；他留下來，更是為了老朋友的女兒愛特拉。

愛特拉美得就如夏日的早晨，是特洛伊西納的喜悅和驕傲，而愛琴斯從來沒有像現在在愛特拉（Aethra）身邊這麼快樂過。

等到愛琴斯的船離開一段時間後，皮特修斯國王的宮殿裡舉辦了一場婚禮。但是他們將這件事保密，因為愛琴斯擔心，姪子們聽到這件事會很氣憤，然後派人來特洛伊西納傷害他。

一天早上，當特洛伊西納的花園都開滿了玫瑰，山丘上的石南都變得青綠，愛特拉生下了一個男娃娃，臉龐清秀，手臂強壯有力，眼睛就如山鷹一般敏銳明亮。

現在，愛琴斯更不想回家了，於是他爬到可以俯瞰全特洛伊西納城的山上，祈禱空氣女神雅典娜賜給他智慧，告訴他該怎麼辦。

就在這個時候，一艘船開進港口，為愛琴斯帶來一封信，告訴他雅典遇到了危險。

「請立刻回來。」長老送來的信裡寫著：「請趕快回來，否則雅典就完了。海外大國克里特的米諾斯國王，正開著船隊、帶著士兵，在前來雅典的路上。他說，他會把劍與火帶入我們的城牆，殺盡我們的青年，讓我們的孩子都當他的奴隸。請快回來拯救我們！」

「我的職責在呼喚我了。」愛琴斯說。

離別的時刻來臨時，他對愛特拉說：「世間最好的女子，聽我說，因為我可能再也見不到你美麗的臉龐了。你還記得山坡上那棵老懸鈴木嗎？還有不遠處除了我就無人可抬起的那顆平坦的大石頭？我把我從雅典帶來的劍和涼鞋，都藏在石頭下面。這兩樣東西要一直藏著，等到我們的孩子力氣大到能夠把石頭抬起來的那一天，這兩樣東西就是他的了。好好照顧他，愛特拉，到了他把石頭抬起來的那天，再跟他述說他的父親，並要他來雅典找我。」

愛琴斯親了他的妻子和寶寶，便上船了。水手吆喝，船槳入水，白色的帆迎風展開。宮殿窗口前，愛特拉目送著愛琴斯的船在蔚藍的海水上，駛向愛琴娜島（Aegina）和遙遠的亞提卡（Attic）海岸。

❷ 鐵修斯舉起重石

p. 177 一年接一年過去了，愛特拉一直沒有從彼岸得到丈夫的隻字片語。

接著，謠傳米諾斯國王已經俘獲雅典所有的船隻，燒掉了部分的城市，強迫雅典人獻給他珍貴的貢物。除此以外，就沒有別的消息了。

此時，愛特拉的孩子已經長成一個身材高大、雙頰紅潤、如山中獅子一樣強壯的少年了，愛特拉為他取名為鐵修斯（Theseus）。他十五歲生日那天，跟著母親愛特拉一起走到山上，眺望大海。

「唉，如果你父親回來就好了！」愛特拉嘆氣道。

「我父親？」鐵修斯問，「我父親到底是誰？為什麼你總是在這裡望啊望的，期盼他會回來？告訴我父親的事。」

愛特拉回答：「孩子，你看到那裡那塊平坦的大石頭嗎？一半埋在地下，表面爬滿了苔蘚和長春藤？你覺得你可以把石頭搬起來嗎？」

「我試試看，母親。」鐵修斯說。他把手指貼著石頭，插進土壤，抓住石頭不規則的邊緣，使勁地又拖又拉，弄得自己氣喘吁吁，手臂痠痛，全身是汗，石頭卻還是一動也沒動。

最後他說：「這個任務現在對我來說還太難了，等我更強壯了，才有可能搬動它。但是你為什麼要我把石頭搬起來？」

愛特拉說：「等你壯到能把石頭搬起來的時候，我就會告訴你父親的事情。」

從這天起，鐵修斯每天都出去鍛鍊跑步、跳躍、丟擲和舉重，而且每天都會練習搬一顆石頭。

漸漸地，他越來越強壯了，肌肉練得如鐵條一般，四肢就像堅固的槓桿。在他十六歲生日那天，他又跟母親來到山上，嘗試把大石頭搬起來。但是大石頭還是穩穩地躺在地上，一動也不動。

「我還不夠強壯，母親。」他說。

「要有耐心，孩子。」愛特拉說。

於是，他又繼續鍛鍊跑步、跳躍、丟擲和舉重。他還練習摔角，馴服平原上的野馬，追獵山上的獅子。他的力氣、迅捷和技巧，是所有人驚歎的對象，而鐵修斯的事蹟更在老特洛伊西納城傳了開來。

然而，他在十七歲生日那天，還是無法把山坡上懸鈴木邊那塊平坦的大石頭搬起來。

「要有耐心，孩子。」愛特拉說，但是這次她的眼中含著淚。

於是鐵修斯又繼續鍛鍊。人們都說自海格力士以來，就沒有出現過力氣這麼大的人了。

然後，在他十八歲的時候，他和母親又一次爬上山。他彎腰抓住石頭，結果石頭動了，啊，看啊，他把石頭搬離地面，然後在下面發現一把青銅劍和一雙金涼鞋。他把這兩樣東西交給母親。

「告訴我父親的事。」他說。

愛特拉知道她等待已久的時刻終於到了。她把劍掛在鐵修斯的皮帶上，又為他把涼鞋穿上，然後告訴他，他的父親是誰，為什麼把他們母子留在特洛伊西納。

鐵修斯聽了非常高興。他自豪的雙眼露出渴望的光芒，說：「我準備好了，母親，我今天就出發前往雅典。」

　　但是老國王難過地搖搖頭，想說服鐵修斯不要走。

　　「在這個無法無天的時代，你怎麼去雅典？海上都是海盜。」他說。

　　鐵修斯問，「哪條路更危險？坐船，還是沿著海岸走過去？」

　　「海路是充滿了危險，但是陸路比海路還要危險十倍。」外公說。

　　「好，如果路上比海上還危險，」鐵修斯說：「那我就走路，而且馬上就出發。」

　　「那你至少要帶上五十個青年，當你隨行的同伴吧？」皮特修斯國王問。

　　「誰都不要跟著我。」鐵修斯說。他站起來，玩弄他的劍柄，對外公的恐懼不以為然。

　　等該說的都說完了，他親吻母親，向外公道別。國王和愛特拉懷著祝福和淚水，跟著他走到城門，一路目送他，直到他高大的背影，消失在海岸邊的樹林之中。

❸ 鐵棒巨人

p. 183 鐵修斯懷著一顆勇敢的心，沿著右手邊的大海，不斷往前走。他爬上一片又一片的山坡，最後終於爬到一座灰色山峰的山頂，俯瞰整片在他腳下綿延開來的大地。接著他下山繼續往前走，最後來到一座陰暗的森林。

在這片森林裡，住著一個叫做鐵棒巨人的強盜。他是當地人民的憂患，因為他常常跑到牧羊人放牧的山谷，不只擄走綿羊和小羊，有時候連小孩和牧羊人也一併抓走。

現在，他看到鐵修斯走在森林裡，便心想這回他要得大獎了，因為從鐵修斯的穿著和舉止看來，巨人知道他一定是個王子。

於是他趴在地上，讓長春藤葉和長草遮住他，抓著他的大鐵棒，準備隨時出手。

然而，鐵修斯有雙敏銳的眼睛和靈敏的耳朵，不管是野獸，或巨人強盜，都不可能讓他措手不及。等鐵棒巨人跳出來想把他打倒時，他迅速地往旁邊一閃，結果沉重的鐵棒，只打到他身後的地上。而巨人還沒來得及舉起鐵棒再下手，鐵修斯就已抓住他的雙腳，把他摔倒了。

鐵棒巨人大吼一聲，想再出手，但是鐵修斯把鐵棒從他手上搶過來，然後在他頭上重重一擊，而這一擊使巨人以後再也無法傷害穿越森林的旅人了。

鐵修斯繼續往前走，肩上扛著大鐵棒，嘴裡唱著勝利的歌曲，一邊警覺地掃視四周，提防樹林裡還躲著其他敵人。

❹ 彎松巨人西尼斯

p. 185 他剛跨過下一座山的山脊，就遇到一個老人。老人警告他，不要繼續往前走，因為他在下山的路上，馬上就會穿過一座小松樹林。小松樹林邊住著一個叫做西尼斯（Sinis）的強盜，他會殘忍地殺害過路的陌生人。

「大家稱他做彎松巨人，」老人說：「因為他每次抓到一個旅人，就會把兩棵又高又有彈性的松樹彎到地上，然後把他的俘虜綁到樹上，一邊的手腳綁在一棵樹上，另一邊的手腳綁在另一棵樹上。然後他讓兩棵樹彈回去，大笑著看旅人的身體被撕裂成兩半。」

「看來，現在是除掉這個惡棍的時候了。」鐵修斯說。

他很快就看到強盜的家，建在一座高聳的峭壁腳邊。屋後是一片石子峽谷，和一條嘩啦嘩啦作響的山溪，屋前有一座花園。但是屋旁的松樹頂端，滿是不幸旅人的屍骨，慘白地掛在那裡，任風吹日曬。

路邊的石頭上，就坐著西尼斯本人。他一看到鐵修斯，便衝過來，手裡甩著一條長長的繩子，大喊：「歡迎，歡迎，尊貴的王子！歡迎來到我的旅店——真正的旅人歇店！」

「你提供什麼樣的娛樂活動？」鐵修斯問：「你是不是準備好一棵松樹，把它彎到地上給我了？」

「是的，而且是兩棵松樹！」強盜說：「我知道您要來，特意為您彎下兩棵松樹。」

他邊說，邊把繩子扔向鐵修斯，想用繩圈纏住他。但是鐵修斯往旁邊一跳，躲過了。

接著兩人開始在樹林裡扭打成一團，但沒有多久，強盜趴在地上，鐵修斯趁機跪在他的背上，然後用他自己的繩子，把他綁在已經彎下來的兩棵松樹上。

「你想怎麼對我，我就怎麼對你。」他對強盜說。

彎松巨人又哭又求，還提出許多好聽的承諾，但是鐵修斯不理他。他轉身，松樹立刻彈起，留下強盜的身體在枝葉間懸盪著。

❺ 派瑞金和蘆筍

p. 185 這個彎松巨人有一個女兒，叫做派瑞金（Perigune）。她跟父親相比起來，就如同美麗嬌嫩的紫羅蘭，之於她依偎著的盤根錯節的老橡樹。強盜家花園裡的花朵與罕見植物，就是她在照顧的。

她看到鐵修斯對父親做的事後，心裡很害怕，立刻跑去躲起來。

「噢，親愛的植物，救救我！」她喊著，因為她常常對花園裡的花說話，所以它們好像都能聽懂她似的。「親愛的植物，救救我。只要我活著，就不會摘你一片葉子，也不會傷害你。」

其中有一株植物，一直沒長出葉子，立在地上看起來就像一枝棍子。這株植物很同情派瑞金，於是它立刻生出毛茸茸的長枝條，枝條上面還長著精美的綠葉，一下就把派瑞金整個包起來了。

於是鐵修斯大喊：「派瑞金，你不用怕我，因為我知道你溫柔又善良，而我只對付陰險殘忍的人。」

派瑞金偷偷地往外看。她看到鐵修斯俊美的臉龐，又聽到他溫柔的聲音後，便發著抖走出來，跟他說話。

那天晚上，鐵修斯便在她家過夜，而她摘了幾朵她最喜歡的花送給他，還給他吃的。但是到了第二天清晨，黎明從東方降臨，山峰上的星光逐漸黯淡後，鐵修斯便與她道別，翻山越嶺繼續前進了。

派瑞金一直留在小松樹林裡那座寂寞的花園裡，照顧她的植物和花朵，而她從來不摘那株蘆筍的莖，也不把它拿來吃。後來，她成為一名英雄的妻子，有了孩子、孫子和曾孫後，她叮嚀他們要好好愛惜這株曾經幫助過她的植物。

⑥ 被大海與大地唾棄的斯克戎

p. 191 鐵修斯無所畏懼地繼續前進，最後他來到一個地方，那兒有清澈的泉水從石縫中流出，而通道變得更加窄小，通向一個山洞的開口。

泉水旁邊坐著一個紅臉巨人，腿上放著一根大木棒，守著洞口，不讓任何人通過。懸崖底端的海水裡，躺著一隻大海龜，灰色的眼睛總是望著上面，等著食物掉下來。

鐵修斯知道這就是強盜斯克戎（Sciron）居住的地方，因為派瑞金跟他說過，斯克戎是整個沿海地區的禍患，他會命令經過的旅人幫他洗腳，然後趁此時把旅人踢下懸崖，讓他的寵物大海龜把人吃掉。

鐵修斯一走向前，強盜立刻舉起棒子，兇惡地說：「每個人都要幫我洗過腳才能過去！過來幫我洗腳！」

鐵修斯微笑說：「你的海龜今天餓不餓？你是不是想把我拿去餵牠吃啊？」

強盜雙眼火紅，說：「我會把你拿去餵給他吃，但是你要先幫我洗腳。」他揮舞著大木棒衝過來，想給鐵修斯重重一擊。

但是鐵修斯已經有所準備。他用鐵棒巨人的鐵棒一擋，強盜的木棒頓時飛出手中，邊飛邊轉，從懸崖邊掉落。斯克戎氣得臉色鐵青，撲上來要跟鐵修斯扭打，但是鐵修斯的動作比他還要快。

他丟下鐵棒，一把抓住斯克戎的脖子，把斯克戎推到他之前坐著的石頭上，然後把斯克戎往尖突的石頭上一甩，斯克戎便被他按住，半個身子懸在懸崖外。

「現在換你來幫我洗腳。過來幫我洗腳！」鐵修斯說。

於是，已經嚇得面色慘白的斯克戎，便開始幫鐵修斯洗腳。

斯克戎幫他洗完腳後，鐵修斯說：「現在，你之前怎麼對別人，我現在就怎麼對你。」

空中傳來一聲慘叫，天上的老鷹也應聲高鳴。然後是一聲落水的巨響，嚇得大海龜也匆匆逃走。

這時，大海大喊：「我不要跟這個惡棍扯上關係！」

　　接著一陣大浪，便把斯克戎的屍體沖上岸。但是斯克戎的屍體一碰到海岸，大地就喊：「我不要跟這個惡棍扯上關係！」

　　接著便突然來了一陣地震，把斯克戎的屍體又丟回海裡。

　　大海氣極了，掀起一陣暴風雨，把海水都攪成泡沫，然後吹起一股巨浪，把那具受人嫌惡的屍體扔到高空。如果不是天空也不屑收留這具屍體，把它變成一塊黑色的大石頭，它現在還會掛在那裡。

　　而這塊人們說是斯克戎屍體的石頭，到今天你還可以看到。它陰森、醜陋、孤獨，有三分之一躺在海裡，三分之一埋在沙岸裡，另外的三分之一，則暴露在空氣中。

❼ 愛摔角的壞國王

p. 195 鐵修斯走下山谷，來到一片美麗的平原。他的英勇事蹟早已傳開了，男人女人都擠在路邊，爭著看看這名除掉鐵棒巨人、彎松巨人和懸崖上可怕的斯克戎的英雄。

「現在，我們可以安心過日子了，」他們喊道：「吃掉我們牲畜和小孩的強盜都不在了。」

「不要踏進伊流西斯城，從山丘上的路繞過去。」一個正帶著一隻綿羊準備上市場的窮人，小聲地跟他說。

「為什麼？」鐵修斯問。

窮人説：「請聽我説，伊流西斯的國王叫做克錫翁（Cercyon），他很會摔角。他要每個進城的旅人，都跟他摔角，但是他的手臂力氣非常大，最後總把對方活活打死。有很多旅人進到伊流西斯城，但是從來沒有一個人離開過。」

「那我不只會進到伊流西斯城，我還會活著離開。」鐵修斯説完，就扛起鐵棒，大步邁向神聖的伊流西斯城。

「愛摔角的克錫翁在哪？」他問城門的守衛。

「國王正在他的大理石宮殿用餐。」守衛回答道：「如果你還想活命，最好現在就回頭，趁他還沒聽到你來之前，趕快逃走。」

「我為什麼要逃走？」鐵修斯説：「我不怕。」他沿著窄小的街道，走向老克錫翁的宮殿。

鐵修斯大膽地走到宮殿大門，大喊：「克錫翁，出來跟我摔角！」

「啊！」國王説：「又來了一個時日不多的傻小子。讓他進來跟我一起用餐，吃完了，他就可以盡情摔角摔個夠。」

他們讓鐵修斯在國王的餐桌前坐下，於是兩人便坐在那裡，邊吃邊瞪著對方，一句話也不說。

等他們吃完後，鐵修斯站起來説：「來吧，克錫翁，如果你不怕的話，就來跟我摔角吧。」

於是兩人走到庭院裡。這座庭院，就是許多青年不敵克錫翁而喪生的地點。他們一直摔到太陽下山，都無法分出高下。

但是顯然鐵修斯受過訓練的技巧，最後能勝過克錫翁粗暴的蠻力。接著，站在一旁觀看的伊流西斯人，看著鐵修斯把巨大的克錫翁整個舉起來，然後往後一甩，讓克錫翁一頭撞到後面堅硬的地面。

「你怎麼對別人，我就怎麼對你！」鐵修斯大喊。

但是可怕的老克錫翁既不動，也不説話。鐵修斯把他翻過來，看著他殘忍的臉孔，才發現他已經死了。

伊流西斯的人民都走向鐵修斯，希望他成為他們的國王。

「有一天，我會成為你們的國王，」鐵修斯説：「但是，不是現在，因為我還有任務要完成。」

説完，他扣上他的劍，穿上他的涼鞋和尊貴的長袍，扛起鐵棒，走出伊流西斯城。所有的人都跟在他後面，大喊：「祝您好運，我們的國王，願雅典娜保佑您、指引您！」

❽ 鐵床拉人魔

p. 199 現在，雅典就在前方不到二十英里的地方了。太陽快下山的時候，他來到一片開闊的綠色峽谷。旁邊的山丘上，有一間石造的大房子，半掩在樹林裡，牆上和屋頂都爬滿了葡萄藤。

鐵修斯正在納悶，誰會住在這個美麗卻孤寂的地方，一個男的從屋裡走出來，急忙趕到路上來見鐵修斯。

「這個地方很荒涼，不常有旅人經過。」他說：「請上來與我一起用餐，在我的屋裡過夜。我會讓你睡在一張很舒適的床上，這張床不僅適合每一位客人睡覺，還能治好他們所有的病痛。我現在進去幫你把床準備好，你就可以躺在上面休息了。」

那男人進屋後，鐵修斯開始東張西望，想看看這到底是個什麼樣的地方。他很驚訝這間房子這麼華麗，好像每間房間都用金啊、銀啊等各種漂亮的東西裝飾著，真的是個可以給王子住的地方。

他邊看邊讚嘆，面前的葡萄藤卻被撥開，探出了一張美麗的少女臉龐。

「高貴的陌生人，」她小聲說：「千萬不要在我主人的床上躺下，因為每個躺下去的人，都沒再起來過。趕快趁他回來之前，逃到峽谷裡的森林躲起來，不然你就逃不掉了。」

「美麗的女子，你的主人是誰，我該懼怕他嗎？」鐵修斯問。

「大家都叫他普克拉提斯（Procrustes），或是拉人魔。」少女說：「他不是說這張床適合每一位客人睡覺嗎？的確，是每一位客人都合適，因為如果客人比床還要高，普克拉提斯就把客人的腳砍掉一截，讓客人跟床一樣長。如果客人比床還要短，而大多數的客人都是比床要矮，他就用繩子把客人的四肢和身體拉長，一直拉到客人跟床一樣長。這就是為什麼大家都叫他拉人魔。」

「你聽！你聽！」少女低聲說：「我聽到他來了！」說完，葡萄藤便把她藏身的地方遮住了。

下一秒鐘，普克拉提斯已站在門前，對鐵修斯又鞠躬又微笑的，好像從來沒有傷害過任何人一樣。

「親愛的朋友，床已經準備好了，我現在就帶你去，你就好好休息一下吧。」他說。

他們走到一間房間裡，裡面擺著的，當然就是那張床架，鐵製的，造得非常奇怪，上面鋪了柔軟的臥榻。

但是鐵修斯機警地環視一周，看到窗簾後面藏著斧頭和連著滑輪的繩子，還看到地板上都是血跡。

「這就是你那張舒適的床？」鐵修斯問。

普克拉提斯回答，「是的，你只要躺上去，它就會自動調整為你的身長。」

鐵修斯說：「但是你應該先躺上去，讓我看看它怎麼自動調整到你的身長。」

「噢，不行，不行，」普克拉提斯說：「這樣魔咒就會消失了。」語畢，他的臉頰變得一片慘白。

「但是我告訴你，你一定得躺上去。」鐵修斯一說完，便抓住已經全身發抖的普克拉提斯的腰，一把丟到床上。

普克拉提斯一趴到床上，就有奇怪的鐵臂伸出來，把他緊緊圈住，使他動彈不得。可憐的普克拉提斯又哭又叫，跟鐵修斯求饒。

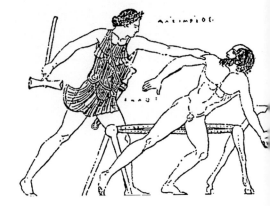

「這就是你要你的客人躺下休息的床嗎？」他問。

但是普克拉提斯什麼話也不說。於是鐵修斯拿出斧頭、繩子和滑輪，問他要這些東西做什麼，又為什麼把這些東西藏在房間裡。普克拉提斯還是什麼也不說，只是在那裡又哭又抖。

「你是不是把上百名的旅人，」鐵修斯接著問，「引誘到你的巢穴裡，就只為了搶奪他們的財物？你是不是把他們綁在這張床上，然後砍斷他們的腿，或是拉長他們的身體，直到剛好適合這個鐵床架？跟我說，是不是？」

「是的！是的！」普克拉提斯哭哭啼啼地說：「現在請發發慈悲，壓一下我頭上的彈簧，放我走，我所有的財物都給你！」

但是鐵修斯不理他，轉身走開了。他說：「現在，你被困在你自己設計的陷阱裡了。沒有慈悲的人，也沒有必要對他慈悲。」他走出房間，讓可憐的普克拉提斯死在自己殘忍的刑具下。

鐵修斯四處巡視著，這時，鐵修斯之前在葡萄藤中看到的少女跑了進來。她抓著這名英雄的雙手，祝福他、感謝他，因為他為這個世界，除掉了殘忍的普克拉提斯。

她說：「一個月前，我的父親在前往伊流西斯的路上，路過這裡。他是雅典的富商，我當時跟著他。結果這個強盜把我們引到他的巢穴裡，因為我們帶著很多黃金。他把我父親拉死在鐵床上；而我，則被逼做他的奴隸。」

鐵修斯把房子裡所有的人都叫出來，那些都是被普克拉提斯逼迫當奴隸的可憐人。他把強盜的贓物平分給他們，宣告還他們自由之身，想去哪裡就可以去哪裡。

❾ 歸鄉

p. 205 第二天，鐵修斯又上路了。他沿著窄小彎曲的小路，穿過高山與丘陵，最後，終於來到雅典城坐落的平原。他看到宏偉的雅典城，中間的岩石高地上，矗立著雅典娜神殿。神殿過去一點點，就是皇宮的白牆。

鐵修斯進了雅典城，走在街上，路上行人都很納悶，這個英俊挺拔的青年到底是誰。但是他的英勇事蹟早已傳遍各地，因此沒多久，就有傳聞傳開，說他就是除掉了山上的強盜、在伊流西斯跟克錫翁摔角、把普克拉提斯困在自己陷阱裡的英雄。

「別胡說了！」幾個推著滿載的推車，正準備上市場的屠夫說：「這小伙子唱情歌給女孩子聽還差不多，怎麼可能跟強盜對抗，又跟巨人摔角。」

「你們看他又亮又軟又黑的頭髮！」一個屠夫說。

「還有他秀氣的臉龐！」另一個屠夫說。

「還有他的長袍在腳邊蕩啊蕩的！」第三個屠夫說。

「還有他金色的涼鞋！」第四個屠夫說。

「哈哈哈！」第一個屠夫大笑說：「我打賭，他這一輩子從來沒舉過十磅重的東西。他這個樣子，怎麼可能把老斯克戎丟下懸崖！完全就是胡說！」

鐵修斯大步走在街上，把這些話都聽進去了，但是他一點也不生氣，因為他到雅典並不是為了跟幾個屠夫爭吵。

他什麼話都沒說，逕自走到最前頭的推車前，在屠夫還來不及反應前，把要推去市場賣的死公牛一把抓起來，往空中用力一擲，公牛便飛過旁邊的屋頂，掉到屋後的院子了。

接著他把第二輛、第三輛和第四輛推車上的公牛，也都一把丟過屋頂，然後他轉過身，繼續往前走，留下屠夫們目瞪口呆地站在街上。

他爬上通往陡峭多石丘頂的階梯，最後終於站在父親的宮殿門口，心跳又急又快。

「國王在哪裡？」他問守衛。

守衛回答：「你不能見國王，但是我可以帶你去見他的姪子。」

守衛把他帶到用餐的大廳，他立刻看到他五十個表哥坐在桌前大吃大喝，狂歡作樂。大廳裡，滿是宴會的喧囂，流浪藝人在唱歌演戲，宮廷仕女在跳舞，喝得半醉的王子們在又叫又罵。

鐵修斯站在門口，為這一幕氣得皺眉咬牙。這時，一個表哥看到他，大喊道：「大家看看門口這個高個子！他在這裡做什麼？」

「對啊，秀氣的陌生人，」另外一個表哥說：「你在這裡做什麼？」

鐵修斯說：「我來這裡，是為了請求受到招待，就如我們家鄉的人，從來不會拒絕招待外人。」

「我們也不會。」他們大喊。「進來，跟我們一起吃喝，當我們的客人。」

鐵修斯說：「我會進來，但是我要當國王的客人。他在哪裡？」

「別管國王了，」其中一個表哥說：「他在享他的清福呢，現在國家由我們來治理。」

但是鐵修斯只是無畏地大步穿過宴會廳，在皇宮裡四處尋找國王。

最後，他終於發現愛琴斯孤單又悲傷地坐在一間房間裡。他看到憂慮在年老的愛琴斯臉上刻滿了皺紋，又注意到他的動作帶著顫抖與遲疑，心裡非常難過。

他説：「偉大的國王，我在雅典是個外人，我來這裡，是請您給我吃的、住的和友誼，因為我知道，您從來不會拒絕高貴的同族。」

「你是誰呢，青年？」國王問。

「我是鐵修斯。」鐵修斯回答。

「什麼？你就是除掉山上的強盜、摔角王斯克戎，還有殘忍的拉人魔普克拉提斯的鐵修斯？」

鐵修斯説：「是的。」

國王聽了心中一驚，臉色都白了。「特洛伊西納！特洛伊西納！」他忍不住喊道。然後他克制住自己，説：「是的！是的！勇敢的陌生人，我歡迎你，我會盡雅典國王能盡到的一切能力，給你住的、吃的和友誼。」

❿ 邪惡女巫梅黛亞

p. 210 這時，國王身邊有一個美麗但邪惡的女巫，叫做梅黛亞（Medea）。她對國王有非常大的影響力，因此國王不管做什麼，都不敢不問她的意見。

於是他轉向梅黛亞，問：「梅黛亞，我這樣歡迎這位年輕的英雄，做得對不對？」

「你做得很對，愛琴斯國王。」她說：「你不如現在就派人帶他去客房，讓他好好休息休息，之後再讓他在你的桌前，跟我們一起用餐。」

梅黛亞已經透過巫術，得知鐵修斯的身分，因此她絲毫不願意鐵修斯留在雅典，因為她擔心鐵修斯一旦跟國王表明身分，她就一點權力都沒了。

於是，她趁鐵修斯在客房休息的時候，跟愛琴斯說，這個年輕的陌生人根本不是個英雄，而是他的姪子派來殺他的，因為他的姪子已經厭倦了等他死去。

可憐的老國王聽了非常害怕，因為梅黛亞說的話，他句句相信為真。於是他問梅黛亞，該怎麼保住自己的性命。

「交給我吧。」她說：「他馬上就會來跟我們一起用餐了。我會在一杯酒裡下毒，等用餐後給他喝，這樣再簡單不過了。」

到了用餐的時刻，鐵修斯便坐下來，與國王和梅黛亞一起用餐。他邊吃，邊敘述他的經歷，敘述他怎麼打倒巨人強盜、摔角王斯克戎，以及殘忍的普克拉提斯。國王越聽，就莫名地越欣賞這個青年，最後更希望他不要喝下梅黛亞的毒酒。

接著鐵修斯停下來，想為自己切一塊烤肉。他依當時的習慣，抽出劍，準備切肉。

他的劍才出鞘，愛琴斯就看到劍上的刻字——他名字的縮寫。

他立刻明白，這就是他多年前埋在特洛伊西納山坡石頭下的那把劍。

「我的兒子！我的兒子！」他喊著。他跳起來，打翻了桌上那杯毒酒，緊緊擁抱鐵修斯。父子倆在這一刻開懷地相認，兩人都有問不完的問題，和說不完的話。

至於邪惡的梅黛亞，她知道自己掌權的日子結束了。她跑出皇宮，吹出一聲響亮刺耳的口哨聲，傳說這時從空中飛來一輛龍拉的雙輪馬車，梅黛亞跳上去，逃走了。從此以後，再也沒人見過她。

隔天早上，愛琴斯派出傳令官，宣告全城說，鐵修斯就是他的兒子，而有一天，鐵修斯就會繼承王位。五十個姪子聽到這個消息，個個氣憤又驚慌。

「這個新人，想騙走我們的王位？」他們大喊。於是他們密謀在城門邊的小樹林裡，伏擊鐵修斯，想把他除掉。

壞心的姪子們，狡猾地設下陷阱，想抓到青年英雄鐵修斯。某天，鐵修斯一個人走過城門邊，幾個姪子立刻撲向他，手裡揮著劍和長矛，想當場置他於死地。對方有三十個人，但是鐵修斯英勇地奮戰，抵擋住他們的攻擊，並大聲求救。

一直遭到這些姪子欺壓的雅典人民，聞聲都從街上跑來，然後在接下來的混戰裡，每一個參與伏擊的姪子都被殺死了。其他的姪子聽到這件事後，都匆匆忙忙逃出雅典，再也沒有回來過。

12 神奇的工匠

❶ 佩狄克斯和鷓鴣

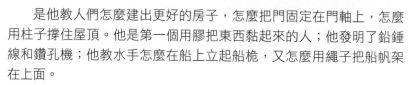

p. 216 雅典還只是個小城市的時候，裡面住著一個叫做戴達魯斯（Daedalus）的工匠，他是處理木材、石材和金屬技術最精湛的工匠。

是他教人們怎麼建出更好的房子，怎麼把門固定在門軸上，怎麼用柱子撐住屋頂。他是第一個用膠把東西黏起來的人；他發明了鉛錘線和鑽孔機；他教水手怎麼在船上立起船桅，又怎麼用繩子把船帆架在上面。

他為年輕的雅典國王愛琴斯，建了一座石造的皇宮，又把矗立在城中大石丘上的雅典娜神殿，裝修得更加美麗。

戴達魯斯有個姪子叫做佩狄克斯（Perdix）。佩狄克斯還小的時候，他就把他收為徒弟，傳授他工匠的技藝。佩狄克斯是個非常聰明的學生，沒多久，他在許多方面就已經懂得比師傅還要多了。

他時時刻刻都在觀察周圍的世界，因此習得了田野和森林相關的知識。

一天，他走在海邊，撿起一隻大魚的脊骨，因此得到靈感發明了鋸子。他看到小鳥在樹幹上啄洞的樣子，因此學會了怎麼製作和利用鑿子。然後，他發明了陶藝工人用來製陶的轉盤；從分岔的木棍，做出第一把圓規，此外還研究出許多其他新奇而有用的東西。

戴達魯斯看到姪子這麼聰明好學，這麼有幹勁，心裡很不是滋味。

「如果他繼續保持這個樣子，」他喃喃道：「他就會變得比我還偉大。大家就只會記得他的名字，而我的名字就會被人淡忘。」

日復一日，戴達魯斯工作的時候，一直想著這件事，不久他心裡就對年輕的佩狄克斯充滿了怨恨。

　　一天早上，他們正在為雅典娜神殿的外牆裝上一具裝飾，戴達魯斯趁機要姪子走上一座狹窄的鷹架，而這座鷹架就高高地吊在神殿矗立的懸崖邊。佩狄克斯走上去後，戴達魯斯只需要用槌子一敲，鷹架就鬆脫了。

　　可憐的佩狄克斯立刻頭朝地往下墜，如果不是雅典娜看到他，可憐他，他一定會摔死在懸崖底邊的石頭上。他還在空中往下墜的時候，雅典娜把他變成了一隻山鶉。他拍著翅膀，飛到山裡，從此永遠生活在他熱愛的森林田野中。

　　直到今天，當夏日的微風吹起，當野花綻放在草原上和森林裡，你有時候還可以聽到草地裡、蘆葦叢中，或茂密的樹叢間，傳出佩狄克斯的叫聲，呼喚著他的伴侶。

❷ 克里特國王：米諾斯

p. 221 雅典的人民，聽説戴達魯斯做的事情後，心中都充滿了悲慟與憤怒。他們為年輕的佩狄克斯感到悲慟，因為大家都很愛他。他們對壞心的戴達魯斯感到生氣，因為他是個自私的叔叔。

他們本來都贊成以死刑懲罰戴達魯斯，因為戴達魯斯罪該萬死，但是他們只要一想到戴達魯斯，是如何使他們的住家變得更舒適，又如何使他們的生活變得更方便，便決定放他一條生路。但是他們還是把他趕出雅典城，永遠不准他再回來。

這時，港口剛好有一艘船準備出航，於是戴達魯斯帶著他珍貴的工具，和年幼的兒子伊卡洛斯（Icarus）上船了。

小船一天一天慢慢地往南開，一直與右邊的大陸保持一定的距離。之後它繞過特洛伊西納和阿爾戈斯的岩岸，勇敢地駛向大海。

最後，他們終於抵達著名的克里特島。戴達魯斯在這裡上岸，並表明自己的身分。克里特的國王以前就聽説過他精湛的工藝，因此很歡迎他來到他的王國，還讓他住在他的皇宮裡。他向戴達魯斯承諾，只要他留在這裡，像在雅典時一樣從事工藝，一定會得到萬貫財富與聲譽。

克里特的國王叫做米諾斯（Minos）。他的祖父也叫做米諾斯，是歐羅巴的兒子。老米諾斯被認為是全世界最有智慧的人，連朱比特都把他選做陰間的法官之一。

小米諾斯幾乎就跟他祖父一樣有智慧，同時也是個英勇有遠見、有手腕的君王。他使所有的小島，都臣服於他的王國，而他派出的船隻，更航行到世界各地，把異地的財寶都帶回克里特。所以，他兩三下就説服戴達魯斯在皇宮裡待下來，並擔任宮庭總工匠。

戴達魯斯為米諾斯國王建了一座華麗無比的宮殿，有大理石的地板，和花崗岩的梁柱。在宮殿裡，他立起一座座黃金雕像，雕像有舌頭，還會説話。全世界再也沒有一棟建築物，比這座宮殿更美更壯觀了。

❸ 米諾陶和迷宮

p. 224 那時候，克里特的山上住著一個叫做米諾陶（Minotaur）的猛獸，世界上從來沒有出現過這麼可怕的猛獸。傳說，這個猛獸有人的身體，卻有野牛的臉和頭，還有山獅一般兇殘的天性。

克里特的人即使殺得了牠，也不能把牠殺死，因為他們以為這隻猛獸是與朱比特一起住在山頂上的眾神派來的，如果殺了牠，眾神就會生氣。

牠是整個克里特的禍患。沒有人想到牠會出現的地方，牠就偏偏在那裡出現。幾乎每天都有男人、女人或小孩被牠捉去吃掉。

「你已經做了這麼多美好的東西，」國王對戴達魯斯說：「那你能不能做個東西，為克里特除掉米諾陶？」

「您要我把牠殺掉嗎？」戴達魯斯問。

「不是！不是！」國王說：「殺掉牠，只會為我們帶來更大的災難。」

「那我就蓋一棟房子，」戴達魯斯說：「讓你把牠關在裡面。」

「但是如果把牠監禁起來，牠會漸漸消瘦，最後死在裡面。」

「牠在裡面會有很多空間能四處活動，」戴達魯斯說：「而且，你只要偶爾從你的敵人裡，抓一個進去餵牠，我保證，牠在裡面會過得好好的。」

於是，神奇的工匠戴達魯斯帶著他的工人，建起一棟絕妙的房子，裡面有好多房間，和好多曲折的通道，任誰走進去，都無法找到出來的路。戴達魯斯把這棟房子，稱為「迷宮」，並狡黠地把米諾陶騙進去。

米諾陶進去後，馬上就在曲折的通道裡迷失了方向。然而，日日夜夜，人們還是可以聽到牠來來回回想逃卻逃不出去所發出的可怕吼聲。

❹ 人類的雙翅

p. 227 不久之後，戴達魯斯做了一件事得罪了國王。

國王說：「一直以來，我讚賞你的技巧，又獎賞你的功勞。但是從現在開始，你就是我的奴隸，我不會給你工錢，也不會許你一句稱讚。」

接著，他命令城門的守衛，無論何時都不准戴達魯斯出城；又派士兵看守港口的船隻，以免戴達魯斯坐船逃跑。

但是神奇的工匠戴達魯斯，雖然從此像個犯人一樣被監禁起來，他沒有為米諾斯國王建造其他的建築物，他把時間都花在如何重獲自由的計畫上。

「我所有的發明，都是為了帶給別人快樂而作。」他對兒子伊卡洛斯說：「現在，我要發明一個能帶給我自己快樂的東西。」

於是，他白天就假裝是在為國王計畫什麼大工程，晚上卻把自己鎖在房裡，藉著燭光偷偷進行自己的工程。

沒過多久，他就為自己造了一對堅固的翅膀，為兒子伊卡洛斯也造了一對小翅膀。某天午夜，大家都在睡覺時，他們兩人便出門，試試看自己能不能飛起來。

他們用蠟把翅膀固定在肩膀上，然後往空中一跳。一開始，他們還無法飛得很遠，不過他們飛得很順，因此兩人深信不久以後，他們就能夠飛得更遠了。

隔天晚上，戴達魯斯對翅膀做了一些調整，然後他跟伊卡洛斯走到屋外，在月光下又試了一次。這一次，他們飛得更遠了。但是，他們還沒準備好進行長距離的飛行，於是他們在日出之前又飛回家。

之後，每個晴朗的晚上，他們都會裝上翅膀練習飛行，而一個月之後，他們飛在天上，就跟走在地上一樣熟練，可以像小鳥般飛過重重的山丘了。

❺ 伊卡洛斯的墜海和伊卡里亞海

p. 230 一天清早，國王米諾斯還沒起床，他們裝上翅膀，往空中一跳，飛出城了。

飛離克里特島一段距離後，他們開始往西飛，因為戴達魯斯聽說，西西里島（Sicily）就在西方幾百英里外處，而他決定要在那裡找個新家。

一切都很順利，兩名勇敢的飛行家飛得很快，在距離海面上一點的地方飛行著，並乘著涼爽的東風，助他們一臂之力。

到了中午，太陽變得特別炙熱，於是戴達魯斯要跟在後面的小伊卡洛斯保持翅膀的涼爽，不要飛太高，但是小伊卡洛斯非常得意自己能飛得這麼好，他抬頭看看太陽，心想如果能夠像太陽一樣，翱翔在雲端之上的藍天裡，該有多好。

「不管怎麼樣，我要再飛高一點。」他對自己說：「說不定，我就能看到拉太陽車的馬，甚至看到駕車的太陽神。」

於是他越飛越高，但是飛在前面的父親卻沒有注意到他。沒多久，太陽的熱度就開始熔化小伊卡洛斯用來固定翅膀的蠟。他覺得自己在往下掉，而肩膀上的兩隻翅膀已經鬆掉了。他對著爸爸大叫，但是已經太遲了。

戴達魯斯一回頭，只看到伊卡洛斯一頭掉進海裡。海水很深，就連神奇工匠的技術，也救不了他的兒子。他只能悲傷地看著無情的大海，然後獨自飛向遙遠的西西里。

傳說，他在那裡住了好幾年，但是他再也沒做過什麼偉大的東西，也沒再建過像克里特迷宮一樣了不起的建築物。

而可憐的伊卡洛斯溺死的那片海，從此以後，就叫做伊卡里亞海（Icarian Sea）。

13 鐵修斯的歷險記（II）

❶ 殘忍的貢品

p. 234 克里特國王米諾斯對雅典開戰了。他帶著一大批船隊和軍隊，燒毀了雅典港口的商船，侵略了整片大地和海岸，直逼西邊的梅戈拉。

於是，雅典國王愛琴斯帶著十二位長老，出城去見米諾斯，跟他談判。

「噢，偉大的國王，我們做了什麼，」他們說：「讓您這麼想把我們趕盡殺絕？」

「噢，你們這些懦弱無恥的人，」米諾斯國王回答：「你們都知道我憤怒的原因，怎麼還問這種傻問題呢？我曾有個獨子，安卓哥斯（ Androgeos ）。三年前，他來到雅典，參加你們為了紀念雅典娜所舉辦的比賽。你們都知道，他怎麼擊敗你們所有的青年，也知道你們的人們如何用歌聲、舞蹈和桂冠，來慶祝他的勝利。但是你們的國王，也就是現在站在我面前的愛琴斯，看到每個人這麼崇拜他，這麼讚賞他的英勇，心生嫉妒，就設陷把他害死了。」

「我們否認，我們否認啊！」長老們喊道：「那個時候，我們的國王正住在薩羅尼加灣對岸的特洛伊西納，對這件事一無所知啊。安卓哥斯不是死於國王的命令，而是死在國王姪子的手下；這幾個姪子，就是想激起您對愛琴斯的不滿，利用您把他趕出雅典，這樣他們其中一位就可以當上國王了。」

「你們發誓所說屬實？」米諾斯問。

「我們發誓。」長老們說。

米諾斯說：「好，那請聽好我的決定。雅典奪走了我最珍貴的寶物，再也無法賠償我，所以，現在我要雅典把他們最珍重、最寶貴的東西獻給我，然後這份貢物會被無情地毀掉，就如同我的兒子被無情地害死。」

「這個條件很苛刻，但是很公平。」長老們說：「那您要求什麼樣的貢物呢？」

「國王有兒子嗎？」米諾斯問。

愛琴斯國王頓時臉色一片蒼白，他想到薩羅尼加灣對岸特洛伊西納城裡，年幼的兒子和妻子，不禁全身發抖。但是長老們不知道愛琴斯有個兒子，所以他們一致回答：

「沒有！國王沒有兒子，但是他有五十個姪子。」

「我跟這些人沒什麼交道好打的，」米諾斯說：「你們要怎麼處置他們，是你們的事。但是，你們問我，我要求什麼樣的貢物，現在我就告訴你們。每年春天玫瑰開始綻放的時候，你們要從你們的人民當中，選出七個最高貴的青年和七位最美麗的少女，讓國王派船送到克里特給我。這就是你們要獻給克里特國王米諾斯的貢物。」

「噢，米諾斯國王，我們同意這個條件，」長老們說：「畢竟我們也願意兩害相權取其輕。但是請告訴我們，這七名青年和七名少女，會遭到什麼樣的命運？」

「在克里特，有一棟叫做迷宮的房子，」米諾斯回答：「你們絕對沒有看過這樣的房子。迷宮裡有一千個房間，和一千條曲折的通道，不管是誰，只要稍微走進去，就再也找不到出來的路。這七名青年和七名少女，會被推進迷宮裡，然後——」

「餓死？」長老們喊。

「被一隻叫做米諾陶的猛獸吃掉。」米諾斯說。

愛琴斯國王和長老們聽了，都把臉埋在手裡，開始哭泣。他們慢慢走回城裡，向人民宣告，這個唯一能夠拯救雅典悲傷而可怕的條件。

「犧牲幾個人的性命，總比全城都被毀掉好。」他們說。

❷ 前往克里特島

p. 238 一年接著一年過去了。每年春天玫瑰開始綻放的時候，七名青年和七名少女，就會坐上一艘張著黑帆的船，被送到克里特，作為獻給米諾斯國王的貢物。

這時候，大海對岸特洛伊西納城裡那個小男孩已經長大成人了。最後，他終於來到雅典找到父親愛琴斯，而愛琴斯國王這段時間一直都不知道自己的兒子是生是死，所以當鐵修斯向他表明身分時，國王開心地歡迎他，而雅典人民也很高興得到一個這麼高貴的王子，而且以後這個王子會統治他們的城市。

春天又到了。他們又把張著黑帆的船配備好，準備下一次的出航。兇暴的克里特士兵，列隊走在雅典街上，米諾斯國王的傳令官站在城門前，大喊：「雅典的人民，還有三天，就是你們獻貢的日子了！」

接著，每條街上的每戶人家都把門關上了，再也沒有人進出。大家臉色蒼白、沉默不語地坐在家裡，心裡擔憂這一年不知又要輪到誰了。

「這到底是怎麼一回事？」年輕的鐵修斯王子喊道：「克里特人有什麼權力，要求雅典獻貢？他要的貢物又是什麼？」

愛琴斯把他領到一旁，流著淚告訴他米諾斯國王興起的戰爭，還有那殘酷的和平協定。

鐵修斯激動地說：「雅典再也不向克里特獻貢了。我要跟著這些青年男女一起去，然後殺了米諾陶，讓米諾斯國王知道，我們不是這樣讓人欺負的。」

第三天早上，城裡所有的青年少女都被帶到市集的廣場上，準備抽籤。兩個黃銅的大桶子，被放置在愛琴斯國王和克里特的傳令官面前。兩個桶子裡的球都是白色的，只有七個球像黑檀木一般黑。

然後，每個少女都閉著眼睛，把手伸到桶子裡，抽出一顆球，抽到黑球的，就被帶到等在港口的黑船上。

　　青年也用一樣的方式抽籤，但是抽出六個黑球後，鐵修斯趕忙走到前面說：「等等！不要再抽了。我就是第七個獻貢的青年。現在我們上船出發吧。」

　　接著雅典的人民，還有愛琴斯國王都走到海邊，跟這些青年男女道別，心想以後再也看不到他們了。除了鐵修斯之外，每個人都在哭，每個人的心都碎了。

　　「我會回來的，父親。」鐵修斯說。

　　「我也希望你會回來。」老國王說：「如果船回來的時候，黑帆上面另外張著一張白帆，我就知道你還活得好好的。但是如果我只看到黑帆，我就知道你已經喪生了。」

　　他們把繫船的繩索解開，北風揚起船帆，七名青年和七名少女便被載向大海，駛向在遙遠克里特等待他們的殘酷命運。

❸ 亞莉阿德妮公主

p. 241 黑船終於抵達航程的終
點。雅典的青年男女被領上
岸，由一群士兵領著走過克
里特的街道，向監獄前進，
因為今晚他們要先待在監獄。

他們不哭也不叫，因為
他們已經不再害怕了。他們
只是臉色蒼白、嘴唇緊閉地
走在克里特一排排的房屋之
間。房屋的窗口門前都站滿
了人，急著想看他們一眼。

「這麼英勇的青年，都要
成為米諾陶的食物，實在太
可惜了。」有些人說。

「唉，這麼美麗的少女，居然要遭到這種厄運！」其他人說。

他們一行人走過皇宮大門，皇宮裡站著米諾斯國王，還有他的女
兒亞莉阿德妮（Ariadne），克里特最漂亮的女子。

「的確，一個個都是高貴的青年！」國王說。

「是啊，這麼高貴的青年，實在不值得去餵可憎的米諾陶。」亞莉
阿德妮說。

國王說：「越高貴越好，他們沒有一個比得上你死去的哥哥安卓哥
斯。」

亞莉阿德妮不再說什麼了，但是她心裡想，她從來沒有看過像年
輕的鐵修斯這麼充滿英雄氣質的人。

看他多挺拔，又多英俊啊！看他的眼神有多驕傲，腳步有多堅定
啊！克里特從來沒有出現過像他這樣的人。

整個晚上，亞莉阿德妮都醒著，想著這個舉世無雙的英雄，為他

死亡的命運感到悲傷，但是不久她就開始計畫拯救他。

第一道曙光出現時，她便起身，趁著大家都還在沉睡的時候，跑出皇宮，趕到監獄。她是國王的女兒，所以獄卒遵照她的命令，為她開了門，讓她進去。七名青年和七名少女都在坐在地上，但是他們都還沒放棄希望。

她把鐵修斯領到一旁，小聲告訴他她拯救他的計畫。鐵修斯聽了之後對她承諾，等他除掉米諾陶後，他就會帶她回雅典，讓她永遠跟他生活在一起。

接著，亞莉阿德妮交給他一把利劍，並幫他藏在他的斗篷下，告訴他只要用這把劍，就能除掉米諾陶了。

「這裡還有一團絲線，」她說：「你一進了迷宮後，就把絲線的一端，綁在門口的石柱上，然後邊走邊放線。等你除掉米諾陶後，只要跟著線走，就可以回到門口。我會讓人把你的船準備好，然後到迷宮門口等你。」

鐵修斯謝謝美麗的亞莉阿德妮公主，然後又一次承諾她，如果他能夠活著回去雅典，一定會帶她同行，然後娶她為妻。亞莉阿德妮向雅典娜祈禱，之後便匆匆忙忙離開了。

❹ 迷宮和愛琴海

p. 244 太陽升起後，守衛來把這群年輕的犯人帶去迷宮。他們沒有看到鐵修斯藏在斗篷下的劍，也沒看到他緊緊握在手裡的小絲線團。

他們領著這些青年男女，走進迷宮深處，一下左轉一下又右轉，一下往前一下又往後，換了上千次方向，一直到他們覺得再也找不到出去的路。然後守衛就從一個祕密通道離開，留下這些人如同過去一樣，在迷宮裡亂走，等著被可怕的米諾陶找到。

鐵修斯對他的同伴們說：「跟好我，再加上住在我們美麗家鄉神殿裡雅典娜的幫助，我就能夠救你們一命。」

他拔出劍，在狹窄的通道裡站在他們前面，然後他們都舉起雙手，向雅典娜祈禱。

好幾個小時過去了，他們站在那裡，什麼都沒聽到，什麼也沒看到，只看見通道兩旁光滑的高牆，和高高在上寧靜的藍天。

接著，七名少女在地上坐下來，把臉埋在手裡，哭著說：「噢，拜託牠趕快出現，結束我們的痛苦和生命吧。」

到了傍晚，他們終於聽到一聲低沉模糊的吼叫聲，彷彿是從很遠的地方傳來的。他們靜靜地聽，很快又聽到第二聲，這一聲比剛剛那聲音量更大，聽起來又兇猛又可怕。

「那是牠！那就是牠！」鐵修斯喊，「準備作戰了！」

他大喊一聲，在迷宮的牆間引起一陣陣回聲。他的聲音傳到天上，傳到山上的石間和峭壁。米諾陶聽到他喊，吼聲越來越大，越來越兇猛。

「牠來了！」鐵修斯喊。他往前跑，準備迎戰。

七名少女開始尖叫，但是她們還是勇敢地站起來，準備面對她們的命運。六名青年站在一起，咬著牙，握著拳頭，準備奮戰到最後一口氣。

沒多久，米諾陶就出現在他們眼前了。

牠沿著通道，衝向鐵修斯，一邊還發出可怕的吼叫。牠有兩個人

高，頭是牛的樣子，有兩根巨大尖銳的牛角、一雙火紅的眼睛，和一張大如獅口的嘴巴。但是青年們看不到牠的下半身，因為牠的下半身隱沒在牠衝過來時揚起的飛塵裡。

　　牠看到鐵修斯手裡拿著劍迎向牠，頓時停了下來，因為以前從來沒有人這樣拿著劍對著牠。牠把頭低下來，邊吼邊往前衝。但是鐵修斯迅速往旁一躍，然後對著米諾陶用力一揮，沿著膝蓋上方，砍斷了米諾陶一隻腳。

　　米諾陶跌在地上，又吼又叫，牠長著角的頭，和蹄一般的拳頭，瘋狂地亂揮，但是鐵修斯敏捷地衝向牠，一劍刺向牠的心臟，然後在牠能夠出手傷害他之前跳走。鮮血頓時從傷口湧出，沒多久，米諾陶臉朝著天死了。

　　青年和少女跑向鐵修斯，親吻他的雙手和雙腳，感謝他救了他們。這時，天色已經開始變暗，鐵修斯要他們跟著他走，然後他邊走，邊收起能夠帶領他們走出迷宮的絲線。

13 鐵修斯的歷險記（II）

他們走過一千間房間，和一千座院子，走過一千條曲折的通道，最後終於在午夜時分，來到迷宮的外門，看到月光下的克里特城在他們眼前展開。再過去一點點，就是海岸，載著他們來到克里特的黑船，便繫泊在那裡。

大門敞開著，亞莉阿德妮就站在門邊等著他們。

「現在風向正好，海水也很平靜，水手正等著待命呢。」她低聲說。然後她挽起鐵修斯的手臂，一行人便穿過寂靜的街道，向著黑船走去了。

黎明來臨時，他們已經在遠遠的海上。從小船的甲板回頭看，只看得到克里特山脈白色的山峰。

米諾斯起床後，並不知道七名青年和少女已經安全逃出迷宮了。他發現亞莉阿德妮不見後，還以為是強盜把她擄走。他派士兵去山裡尋找她的蹤跡，壓根沒想到她正好好地在前往遙遠雅典城的路上。

好幾天過去了，最後士兵回到皇宮，報告說他們到處都找遍了，還是找不到公主。

國王用手抱著頭，開始哭了起來，說：「現在，我兩樣寶物都沒了！」

這個時候，雅典的愛琴斯國王已經在海邊的石頭上坐了好幾天了，他一直望著大海，就等著看到從南方駛來的船。最後，載著鐵修斯和他同伴的小船終於出現了，但是小船還是只揚著黑帆，因為他們一行人高興得忘了把白帆升起來。

「唉！我的兒子還是喪生了！」愛琴斯呻吟道。他昏過去，掉進海裡，溺死了。

而那片海，從此就以他為名，稱之為愛琴海。

然後，鐵修斯就成為了雅典的國王。

國家圖書館出版品預行編目資料

邂逅希臘神話：英文讀本 / James Baldwin著；羅慕謙譯. --
初版. -- [臺北市]：寂天文化, 2016.06印刷

　面；　公分
ISBN 978-986-184-685-9(25K平裝)
ISBN 978-986-184-670-5(25K平裝附光碟)
ISBN 978-986-184-797-9(25K精裝附光碟)
ISBN 978-986-318-464-5(精裝附光碟)

1.英語 2.讀本

805.18　　　　　　　　　　　　105009447

作者	James Baldwin	電話	02-2365-9739
譯者	羅慕謙	傳眞	02-2365-9835
編輯	鄭家文	網址	www.icosmos.com.tw
封面設計	林書玉	讀者服務	onlineservice@icosmos.com.tw
製程管理	洪巧玲		
出版者	寂天文化事業股份有限公司		

出版日期　2016 年 6 月　　　初版五刷（250101）
郵撥帳號　1998620-0 寂天文化事業股份有限公司

語言程度		
CEF國際語言 能力指標	GEPT 全民英檢	TOEIC 多益測驗
B1 (進階級) Threshold	中級	550